INGRID JOHANNSEN

EMERALDS
AND
AQUAMARINES

A Novel

MINERVA PUBLISHING CO.

MIAMI

LONDON   RIO DE JANEIRO   NEW DELHI

EMERALDS AND AQUAMARINES
Copyright © Ingrid Johannsen 2001

ISBN 0 9676053 6 9

First Published 2001 by
MINERVA PUBLISHING CO.
1001 Brickell Bay Drive, Suite 2310
Miami, Florida 33131

Printed for Minerva Publishing Co.

EMERALDS
AND
AQUAMARINES
A Novel

*Dedicated to my husband
and this great land of ours – Canada*

Arne, shortly before I met him.

Contents

Lake Ontario

With even strokes, my body glides through the warm waters of our inland sea, as I swim aimlessly for the pure joy of it. I am relaxed and happy. With the southerly winds, the water today is unusually tepid for this otherwise somewhat cool lake. I call it "my lake" for it is part of my childhood, my youth – my Lake Ontario.

I keep looking south, to the vast expanse of water and sun. The sky is so blue! Just a few white patches of lofty clouds, like puffs of cotton here and there. My mind is free. I am in harmony with nature and life…

A sudden collision brings me to a splashy stop. My head surfaces and here it is, right at my chin, something that looks like an oversized ironing board, with another head looking at me over it.

"I am sorry, very sorry that I was in your way!" apologizes the other head in a masculine voice with a delicious accent.

"Well, I didn't look where I was going!" I laugh back.

"Did you hurt yourself?" asks the young man.

"No, not much, just my left hand, a little."

By this time, I realize my situation. I'm bobbing up and down a little with my feet touching the sandy bottom. The man's shoulders are out of water. He turns the out-of-place board right side up and asks me if I would care to rest on it.

"I found it floating here without an owner and have to cool down anyway, but you were swimming." He smiles at me while I wipe water out of my eyes and off my face.

"Why not? I haven't been on a sea horse before!" I do not know what made me say these words; they just came.

His presence is very wholesome and dignified. I'm instantly attracted. Here's someone I have stumbled upon and should take care not to lose. Most unusual for me. He holds the board with his hands on its edges and I slide on it between his arms, putting

9

my hand on his shoulder for balance.

Then it happens! As he is helping me, sunlight reflects on his handsome face. Our eyes meet for the first time and remain locked. In his greyish-blue eyes, I see a soul so deep that I fail to fathom it all. I know I've met my fate for better or for worse – or am I an impressionable young girl and have lost my head? What does he see in my eyes? The same as I? That there is more to it than just a chance meeting? Is it possible that he looks at me as a falcon on its prey? No, not this man! Not with those eyes! Not like some schoolboys I know! This is a man I can trust, and I realize that I have never been between a man's arms so close, with so little on. He does not touch me, just holds the board. By this time not only my hand, but my arm is over his shoulder as well. I feel the warmth of his muscular body, sunlit and strong. All of this during the few, all too brief seconds our eyes are greeting and exploring each other. I see clean thoughts and a clean life. I am sure I see my destiny... I feel him in the whole of my body... There is no escape – even if we do not meet again, I'm his for life. There will always be a secret corner for him in my heart...

He disengages this eye lock and I lean my head backward to rest it on the board, letting my arm slide off his shoulder.

"Let me see your left hand. Does it still hurt?" he asks and gently picks it up. "I do not see anything serious. Where does it hurt?"

I flex my fingers. "There, the upper part. I must have hit the board with them," and suddenly I realize how disorientated I am. I could not have hit anything else but the board, or him, and it did not feel like him at all.

"You're not as hard as the board, are you? And they do not hurt much any more!" as I try to salvage what I can.

"I am hard, but not that hard!" he laughs and looks at my fingers closely. "No, there is no harm done. What little pain there is will be gone by tomorrow or the day after. Examine them with your right hand," and he joins both of my hands. At that instant, our four hands meet gently and with care.

"You have the most beautiful green eyes I have ever seen, but what I saw in them is more important. I saw horizons far beyond what we can see now," and as he tells me that, he looks in my eyes again – very, very close – and I in his...

"Pardon me, I do not even know your name and here I am drowning myself in your eyes and thinking about the flight of souls! Pardon me, I did not mean to intrude," he apologizes, just as he did when I woke him from his dreams and plunged him in water.

"Oh, yes, my eyes have created problems for me, but nothing that I couldn't handle, at least not so far. I hope that your attention is not because of my eyes?" I reply, avoiding the question of my name.

"No, no!" he responds quickly, "I saw the colour of your eyes only when we... when we... when I helped you on the board..."

I rejoice. This "...when we...", "...when we..." is a clear sign of victory. When our eyes met, we responded to each other, recognizing the beauty and depth of our feelings – not just mine – ours! Perhaps fate intertwined us with each other? How beautiful it would be if it turns out to be true! How singularly beautiful!

"My name is Ingrid. Ingrid Johannsen," and I lift my right hand to meet the man I do not know yet.

"My name is Arnis. Arnis Petersons. I am a Latvian, and you are Swedish, are you not?" he introduces himself and asks me, all in one breath as if with great expectations.

"Yes, I am Swedish. My parents are Swedes and my grandparents too, both sets of them. Your name is Arnis? A-r-n-i-s?" I spell it out.

"Yes!"

"We Swedes have Arne – that is: A-r-n-e."

"Yes, you do, but there is more to it than that, much more," he replies very slowly and deliberately, as if holding something back. There is silence for a while and then he continues:

"My last name is also Swedish and comes from Sweden in the person of an officer in the Swedish army. With the king's permission he married a Livonian girl in the mid-1600s and settled in north-western Latvia at the foot of a beautiful and famous mountain – the Blue Mountain."

"...you do..." and as this "...you do..." comes over his lips, a thought hits me. I try to control it, but the more I try, the worse it gets. I explode in laughter and over the edge of the board I go.

11

When I surface and try to get water out of my eyes I see that the board is no longer between us. Arnis has pushed it aside and stretches out his arms for me to hold on to and steady myself. Again, he does not touch me, but is there for me to hang on to, if need be.

"What happened?" he asks with justified surprise. "What happened, Ingrid?"

I can't answer that right now and, with the support of his arm, try to wade out to shallower water toward the shore, still snickering.

After we are on dry land, he wades back to pull the board out as well. I look at him quickly and see puzzlement on his face, but no more questions.

"I'm sorry, Arnis! I'll tell you, but do not ask just now," and with some control in my voice again: "Should we get dressed? Or are we going back in the water? What do you say? Where are your things? Oh, right here! Wait – I'll get mine! Do we get dressed?" I ask.

"Yes, of course, if you wish. I shall be in the shade on that street corner," pointing it out to me.

When I return, all freshened up, he is waiting in light-brown sports pants and fitting shirt. Only now I notice how tall and slender he is. How could I not have noticed? We were in the water and so close!

As I approach, I feel that I should run and throw my arms around his neck and hang on – just hang on, but I do not want to scare him away – I must be worthy of him, and I remember the studies I'll undertake in the fall.

Now I look at his face, and soon enough, directly and softly in his eyes – just a step away; and he looks into mine, but not in the way we looked the first time. This is intentional, and I am not surprised any more – it is a greeting, a confirmation… Will it be our destiny? He is already in my heart – am I in his?

"Ingrid, you are not a girl. You are not even a woman. You are a goddess with two emeralds and a ruby in a crown of gold," he whispers, as if to himself.

I realize now that he had not seen my deep golden, below-the-shoulder-length hair, with slender inside curls. I had taken good care of them while dressing. As for the ruby – I do not use cosmetics yet, but I bit my lips a little.

"That board was outright dangerous. Are such boards allowed?" he asks, now louder, and with a smile I'm already in love with.

"Sure, but remember, everything in life has a purpose. That board may have served its purpose today and changed destinies," I smile back.

"Destinies? Yes, it may well have... There is nothing in the world that I could wish for more ardently right now than to know you before you are lost in the sea of people around us," he answers quietly, but does not ask for a date. Well, it may come...

We walk very slowly and soon enough I notice that imperceptibly he makes sure that he is always between me and the street. This confirms my initial impression – I have met someone rare.

"Destinies... Destinies... Without that board we probably would not have met... Well, here we are! What do we do now?" he tells me quietly to start with, and asks laughing sincerely at the end.

We decide to walk towards the Centre Island ferry wharf, and soon we are having delicious hamburgers and French fries. Time flies. It's early evening when we leave the ferry and he starts to head for the streetcar loop. There is a crowd of people, but we just do not see them.

"Arnis! What do you plan to do now?"

"Today I am your servant, Ingrid," and he stretches out his arm as if taking me in his protective custody, towards the streetcars.

"Now then, follow me, my knight! We shall ride the same horse today, just you and me!" I laugh and take him to my car, dropping a small bunch of keys in his hand.

"Now you have surprised me in a way I did not expect. I do not know how to drive! I do not have a driver's licence, let alone a car!" and he looks at me.

"I wouldn't throw a new woman and a car at a man on the first day, and it isn't even a date. We collided, don't you remember, and got stuck, so to speak!" I laugh in a most girlish way and yet –

there's an awakening woman behind that voice of mine. "Oh, just unlock the door, please, as a gentleman!"

"But, but... which key? There are so many!" he asks.

Since we met, this is the first time I see him puzzled, but he does not even try to hide his ignorance of the simplest things I take for granted. In the last few seconds, realities of life have hit him. Realities of life as they are on this continent, in this country. I did not plan it this way, it just happened, and he's just the man I thought he was – not afraid of new situations, facing them directly and honestly, and that is worth more than a hundred or a thousand lesser men.

"Here, Arnis," and I pick out the right key.

While we let the car ventilate and cool down a little, I ask him whether he has seen the movie *The Bachelor and a Bobby Soxer* with Cary Grant, Myrna Loy and Shirley Temple, presently being shown in Toronto. No, he has not.

"I would like to see it again! Would you escort me?" I ask boldly.

"Yes, of course, Ingrid, but you do not know me or anything about me. We have not been properly introduced! You, of course, can trust me, but still…"

"Arnis, I have trusted you since we met 'improperly' in rather wet circumstances. I'll tell you all at another time, if there shall be another time." I hint for a date again, but still there is no bite.

"In the meantime, I owe you an answer to the question you asked and were polite enough not to repeat. Shall we go?" But to myself I say: What am I doing? This is foolish! Our ways should separate here! But then I may not see him again, may not learn to know him. Is he as I perceived – all good and noble and therefore worthy of not being lost? Is it fate and my good fortune? I must find out! I trust him! I trust him!

The movie breaks some other barriers of common cautiousness. Laughter unites many people and helps us to recognize or find out our inner selves. So it is with us, and indirectly brings to the surface our very situation, but without the age gap. That was another reason why I wanted to see this particular movie with him.

"Now, do you have the answer to my inexcusable laughter

when I fell off the board?" I ask as we walk back to the car.

"No, Ingrid, I don't!"

"Well, listen to me carefully. The magic circle conversation goes like this:

"...Hey! You remind me of a man.

What a man?

The man with the power.

What power?

The power 'Who Do'.

Who do?

You do!

Do what?

Remind me of a man!

What a man?

Etc., etc., etc...

"Do you remember that in the movie?" I ask.

"Who could miss it!" he answers.

"Now, do you remember, when you said: '...you do...' that's when you told me of our common ancestry – for you going back to the mid-1600s? Your '...you do...' somehow, at that very moment, reminded me of this silly '...Who Do...' and..."

"Of course, Ingrid, of course! The '...you do...' – '...Who Do...' connection! It is a lady's privilege not to answer questions. I had not forgotten, but felt that I have no right to pester you with it," he answers.

I feel a little let down. I expected an instant explosion of laughter, but let it be as it is. The other point of this movie was also important, I think to myself, as we continue to walk to my car... Arnis is snickering a bit and then I see his shoulders shaking until he breaks out in laughter. It has sunk in. Yes, he is in tune with me!

"Oh, Ingrid, I am sorry that it took me so long! Since I met you, I am somewhat lost!" he exclaims.

There is no need for a snack. We were true Canadians at the theatre, munching on popcorn and enjoying soft drinks. Here is my car. What now? But, before I can answer that question to myself, Arnis offers to see me home.

"Thank you, Arnis, but I think that I should go home alone.

Without a car it would be different," I say with concern in my voice.

"I understand you perfectly, Ingrid. At least, would you grant me a date? I do not want to lose you," he asks humbly and quietly.

"Yes! Yes, Arnis!" I exclaim, to my own surprise and then, under better control of myself, "I've been waiting for these words all evening. Just before you spoke, I felt that, perhaps, I'd have to ask you for a date and for the same reason. I do not want to lose you either! Would 2:00 p.m. tomorrow be okay?"

"2:00 p.m. it is! How about at Queen's Park to watch the squirrels, just south of Bloor?" he asks.

"Will see you tomorrow," and I get in the car with him gently helping and closing the door.

"Ingrid, if you cannot and do not come – I will be waiting there for you every Saturday and Sunday afternoon at 2:00 p.m., rain or shine," he promises.

"Dear Arnis, there shall be no need for that. Ladies do not give out their telephone numbers, but here is everything. It is my social card. I shall be there, but call me if, by 3:00 p.m., I'm not. Do you promise to do that?" I ask.

"Of course, Ingrid! Of course!"

As he takes my hand, I offer him the other as well and he kisses both. The manner in which he does it is elevating and dignified, but it's not the custom of this land. I shall do something about it tomorrow in a way that does not hurt him. I think I know how. Yes – that should do it! An idea blossoms in my mind.

I still see him standing and waving, as I drive off.

Tomorrow is so far away…

That is all! So little and yet – so much! I have lost my heart and my head! Or is biology playing tricks with me? Was it to come, regardless? Could it have been anybody? Anybody at all! And Arnis happened to be there? No, I do not believe that! His eyes! His eyes, body and deportment did it.

I know only too well what I do to men, particularly those who know of our comparative wealth. Arnis knew nothing of that and I am sure his attraction is pure – just like mine for him. Where does he live? What surrounds him? I must see that, for there may lay the confirmation of my feelings for him.

Tomorrow is so very far away. No, it's already "today" – 2:00 p.m. is far away... Must have some sleep now...

★

Mother closes the diary and lets it rest on her lap. I'm sitting wide-eyed and quiet. It's late morning. It took me hours to write what was yesterday and it still was yesterday when I started. Mother's polite concern about being so late prompted me to show this entry and let her be the judge.

Our family is liberal, but within the confines of dignity and family honour. This is the very first time I have shown my diary to anyone. There was no need for it earlier. Nobody asked! Nobody knew I have a diary. Mother would have taken my word. There is no lying in this family. Just for these reasons I decided to assure Mother, Father, family – that there is no cause for concern.

"So, you are seeing that young man today at Queen's Park?" asks Mother.

"Well, that's where we shall meet. After that, I don't know. Being late yesterday was not planned, but I shall be late tonight. I must find out the truth as soon as I can. Otherwise, it would be a torture to live and not know. Mother, there is no need to worry and do not wait up for me! I can assure you – I have not yet belonged to any man and I will come home tonight as I am now. Trust me, Mother! You know some of the experiences that I've had in the past..."

"I know, Ingrid. I know, but I also know that the time will come when you will weaken and become a woman. It's inescapable!"

"Mother, I know that too, but it will not be tonight and with this man! It will not be before our wedding!" Oh, what did I say? Our wedding! I stop the flow of words, stunned by myself.

"I didn't realize, Mother, how far my subconscious mind had 'worked it all out' for me. Is it the beautiful dream I had and woke up with this morning?" I ask as if to myself. "Is it an acute case of infatuation? Is this love?"

"My dear, dear Ingrid, I have never seen you like this. You most certainly seem to be in love. You are very vulnerable now, very vulnerable. I do not want to hurt you, but think once more, by daylight, about the words you used to describe him: '...Masculine... handsome... delicious... wholesome... cultured... elevating... dignified... etc.' Think about them now... Think about them when you see him today..."

"Yes, Mother! Yes! All are true! Am I in love? Perhaps tonight I may find out – or maybe the sunrise tomorrow will answer that – or will it be a rainy day full of remorse for a shattered dream? No – that cannot be! Theoretically, anything may happen, but I am dealing with a tangible reality. Yes, you are right, Mother – I am very vulnerable now, but do you remember what you once said: '...gold is gold – no matter how you look at it...' Remember? If he is that, why should I break my heart and worry you that he might not be? I simply must find out, and the sooner the better!"

Mother gets up, comes to me, returns the diary and, putting both hands upon my head, prays quietly: "God be with you, Ingrid. May God be with you," and leaving the room she remembers, "We will not be waiting up for you, but you know that we will be waiting...

"Give him my greetings. Tell him that Mother's eyes are looking upon both of you."

Queen's Park

I park my car in the shade of trees on a side street and walk to Queen's Park. Yes, Arnis is there and sees me as I cross the southbound lanes. He comes to meet me and stretches out his arms. So do I and, taking both his hands, I reach up and give him a peck of a kiss on the lips. Oh, I am so happy! So happy!

"Arnis, Mother sends you greetings and told me to tell you that she is watching over us."

"Thank your mother for me, Ingrid," is all that Arnis can say – still holding my hands, or am I holding his? It does not matter – 2:00 p.m. has arrived and we are here!

Arnis is in a light summer suit with a dress shirt and tie. Good! I shall put that to good use. I am in a conservative pleated summer dress. I press his hands a bit harder and suggest, "Arnis, let's make a pact! When we are in public, let's greet each other with a quick kiss on the lips. The kissing of hands is not entirely out of style in this country, but reserved for solemn occasions! Remember yesterday? Oh, yesterday! How much has happened since then! How very, very much!"

"Ingrid, I feel as if life itself is flowing through our hands, and your kiss was so unexpected! It struck me as lightning – to my soul! To my very soul!" he whispers and lifts my hands a bit, looks and pets them lightly. "So be it. I shall kiss these hands in public on solemn occasions only, but if it should come to pass that we are alone, are we still bound by the 'pact'?" he asks, looking in my eyes.

"Oh, no, Arnis! No! That 'pact' is for public places only, and I wish it would come to pass that you may kiss me as long as you wish, wherever you wish – whenever we are alone. I meant what I said! I'm in love with you! I want to be your wife!"

"Ingrid! Ingrid! What are you saying? What are you trying to run away from? A personal tragedy? No! Don't answer that! It was not a question, only a form of speech! Do not tell me anything! But are you sure of what you just said?"

"Yes, Arnis, it sounds as if I proposed to you, although in a direct roundabout way."

"Ingrid, '...a direct roundabout way...'?"

"Yes! A 'direct roundabout way'!" spurt I, and Arnis joins in.

Our hands separate, and when we stop laughing, we realize that we are in each other's arms, closely and firmly. I put my cheek to his and whisper in his ear: "Let's go and feed our kids, the squirrels!" and we disengage.

"Ingrid, your temperament, your honesty in saying what you think, has broken all conventions! It has swept aside all barriers; eliminated all concerns!

"Last night I counted my blessings, and could hardly believe myself. I pondered: If? When? Where? and How? I may ask you for all that you just gave me.

"You do not know me, Ingrid! You do not know my past, or the inhibitions I am facing in this land. I just arrived this year and have been less than a month in Toronto.

"You want to be my wife? How would I be able to support you in the way you are accustomed to? You are using your father's car now! There would be no car for us in the foreseeable future! Will you sacrifice all of that for me?" Arnis asks in a most concerned way.

"Arnis, how about me? Do you care and crave for me just as much as I do for you?" and I face him – this time with a penetrating look. "This is the only thing that is important – do you love me?"

"Ingrid! Ingrid! I did not dare to speak about that so early for it may frighten you away before you have a chance to like me. Now the shoe is on the other foot. Now you may scare me away!"

"Is that the truth? I had to risk it... It was worth it to know the truth... The way I am – *do* I scare you away? You *cannot* see me as your wife?" I say with a sinking voice, looking down, clasping my little handbag with both hands in front of me. I can hardly hold back my tears. Is all lost?

"Ingrid! Ingrid! Dear Ingrid! I have hurt you. I am so sorry! I did not mean to!" and Arnis takes me in his arms and caresses my hair.

"Am I truly afraid of you? Do you really frighten me away? Am I afraid to admit that I love you? No, Ingrid, no – none of those... I am falling in love with you... No! Not correct either... I do already love you, but I will never be able to afford you. It will take years and a lot of prodding and trying to find my place in this great land, this great city. I am sure there are men who would lay all their fortunes at your feet in return for your hand. That is where a lady like you belongs. Just tell me, Ingrid, honestly – how long could I be able to hide you in my bed-sitting room from the world that is yours? With these jewels in this golden crown?

"What I said before was a cliché of a man lost in you. Shall I ever find myself again? Are you my destiny? Or are we 'our destinies'?" and he tries to lift my face by the chin, ever so tenderly...

These words settle in me as droplets of the most precious and rare wine. I was right! I have to break all the rules now, before he knows of my wealth. But he's also right: how would I look at him if I were poor? A nice guy? Fun to be with, against the background of dark, grey days, months, years – a lifetime? He's right, with my looks there would be many with money after me. I'm so very young yet. I've plenty of time – but I burn in the flames of love and passion *now!* How *would* I look at him if I were poor?

No, I can't speak for a person I do not know! I'm glad that I'm not that person. Arnis is, but he's also of the opposite gender, and I love him, and that makes all the difference.

Am I so spoiled that I think that I can buy everything with money? Am I? No! Not really, but it gives me confidence, because I can nullify all the arguments Arnis posed for himself and me. I feel good all over! He did say that he's falling in love with me – that he does love me! What else am I waiting for? Yes, I know! I'm waiting for the expiry of this day – my day of trials and, I hope, confirmations, cold calculations... Cold calculations! What am I doing to this man! What am I doing?

"Ingrid, you are so quiet, but your face did not show worry – you were smiling an invisible smile. Only now there is a cloud over you. Do you see a way that you can live with all those hardships just to be my wife?

"Yes, Ingrid, I love you, but my conscience does not permit me to exploit a time of weakness in a girl or a lady. I know war, and I have known women, several of them, but I have refused to accept or take something that does not belong to me. No husband can raise his finger, point at me, and say that I have taken what rightfully belongs to him, but he can never have. No one! Do you understand me correctly – Ingrid? It is a code of honour I will never break!" Arnis stops and returns my penetrating look. Now his eyes are piercing mine. It is a complete victory and so early in the day, the very place he met me! We're still here. I have my answer and there's no point in torturing him further.

"Arnis, I see a free bench now. Shall we go and sit down?" I say quietly.

"Sorry, Ingrid, I should have watched out for that, but you mesmerized me and nothing else existed – just you and me," and he takes my hand and escorts me to the bench.

"How does your left hand feel today?" he asks.

"Not a hint of pain. All gone," but I change the subject.

"You are the first man who has spoken to me so. Are you prepared for the worst? You said that you are falling in love with me. Will you listen?" I press on.

"Yes, Ingrid, I will listen, but there are three conditions: do not make confessions – I am not interested; do not plead for mercy – you have it all; do not offer sacrifices – as a man I cannot accept them although I may stand to gain."

"Agreed, Arnis!" I reply immediately. "If your financial and social insecurity would not exist, how would it be then with you?"

"I would fall on my knee and respectfully request your hand in marriage, but I would not beg for it, nor make excuses," he tells me with the greatest of care and sincerity – thinking at the time that this is our first and last date. That, I shall find out much later.

"Then do it and see what happens!" I reply with the greatest of admiration for this man. Now! Now! This is the threshold… And Arnis gets up, turns to face me, and kneels on his right knee, lifting his right hand so that I can place mine in his: "Will you, Miss Ingrid Johannsen, give me your hand in marriage?"

"Yes, Arnis, my darling – I most certainly will," I reply slowly and quietly. He kisses my hand and helps me up. As I put my hands on his shoulders, he embraces me and our lips meet in our first real kiss. A brief trembling runs over me. I hold him tighter and press my body against his. Electricity runs through our lips like the very first bolt of lightning from a gathering storm. We part and quickly look in each other's eyes, and kiss again – this time a sensual all-fulfilling kiss between a man and a woman. Time does not exist…

I do not know how long it took, and of all places – in a public park – but it cannot be torn down. We will always be able to come back here: summer or winter, with children or without. That reminds me:

"Arnis, we've to feed our kids!" and with this I take out of my handbag a small, flat paper bag with nuts. The very crackle of paper has served as a signal, and a couple of squirrels are already heading our way. In no time at all we are surrounded.

Some are young; some are old; and some in their very prime of life, with the best possible coats and bushy tails. There are so many black, shining, round eyes following our every move. One has come to Arnis's left leg and is looking straight up, but all the nuts are gone. Arnis lets the empty bag fall. There's a scramble for it, but soon enough all we see are their tails and we are alone again. Alone? No – with us is also love and Mother's eyes. Arnis picks up the empty bag and we sit down again…

"Ingrid, can you imagine? Yesterday, at this time, we had not even met yet – now we are engaged! It's Sunday. I cannot take you to a store for a ring, even the simplest, but even in its simplicity, it has to befit you. I will mortgage my future – you deserve the best!"

"Arnis, thinking of that, let's go for a feast of eyes – the mineral exhibit on the first floor of the Royal Ontario Museum. It is right here, to the left."

"I know, Ingrid! The high ceiling, tall windows and general atmosphere breathe the very essence of this land, its beauty and its riches. It is a cathedral of this land and for this land."

The clouds of doubt have disappeared. We are so happy with each other that we look at the various exhibits with the eyes of children – innocent, unspoiled. As we bend over emeralds, rubies, diamonds, sapphires, etc. – we turn our heads and look at each other.

"Ingrid, I do not think that we are as poor as I felt just a little while ago. We can always come here on weekends and look at what we, in fact, have. This belongs to all – us too! Not so?" he exclaims.

I know too well that in his heart he's happy, but also concerned. He does not show it, but I know this man by now. He worries about me, and the kind of life he can give me, now that he has proposed marriage. This good man is giving up the plans of his life and dreams, to fulfil mine, but to attain that I've committed a cardinal sin – the first so grave in my short life. I've gone too far, too quickly. How do I plead for mercy? How do I plead for atonement?

On the way back to my car, I ask him to come to the park again. It's our luck, our bench is free and we sit down. Our knees meet. He tries to avoid that and looks up at me. I just turn my head from side to side saying a quiet "no". He understands, and our knees remain touching.

"Arnis, I am deeply in love with you. Only one day has passed since we met. I can't explain it, nor expect you to understand it all, and love me as much as I love you – and so quickly; but you do love me? Even if only a tiny bit?"

"It is not a tiny bit, Ingrid! It is more than that. I am not a novice in love. I was married, but it ended in tragedy. There was a divorce and I thought that I should never fall in love again, but now I am exposed to someone like you, and you have taken me by storm. I was cautious and slow to admit it. Yes, it is only one day since we met, but I know that it is love, and it is you, Ingrid! Deep in my soul, I have a proof of it – to and for myself: I would give my life to save yours…"

I jump up – and so does he – but I just grab him and kiss him and put my head on his chest.

"You would give your life to save mine! You would give your life?" I whisper, but I want to shout these words at the top of my voice!

After a little while I've regained myself and say very quietly: "Let's sit down, Arnis. Let's sit down again.

"I'm ashamed of myself for what I've done – for my frontal assault on you with *my* love. I've wronged you. I've forced you. Do you find it possible to forgive me?"

"There's nothing to forgive, Ingrid! Nothing! You only made me think and realize my love for you faster! You made me admit to it earlier! You are a most extraordinary girl and as such – can you forgive *me* for not mentioning my previous marriage before? I did not want to lose you... Can you forgive me?"

"Oh, Arnis! Now I understand you much better – much, much better! Was it difficult? Was it painful?"

"As painful as could be, but I do not want to talk about it ever again. Though, can you forgive me for not telling you before I asked for your hand? After all, I shall be a slightly used husband."

"I have nothing to forgive either. It was your privilege not to talk about it, but I'm glad that you did – not for me to know, but for you to relieve your mind of the burden that was surely resting on your shoulders. It's a custom in our family not to carry such burdens. You'll see..."

Silence...

"You have suffered in love and poor little me shall reap the benefits of that – for you have been forged in fire and water... Water! That's where we met! Didn't we?" and I start to laugh, but realize immediately that my laughing is out of order here and now. "Sorry, Arnis," and I take his hand.

"I swear by everything that is sacred to me, that now I love you even more, and beg of you not to judge me too harshly for what I have done, and for what I am about to disclose... The time has arrived when I do have to tell you, just as you felt you had to tell me, but first – thank you, Arnis, for your patience with me. Thank you. In my mind, I had a very good reason to behave as I did – or so I thought at the time, but now I've no excuse for it. It was most selfish of me. I forced you in all of this so quickly. Now listen, please, and try to understand me.

"You have a worry that need not be there. I'm a wealthy girl from a wealthy family. The car I drive is not 'the family car' borrowed from my father. The 1948 Pontiac is mine. It's the top model and I don't want a heavier one. We live in a mansion and have a number of servants. Besides Father's and Mother's, I have my own safety deposit box with jewels."

"Then why...?" Arnis tries to interject, but I stop him by putting my finger on his lips.

"Listen, Arnis! Relax and listen... This isn't a guilt-ridden introduction to a confession. No man can claim me! No one! Therefore there are no confessions; nor will there be pleas for mercy; and I'm making no sacrifices, nor asking you to make any. We both are victorious!

"For me, it was important that I love the man who will be my husband, and I do love you. It was also very important that my husband loves me, as what I am: a girl; a woman; or a lady made of flesh, blood and bones – just like any other woman; and not for the comparative wealth. You didn't know about that, did you?

"That's why I desperately tried to find out from you your feelings about me, before you learned of my wealth. And, considering the customs in our family, I couldn't pretend or behave differently than what I am.

"We have a standing in society that most can't even dream of. My husband would have to fit in. Up north, we've a private lake and a shady trout stream, with all the countryside around it also belonging to us. We intentionally do not have 'cottages' on Lake Rosseau nor in the Muskokas, where the 'rich' are supposed to be. We like privacy, peace and quiet. That's how Father grew up – that's how we grew up. Oh yes, I have a younger sister, Astrid, a bobby soxer, remember?

"I've spoken a lot, but you have the right to know and slowly get accustomed to the fact that your financial worries do not exist. They did, in your mind, but in fact, they didn't."

I stop and look at his face and eyes while feeling for a handkerchief in my purse, but Arnis quickly takes one out from the inside pocket of his jacket, an extraordinarily fine, brilliantly white handkerchief, letting it drop open. Even in our circle of friends I have not seen so fine and fresh a handkerchief offered to me so quickly and elegantly, as an everyday matter of routine. Etiquette is something he will not have to learn, it is in him.

Now I know! Now I know! It was his etiquette that matched the depth of his eyes! *That* is what attracted me yesterday! That's what made us "stuck"! And I remember the saying: "Birds of a feather..." etc.

I wipe the corners of my lips, pat my cheeks and forehead and return his handkerchief. Arnis is silent, but observes every move I make, every wish that I might have.

We sit silently and I intentionally push my knees harder at his. He lifts his eyes and a smile rises in his face. That is the sign I was looking for. No! It is not going to be a dull and rainy day – ever!

"Ingrid, you have left me speechless. Such honesty and straightforward execution of carefully made plans is most surprising. I was a young officer. Completed my course as first. I know the difference between strategy, tactics and operations. Had you been in our course – you, not me, would have finished as the very first. You did it all, from the conception of thought to operational victory!"

"Would you believe me, Arnis, it all comes naturally?" I ask. "You see, in your course you probably didn't study the subject of 'Women'. When it comes to selecting a mate and father of her children, no military school can teach that. To us women, it is all a part of nature. Be strong against those who will try to rob me of you! Be strong!" I warn him with a smile.

"I understand you now, Ingrid... I understand you now... You did not want me to be blinded by your wealth – you blinded me by yourself instead, and in a big hurry..."

"Yes, Arnis, it has happened that way, hasn't it? I am so happy – so very, very happy!

"Let's get the car and have lunch! What time is it? Well, we'll have an early supper. Today you are under my care. Let's go!"

I take him to the Granite Club and, as we enter, I suggest that we go and freshen up before we eat. When I return Arnis is already waiting, as a gentleman should, discreetly standing.

After my long speech in the park, he has been very quiet. In the car, he turned sideways, watching me drive. Right now, I'm sure, he has no idea where we are. I'm glad he came dressed as he is, we can go in the formal dining room. My friends, the waiters, greet us and we get a very good table. It's true, we are way early, but I have my own schedule. I am entertaining my guest and we have hearty steaks and non-alcoholic beverages. I have to drive, and poor Arnis tells me that he wants to keep a clear head! I do not blame him – with me around...

Have I scared him out of his wits? No! By a long shot, no! He's confident, polite and witty, but quiet and very brief. His table manners are impeccable. I didn't expect anything less. I'm sure Arnis has used silverware properly from his very childhood. It is natural for him. I can show him to my family.

I sign my chit and we go, followed by a number of surprised pairs of eyes. Oh, there will be some talking.

"Arnis, I know that you didn't expect visitors today, and if it isn't convenient, please don't hesitate to say no, but I do want to see what surrounds you – so that at night I may think of you and see you in the sight of my soul. Is it possible? The evening is still young. I would like you to tell me all about yourself. Is it possible?" I repeat.

"Of course, Ingrid, of course! I have nothing to hide. I live in a clean, well-kept Macedonian home. My windows are facing west, over the Don Valley. Come, I will show you. It is north of Danforth off Broadview – where the large 7-up sign is."

"Hey! Then we can look at each other over the valley. Our home is in Rosedale!"

We arrive well before dusk. He leads me upstairs and opens a door: "Please, Ingrid! This is my 'burrow'. I was lucky to find it so convenient to street cars, and so clean in a good neighbourhood," he tells me as we enter and he opens the windows.

It's a bed-sitting room with an expensive, queen size, brass bed and two massive club chairs. He has five suitcases. Four of them are full of books in three languages. While I'm looking out of the window he comes close behind me and puts his arms around my waist – ever so lightly. I feel good... Arnis, do not fail me now, do not try to take advantage of me – that would spoil everything... everything... I find myself begging. I must be able to trust you with the most beautiful women – always, always...

"Can you imagine, Ingrid, the truth of what you said a little while ago? We have to tell each other who we are – yet, we are engaged. This continent is a bit too fast for me. Am I taking advantage of you? Or you of me? Yes, we have to talk. May I take off my jacket and tie? We have a lot of talking to do."

"Yes, Arnis, take them off. Feel comfortable. Yes! Let's get rid of the shoes too and sink into these chairs for the evening," I invite myself.

We turn the chairs, facing each other, out of reach of hands. Arnis starts first:

"Ingrid, even if you were not who you are, even if we both were poor, there are things that I can promise you: the walls of our home would be covered, floor to ceiling, with bookcases full of books of the world; and paintings of great aesthetic value; well-recorded classical music – all that can be obtained. Our home would be all of that, regardless whether we are poor or rich. It is food for one's soul. Now you will be filling it with love and the needs of the body. We shall be rich within ourselves.

"I hope that you understand that our engagement fell out of the sky. I must talk to your father and request his blessing, and your mother's too. Without the blessing of your parents, we cannot marry. This, our engagement, although beautiful for us to experience – is an empty shell without your parent's love..."

"Arnis, do you not have someone close to ask for blessing or support?"

"No, Ingrid, I do not. My parents were killed in the bomber attack on Dresden. I am as alone as anyone can be. I have no one—"

"But me, Arnis! Isn't it so?" I interrupt.

"Yes, Ingrid, it would be good to have your parents' acceptance of me. Then I would have a wife."

"That's why I can't see you tomorrow at all. I'll tell Mother all about today. In the evening, after supper – we call it 'supper' at our house: breakfast, dinner, lunch, supper; the European tradition has stuck with our family through the generations – it will be Father's turn. I think that he'll see in you what I have, and accept the inevitable: love and goodwill, or a miserable daughter. I'm willing to leave them and everything – just to be your wife..."

"No, Ingrid! I am not willing to accept that! No! Under no circumstances should you offer such a sacrifice! Do you remember the third condition – 'no sacrifices'?"

"Oh, yes! I do... I agreed... No more talk about that. Wait and see. Now, give me some facts to work with – tell me all about yourself," I ask.

"I was born on December 31, 1923, in Riga, Latvia. My father, situated in Riga, was the manager of a technical brigade responsible for all trains across the land. My mother died when I was just eight years old. After two years, Father married my nanny. They both perished in Dresden.

"I had a beautiful childhood. We lived at the very outskirts of Riga, with water, sand, forests, sun and wind around me. Summers I spent in Northern Latvia at my grandfather's farm, in one of the most beautiful and historic areas of Latvia. A deep and long lake, rivers, forests, meadows and fields – all for me to explore. This is where the Petersons come from. I am the lucky one. I was born, grew up and was educated in free and independent Latvia.

"Then came the war – Russian occupation, torture, murder, enslavement and deportation of our people to Siberia. I was drafted by the Germans and spent the winter of 1943/44 in the very first lines of the Eastern front. Orders came for us to be butchered, and after needlessly attacking Russian positions on 14 and January 15, 1944 – only sixteen enlisted men and two combat non-commissioned officers were left in our company – out of some 133 men. Thereafter I commanded a half of our company as one of the two NCOs. What spared me? I do not know. Sometimes, later on, I will tell you about the war, but you should know now that I carry in me deep, invisible scars.

"I was a POW for almost a year after the war. Then studied medicine at the Goethe University in Frankfurt/Main, and Heidelberg. Completed my studies of the human body as a healthy living organism. Pathology would follow, but there was an opportunity to come to Canada as an experienced 'hard rock' miner. By the way, you had better know, I am an official 'Displaced Person' – a DP, so to speak. We did not know what hard rock mining is, let alone be experienced in it. The officials should have known that there could not be hard rock miners among the Baltic people.

"We left Genoa, Italy, and in two weeks landed in Halifax, Canada, on April 3, 1948. On the train, we found out that we will be gold miners in our new land. How romantic! How poetic!

"After two weeks, I was poisoned by the smoke of charges that had been just exploded. Four arrived at the hospital that night – myself, and three from another mine. Two died, two survived. The next day my roommates told me that they thought I would most certainly die – blue in the face and fighting for breath, but I survived.

"The doctor would not permit me to go back underground, and the union would not permit a DP to work on the surface. I had a one-year contract with the company, but it terminated the contract, and I was 'laid off'. The employment manager visited me at the hospital and told me so. There is also an ugly lie in the official records of the company: it is stated that I quit the company right there and then – without completing my part of the contract.

"The company did that behind my back, presumably trying to cover up the accident and to avoid reporting it to the Workmen's Compensation Board. I did not qualify for Unemployment Insurance yet, and did not know of the existence of Workmen's Compensation – nobody told me. It is a company town and everybody was afraid of losing his job, even the local Unemployment Insurance officer, I suspect. I learned to know him and even he never mentioned that there is such a thing as Workmen's Compensation, and that I am covered under it.

"Had it not happened – we would not have met – I would still be up north in Timmins. Everything in life has a purpose, Ingrid, you said so yesterday – even this…

"It was a difficult time, but eventually I arrived in Toronto. Some old-timer Latvians extended a helping hand and with their assistance, I found this room.

"I am now working in a well-known dry-goods wholesale warehouse on Wellington Street West at $25 a week. I started at $20 a week. In the evening of the first day, I received a call from a Toronto company for an out-of-town job, with an offer of $50 a week with free room and board. That was a lot to turn down, but my reason was simple: I must stay in Toronto and continue my studies. Not medicine – financially out of reach. I have to start something that can be done by correspondence or at nights. Had I accepted that offer, again, we would not have met. I would not be here…

"Now – enter Miss Ingrid Johannsen, and she turns my world and plans upside down – I do not know what will become of me and my dreams," concludes Arnis: "Will I be your pet, Ingrid?" he asks jokingly.

I sit stunned. Now I understand why Arnis so suddenly became very quiet and spoke so little in the car. The tragedies that he touched upon in the park and now, here – and his dreams for life, an active life, with studies, books, paintings, music! And then – me!

"Now that I have looked at my life in a nutshell, there is also something that you should know, and not be jealous about. First and foremost in my life stands the freedom of my country, Latvia, and its people. You, Ingrid, come after that," he adds.

This gives me an opening; I've something to say:

"Arnis, it's an honour and a privilege to be placed so high on your scale of values. To come in second, after a country and its people is a great honour indeed. Jealous? How could I possibly be jealous of someone's country and people? I also place Canada and its people above everything else. Are you jealous of Canada?" and I get up, walk over and sitting on the armrest of his chair, take him in my arms.

"Now rest! Rest and listen to me," I say, gently caressing his forehead and hair for a brief while in complete silence. I then return to my chair and start to tell him something about me, my family and background:

"Now, this is what you should know. My great-grandfather came to this land and brought with him the famous Swedish steel. He returned home to marry and then came back. They were successful.

"My grandfather by wisdom, foresight or serendipity sold all his shares a month before the stock market crash of 1929. In time he got all of his stock back for peanuts, and thus became wealthy beyond his wildest dreams.

"My father inherited all of that and the company. We lead simple lives – well below the level of our income. For all practical purposes, there's no limit to what we can afford – within reason, of course.

"I'm the fourth generation of business people and have grown up in its environment. We're trained to recognize values for what they are and act immediately – just as in the stock market. Either *we* take it without delay, or someone else will. No, Arnis, neither of us is taking advantage of either of us. I recognized in you immediately what I thought you were, and tried hard to hold on to you before losing out to some other woman. That is why I so desperately wanted to be with you today and do what my mind and heart told me to do.

"Yes, I proposed to you, for all practical purposes, but you put up a valiant fight – not to protect yourself, but to protect me! Do you realize that? To protect me! You are more of a man than I thought yesterday.

"Honesty is a virtue in our family and I have to tell you this – today was your day of trial for both of us. Am I infatuated with an idol that does not exist? But for me it would have been too late anyway – I already loved you.

"What I did not know was: are you in love with me? Even if only a tiny bit – truly and honestly in love? Thus, my mother sent her greetings to you and her message – that her eyes will be upon us both.

"I'll be eighteen this December and shall begin my studies at the University of Toronto, Faculty of Household Science. It's a two-year basic course plus one or two years of specialization.

Father was blessed with two daughters. I have to study to be a perfect hostess, as the wife of the man who will, in time, take over from Father. It would be my pride and privilege to be known as your wife, and I shall not let down our guests; and never ever shall you be ashamed of me.

"I hinted in the park that I haven't yet belonged to any man. It's true – I have not, but think now about the practical aspects. Being me, and as I am, how long do you think I could hold out as I am? I would have to succumb to a man just because he is there for me, my money, or both. I would succumb to wed a man out of necessity. Youth and years of ardour go by," and I get up, stretch out my arms to Arnis and, to his surprise, pull him up as well, taking him to the window to watch the sky darken. Night will soon be upon us.

Arnis stands behind me with his palms on my shoulders. I

take his hands and pull them around me. His body is close to me now. I feel him. I feel all of him. He buries his nose in my hair and whispers: "Sorry, Ingrid."

"What for?" I whisper back, and after an unforgettable moment of silent enjoyment, I continue, "Yesterday, at the lake, you unknowingly gained a secret corner of my heart for life. No matter what would have happened to us; and, I felt then – no matter whom I may eventually marry – there would always be that secret corner for you.

"Now, right now, Arnis, that secret corner is so fortified that no man – no one – could even touch it. I'll never forget these moments here with you at this window."

I turn around quickly and his palm inadvertently touches my breast. I fall around his neck kissing him madly. Shivers of pleasure run through my body and I can't admit, even to myself, what I have experienced just now. It couldn't be hidden, but Arnis discreetly ignores my momentary trembling.

"But not farther... Not farther before our wedding night..." I whisper and break the embrace.

Arnis holds on to my hands as we now face each other, and whispers back, "I do not know, Ingrid, how long it would have taken me to try to kiss and touch you so.

"What has just happened confirms that you are honest; you speak the truth and are not afraid to disclose your desires to a man you love and trust – to a man in whose arms you will put your body for life. I have no doubts now – you love me and I love and trust you.

"Yes, Ingrid, yes! Let us save everything else for the wedding night and our entire lives. Let us remember this, as you wished to," and he pulls me close again and kisses my neck just lightly and then our lips meet in a soul-searching kiss, gentle, heavenly, a gift of nature...

Our lips separate, but the embrace remains until he whispers again:

"Now? What do we do now, Ingrid?"

I wake up. "Arnis, let's put these chairs close to each other. I'll sit in mine with my feet on your chair and you in yours with your feet on mine." When it is done, I whisper: "We shall be out of arm's reach and harm's way now. Let us enjoy the twilight of this memorable day in silence. Do you agree?" I ask as we settle in.

Arnis only nods his head in agreement, holding his hands as if in prayer, and resting his chin on his fingertips. I wonder what he thinks now?

And so we sit looking at each other, observing how darkness slowly makes everything colourless, until there are only reflections of the city lights. These are unforgettable moments...

Moments? It must have been hours! He has his hand on my feet and mine on his. Then, suddenly, he tickles the sole of my foot a bit. I respond in kind and we end up laughing. We are in love. My heavens! We both are in love! And what is more wonderful – we are in love with each other!

"Arnis, my diary just died. There will be no entry for today. I cannot write what I experienced here with you. This is for us to know and no one should ever be let in on it. No one!"

Arnis just nods his head in agreement.

"Ingrid, I have to admit that your wealth did influence me – and you – a most beautiful woman as my wife... and... and... I need a woman badly...

"But something is happening to me... something... Love has taken precedence over passion. If I have to choose between the two – I would choose love. I would want to protect rather than to have you.

"Love? What is love? A chemical reaction in our brains caused by secretions of glands, and we are lost in a maze of feelings that govern us for the rest of our lives...

"Yes, love can manifest itself slowly, but, as you can see, it can also conquer suddenly and quickly, in seconds, as a storm – and nothing can resist that. Nothing! Both of us, Ingrid, are victims of love, beyond the ability to defend ourselves – even if we wanted to..."

"No, Arnis! No! It's quite the opposite with me! What you just said is fuel on an already rampant fire! I have to get away from you, dear Arnis! I have to get away! I must run! I'm not sure of myself anymore!" and I jump up from the chair, and so does Arnis, topsy-turvy.

He's offering to see me home. There's no need for that – and he has to go to work tomorrow. He gives me his telephone number and sees me off instead. We part with a quick kiss that is known to both of us now. It's a bond not to be broken – it's a promise of return...

I'm still trembling while driving across the Don Valley Bridge. What has happened today is nearly unbelievable! In love! Engaged! Overpowered by passion almost to the point of no return!

I didn't think that it could happen to me, but it has – and nagging questions pester me: haven't I bought a husband and a *man* for myself, between yesterday and today? Have I? No, not true, but... still! Haven't I been at an auction of racehorses and ended up with the most desirable stallion? Even a used one...

Perhaps! But I'm a woman, and fighting not only for the man, but also for the father of my children. That is what being a woman is all about. Go and get him! If you don't – some other woman surely will. That reminds me: some other woman did, but foolishly did not recognize her fortune and let him go. It's clearly her loss, my gain...

I have done nothing wrong, and since I have created love in Arnis as well – that's what life is all about! Love and be loved!

Or is it passion? Could it be that it is passion only? Tomorrow or the day after shall, perhaps, answer that.

...No! It *is* love! I'm sure of it now!

*

As I get ready for bed, there is a knock on the door. I recognize it – it's Mother. She's in her dressing gown and I can see that she has not slept. I get in the bed and Mother sits on it, close by, taking my hand into hers. She asks nothing. I tell her what happened, and, freeing my hand, pull out my diary from the night table and give it to her.

"There will be no entry for today. Read it all now and give it to Father too. My childhood and youth is in there. I have nothing to hide, but do not show it to Astrid – let her develop in her own way. Keep it, dear Mother, there will be no more entries ever..."

With a kiss on my forehead and a gentle, "Goodnight, my

dear," she leaves me with my dreams.

What will Father say? I'm sure he'll trust my judgment... He always has... So it shall be now – I'm sure of that too...

My dear diary, do your work well...

Blessing

"And here comes Her Majesty, Miss Ingrid Johannsen, herself," I hear Father's happy voice and, with outstretched arms, he comes from the farthest corner of our living room to greet and receive me.

I was walking slowly, full of unresolved thoughts about today, its hurdles and my ability to overcome them, but Father is home and, in his voice, I sense his usual wholesomeness and positive outlook – I will not have to spend the day in miserable desperation. The battle shall be here and now, but I sense that I have already won. Have I?

"Father! You are home? You are home!" that is all I manage to say, throwing my arms around his neck and planting a kiss on his cheek.

"Where else did you expect me to be, Ingrid? Where else? Come now, come…" and we sit down in Father's favourite place, in the sunny corner he just came from.

Yes, our living room is very spacious, with a number of intimate niches: one for Mother – that is where she spoke to me yesterday morning; one for myself; one for Astrid; and this one for Father. As we grew up, we kind of settled in unoccupied territories as our favourite spots. I notice my diary. It's closed – top cover up. I wonder.

"Here! Now! Let me see," and with these words he takes my hands and lets them settle down on my knees as we sit down. Father pulls me closer and looks in my eyes – and I in his. I see him, as I have always known him – honest, fair, and loving.

"Yes, Ingrid, I do believe that you are truly in love and you know me – I have never wilfully destroyed anything beautiful; and love is, perhaps, the most beautiful thing of all: it takes all; it gives all; it consumes; it creates. No! I have no right to even touch it, particularly in my own daughter – nor shall I," he assures me in his usual sincere voice and a serious smile.

"I have read your diary and Mother told me about yesterday. We had a long talk. It's good that you slept in. It gave me time to awaken to the fact that we have a grown-up daughter. Mother is in the garden. She longs for the beauty of flowers today. Astrid has gone to a rehearsal. We are alone," and with that he pats my hands and releases them.

"Yes, we have a grown daughter and are about to lose her, but also gain a son. Your diary disclosed so much love for everything beautiful, as well as honesty, as we have tried to instill it in you. For that we are proud, Ingrid! Be at ease, we are not going to step in between you and your man. I am not going to try to see reasons 'why not', but rather – 'why yes'."

I jump up and taking his head in my hands, kiss him on both cheeks and his high forehead. I put my arms around him and settle right beside him as close as I can, without saying a word.

"But you do understand me, Ingrid, Mother and I must meet him and spend a bit of time with him before giving our blessing. Do you agree with me?"

"Yes, yes, yes, dear Father! Yes! I secretly planned to introduce him to you and Mother, just as soon as I have your permission to do so!"

"What was your battle plan? I know you had one."

"Tonight. After supper."

"No need for that. You had won before you got up. Your diary and Mother did it. Now, listen carefully," and Father continues:

"For a number of years I have planned our company operations so that, eventually, I can turn it over to you – should you decide not to get married, or your husband not be able to continue our family tradition. Therefore, the step that you are about to take will have an incalculable influence on all of us – the family, the company. Is there anything that you want to add to that?" asks Father.

"Father, your long-range planning approach and ability is also in my blood. Astrid already has her career and life laid out for her—"

"Yes, yes," interrupts Father, "that's why I didn't even mention her."

"The passion of a woman is waking up in me, Father, and the

possibility of not getting married is out of the question. Tell me, Father, how often does one fall in love?" I ask.

"Truly in love? Once, twice – some never... Infatuations and passions may come and go, but love? It just may be that in a lifetime, eventually, there may be only one true overwhelming, never-ending love, but we may recognize it much, much too late. We have lost it or thrown it away... 'It is better to have loved and lost, than never to have loved at all'. Who said that?" asks Father.

"Tennyson."

"During your high school years you had a couple of 'crushes', didn't you, Ingrid?"

"Yes, Father. I remember, but this is not a crush. I feel it in every cell of my body. I long for him. I shall belong to him," I whisper.

"Have you discussed marriage plans?"

"No, Father! How could we? Without your blessing! And Arnis won't have me without it. I offered, and he refused. Last night, Father, he could have tried to have me and almost everyone I know would have tried – single or married – particularly the married ones, but he has a code of honour that transcends the mere mortals around us.

"How I desired him! But we pledged to each other that even petting must wait until after we are married. It doesn't sound realistic, but, in so many other words, that's what was said and understood. If one of us weakens, the other one will come to the rescue. Dignity, self-respect and reliance on each other binds us with bonds made in heaven.

"He's not a stuffed-up Victorian pretender, nor will I ever be such a wife," and I put my head on Father's shoulder. "We will take all that love has to offer – body and soul... It will be beautiful..."

Father caresses my hair ever so lightly and lovingly. "When do you plan the wedding, Ingrid?"

"End of this month, Father..." and dreams are in my voice.

"End of this month!" he exclaims, and my head no longer has his shoulder for support. "That's in less than three weeks, Ingrid!" and Father becomes silent for a while, looking at me seriously. I've never seen him so surprised.

"Ingrid," he continues quietly again: "I visualized a big church wedding for you with a reception, dinner and ball.

"Well – not now, but in the past I have thought about it. I know, I know it would be contrary to our family traditions of peace, quiet and no glamour, but with a daughter as beautiful as you, I indulged in some daydreaming. I think that every father should be entitled to some of it. Don't you?" he asks with a wide smile and love in his eyes.

"Of course, Father! Of course, but look at the facts. I could marry Arnis tonight! No! Even better, now! But he has to acclimatize to the new life that is waiting for him. He has to register at the university; get various suits made and all that comes with it; learn to drive; get his driver's licence and a car; and so on. All of that can be done in three weeks, even two! Our honeymoon should be at least a month long, somewhere far away.

"That would take care of August. Then, September – get ready for studies. Not so?" I borrow an expression from Arnis.

"Yes, Ingrid! According to your schedule, it can be done – but aren't we a bit ahead of schedule?"

"Not mine, Father! I need him – body and soul," and then I whisper, "Three weeks is an eternity for me! Father, dear, dear, loving Father... I have never hidden anything from you and Mother... Now you know..."

"Yes, Ingrid... I know... Your diary is proof of that... Oh, my dear, dear Kitten... The flames of passion are reaching out from your body, but your soul is pure; and your mind, clear and logical... Blessed is the man for whom such flames burn... Blessed is the woman capable of such love... All of it...

"But that's not what I meant when I mentioned being 'ahead of schedule'! We have not seen your 'Prince' yet and there is so much to decide and so much work to do. Believe me – you, Ingrid, have our blessing, but he needs it too and I hope that we can give it to him. What are your arrangements?"

"Well, I told him yesterday that today I cannot see him at all – that I'll be busy with you..."

"Ah, nonsense! Can you get in touch with him?"

"In the evening, yes! Did you mean, now?"

"Of course I meant 'now'!"

"Wait! I may find him at work. He told me where he is. Just a second, Father!" and I run to get the nearest telephone book... "Yes! I found it! Should I call? What should I say?"

"Tell him to get home double quick, change and telephone you immediately. I'll send the chauffeur." Father is in action and once he is set in motion, things happen at home and the company...

Arnis arrives in the early afternoon wearing the same suit, perhaps the only one he has. After a short, but so sweet a kiss, I take him by the hand to Father and Mother.

It's my turn now to go to the garden. It's peaceful. Each and every blossom is so beautiful that I remain in our rock garden wondering about the beauty of nature in the plants and flowers, and as I feel it in myself.

I am not lonely – I am with God...

And then I see Mother coming. She has not sent the maid; she is coming herself. I try to read her face, but I see only her silhouette. It's better to remain with these blossoms – we both can sit down here, and I wait for her... She stretches out her arms; and grasping my hand presses it hard and repeatedly; and then I see – she cannot talk – she is crying... Tears of happiness run down her cheeks... We do not speak... There is no need for words... All is well... All is well... And we return to the house hand in hand.

"Come, Ingrid... Come... And you too, Arnis..." says Father, with hands raised invitingly. "Now, come here and both of you kneel beside each other," and I feel that first Mother, and then Father, place their hands on our heads... Silence...

"Blessed is this house with such a daughter and such a son..." Silence again...

"Now, children, get up and give your Mother and Father a kiss."

I hear Father's voice somewhere far, far away... I'm ecstatic, but feel that just now I've spent the last bit of my strength... The kisses and mutual best wishes took place, I presume, for only kissing Arnis wakes me up and I come to realize, the sun has risen again! It is true – there shall never be a dull and rainy day ever! Now I am in charge of it! Now it is entirely up to me to see to it!

I shall devote my life to it!

"May I call you Arne?" asks Father, while I am still holding on to Arnis with both arms around his neck, and over my shoulder, I hear the answer:

"Of course you may, Sir!"

"Oh, nonsense, 'Sir'! My real first name is Larf, but everyone calls me Ralf. Now, Arne, you are very officially engaged and, with Father's blessing, you may kiss your bride. Women like to be kissed and fussed about. Isn't it so, Gunilla?" asks Father, and only then I let Arnis – no – "Arne" now – out of my tender clutches.

"But Guna for short," I interject, fully awake by now. "Father, did you say that he might kiss me?"

"I did!"

"Well, darling, what are you waiting for? Up till now I've had to kiss you!" and we have our "official" engagement kiss supervised by Father and Mother. With it over, I run to Father and Mother and kiss them again.

"If you wish," says Arne, "both of you may call me 'son', but on my part, I have to forego 'Father' and 'Mother', at least for now. I hope that you will understand," and he kisses their cheeks tenderly.

"For that, son, you have our greatest respect," quietly come these words from Mother. "Call us Ralf and Guna."

"Somehow I do not think that I can see myself calling you by your first names yet. May I be permitted to call you Mr and Mrs Johannsen? For the time being? Just for a little while?" pleads my poor Arne.

"Of course, son, take your time, that's all right! I fully intended to call you 'son' just as soon as I laid my eyes on you – just as quickly as Ingrid spotted you, I pretty well approved of you. Now, Mother, the Johannsen family will, for all practical purposes, become 'The Petersons' in time… All in good time… Not so?" jokes Father.

"But now let's make ourselves comfortable. Let's sit down – there is much to be done," invites Father, and, continuing in the same breath: "Arne, by the way, did you happen to know that you will be a married man by the last day of this month – Saturday,

July 31, 1948?"

Arne looks at me and knows where all of that has come from, but before he can answer, Father continues: "Oh, that reminds me, first things first!" and reaching for his telephone he asks me whether Prince Edward Island (P.E.I.) would be all right for our honeymoon or do we, meaning me, have something else in mind. I had nothing specific in mind, but to be alone with Arne somewhere far away from everybody – anywhere.

"Do you mean Summerside?" I ask. Father replies with a nod. I know the place that he probably has in mind, but could it be done? I answer "yes" with a nod – just like two horses, I think at the time, and almost start to giggle... Father is busy with the operators and the party called.

"You are in luck, kids! You have the month of August in a very special place. I am making reservations. Okay?"

I nod okay.

"Done!" announces Father in a matter-of-fact voice, hanging up the phone.

"Now then, let's talk about you, son! A new life starts for you here and now. Do you want to pursue medicine?" asks Father.

"No, not any more. That door is closed and shall remain closed. I was planning to enrol in a business course – accounting, management, or similar."

"What do you think of Business Administration at the University of Toronto?"

"That would be splendid! Is there such a course?"

"Oh, yes! You can go to a Master's degree in it – or even a Doctorate later on, if you specialize."

"Yes, I shall take that, and right from the start – Philosophy as well! Is that possible?"

"I am delighted! Philosophy! That's what we need in business more than we realize!" and I can see immense pleasure in Father's face as he says these words.

"Ingrid, tomorrow you take Arne through the routine at the University of Toronto, and then without delay to our tailor. On Wednesday, I'll have the best driving instructor at our door. He will be with Arne until he passes the tests, say, 10:00 a.m. till 3:00 p.m. everyday. There's a lot of shopping to do. Try to get that done between 3:00 p.m. and, say, 6:00 p.m. Supper is still at 7:00 p.m. sharp. I'll take care of Arne's obligations to his employer and landlady.

"Wait a minute, I forgot. Arne moves in today, before supper – no later than 6:00 p.m. Ingrid, you give your time to Arne today and tomorrow. After that, while Arne learns to drive, you and Mother can go shopping. Arne will meet you at appointed places shortly after 3:00 p.m. – after his lessons. All bills are to be sent to our accountants, and I mean 'all'. Now, here is something for incidentals, say, daily cash spending money, and Father writes out two cheques from his wallet chequebook.

"Son, here is $10,000. Carry enough cash with you at all times until you become known in our circle of stores and services. You, Ingrid, have plenty, I know, but here is the same for you. Later this week we will set up your finances properly. This should do in the mean time. Okay? But remember, all charges to the accountants!" and Father sets aside his wallet.

I jump up and kiss Father and Mother. Arne expresses his appreciation very quietly.

"Kitten! When she was little I used to call her 'Kitten'," he explains to Arne, "Kitten, will you have a pet name for 'Mr Peterson'?" asks Father.

"I already have! It's 'Pet'!" I answer.

Arne looks at me with a broad smile on his face and in his eyes.

"Sure! It's 'Pet'! Isn't it, darling? Remember?" I ask.

"A very expensive one at that, as I can see," he replies, and the timbre of his voice is full of masculine promise for all my desires, but I must earn what I'm about to receive.

"Well, well, well – take my advice: 'Don't pet until wed'," laughs Father with all of his sincerity and pleasure to disseminate happiness.

He is happy. I see that so clearly and it makes me happy also. I run up to him, sit on his lap and embrace him. I cannot say anything – I have tears in my eyes. Arne notices it, and there he is at attention – with his handkerchief. Oh, my dear, dear, beloved Arne!

"We will not go beyond kisses and embraces," assures Arne

and I again nod my head in agreement.

Father pats me on the back and releases me to Arne. Yesterday I thought that I loved this man, but now I realize that the love of yesterday is nothing in comparison with the love I have for him today. How much more can love grow? Is there no limit?

"Mother, I feel like a young man again, when I was courting you," and Father pats Mother's hand and looks in her eyes.

"It seems to me that here are two very happy couples," says Mother, "both of them and both of us! Not so?"

I break out laughing. This "Not so?" is going to be a permanent fixture in our home now – Not so? I ask myself. This is too much, I shall die laughing, but a loud slam of the door saves me – Astrid is home and heads for upstairs in a hurry, like a whirlwind.

"Astrid!" calls Father, "come here for a sec," and the whirlwind changes direction and heads for all of us, but it freezes in its tracks as she notices Arne. Her neatly and closely combed red hair, held by a small matching ribbon at the back, and beautiful locks in a ponytail, and greenish-blue eyes, excel in the sun. She stands frozen as if smitten.

"Astrid! May I present to you Mr Arne Peterson – Ingrid's fiancée! And this, Arne, is our daughter, Astrid," Father goes through the formalities.

There's no change in Astrid's face, as if the words were not spoken. She lifts her right hand a little, still staring at him – his eyes, I believe, and it strikes me – is this another eye lock? Is it? Could it be? If so, my dear little sister has confirmed my choice! My dear little sister! And my heart fills with love and admiration for her.

Arne kisses her hand and Astrid's face changes from dead serious to joy.

"How do you do, Mr Peterson! You are the first gentleman who has kissed my hand... I shall never forget that..." she replies, and ends her sentence in a whisper, and then repeats again, "I shall never forget that!"

"Well, aren't you going to congratulate him and give Ingrid your best wishes?" asks Father.

"What for?" asks Astrid.

"They are getting married! Didn't you hear?" asks Father.

"No! I did not hear that!" comes Astrid's surprising answer.

"Did you hear anything?" asks Father again.

"No! Did anyone say anything? All I heard was 'Mr Arne Peterson'!"

"You have beautiful aquamarine eyes and your face is so fair and clear. Most unusual for a redhead!" Arne comes to Astrid's rescue with well-deserved compliments.

"I have no freckles at all anywhere, if that's what you meant?" asks Astrid.

"That is what I meant. You are a piece of non-existent art. I say that in the presence of your parents and my fiancée. It is so obvious! Light radiates from your face!" answers Arne in a most sincere and friendly way.

"You wish us well, don't you?" Arne asks.

"Oh, yes! You two are getting married? Why didn't anybody tell me?" she inquires insistently.

"Because we ourselves didn't know that until today," answers Father.

"So sudden! Are you in trouble, Sis?" asks Astrid innocently and we all start to laugh.

"No, Astrid, no – they only met on Saturday!" comes Mother to our aid.

"Saturday?" asks Astrid. "That's only two days ago!"

"Much has happened since then, Astrid. The last two days are more like two years," I interject. "Come! Wish me well," and Astrid does it in her own sweet way – kissing me on both cheeks. Then she walks up to Arne, puts her hands on his shoulders, lifts herself up on tiptoes, and with her lips slightly open gives Arne a long, long kiss, right on his lips.

"You are the first man I have ever kissed, and remember – we share everything, my sister and I," she spurts out in a most adorable way, and is gone to wherever she was going to start with.

"Our daughters did not have a brother. You may just be a brother image for Astrid. She is still young enough. But now, back to practical matters," invites Father and surprises us with:

"Do you realize that we haven't discussed the wedding itself? According to our schedule you're already back from your honeymoon, but not wedded yet!" he laughs. "It's me! I jumped over it by calling P.E.I., and after that everything followed, but the wedding!"

"Arne, darling, let's discuss our wedding with Father and Mother present," I say to Arne, and he nods in agreement.

"We haven't touched upon religion," I continue. "There is no pretence in it either. Our annual donations to various churches are considerable. We go to church individually as our hearts call us, and we go to the ones our hearts tell us. We are not bound by any one of them. Our family comes from Lutherans and we consider ourselves Lutherans, but we do not pretend to be better than others. How about you, darling?" I ask.

"I was born Lutheran, but have lived my life according to the wisdom of our ancestors going back more than 12,000 years. I find God in nature, the sky and the stars, and now in you, Ingrid, but I respect all religions equally.

"Whatever you want, dear. Whatever you want. It is the most important day in a woman's life. Particularly in the life of a woman such as you are," answers Arne quietly.

"We are fortunate that our religious roots are the same, but it would not have mattered had they been different," I assure him.

"My belief is that God knows everything – even if it is only a thought in our minds – just an unspoken thought; He understands everything; He forgives everything at the end, regardless of us.

"There is nothing that one can hide from God and no one can avoid or escape Him, because He is all around us…"

I listen to these words from Arne with pride and joy. He is one of the family! He is! I have a quick look at Father and Mother. Yes, I can see them rejoicing. I have picked the right man out of the crowd, not only for myself, but the whole family… I am so happy…

"Arne, I would like a private ceremony in our rock garden – just us – and the essential parties. What do you think?"

"Yes, let the infinity of the sky be over us when we are given to each other for life. Let it be so, Ingrid!"

"Could we leave it up to my parents to choose the minister?" I ask, knowing the answer.

"Yes, Ingrid, yes! It is of no consequence to me and I am not acquainted with any."

"Do you have someone that you would like to have as your 'Best Man'?"

"What is a 'Best Man'?"

"Well, someone close to you. A close friend to give you to me."

"Yes! All around the world, but not here..."

"To have a 'Best Man' is not compulsory. What do we do?" I ask.

"Better nobody than a stranger," Arne answers with decision in his voice. I consider that matter closed.

"Astrid will be my Maid of Honour and Bridesmaid all wrapped in one," I mention, and continue on.

"Here is something very important, Arne. If we are to have a private wedding, we must abstain from invitations. If we invite even one person, we must invite many and it mushrooms out of proportion. Then we could not be married by the end of this month. It would take months just to organize it all. This will hurt my girlfriends, but they will understand, being girls themselves. I hope they will, but there is no other way out!" I explain.

Now Father comes with a caution: "Kids, particularly you, Ingrid, must be prepared for the inevitable gossip and rumours so well expressed by Astrid and her innocent question. Everyone expects me to give you and Astrid big weddings. Not only in our social circle, but in the business world as well. How do we explain?"

"Tell them, Father, that I would not wait. It's the bare, honest truth. Could you wait, darling?" I ask Arne.

"Not if you can't!" comes Arne's assurance. "That is something that cannot be done by one party only. In marriage both become one."

"That's even better! Tell everybody that *we* couldn't wait, and mail out the social announcements accordingly! You know how to compose one to snuff out the tattle tales...

"Thank you, Father, for the advice. We shall mail them when we return. Would that be okay with both of you?" and Father and Mother agree.

"Could we ask Astrid to invite the witnesses from her profession? It would make her happy to be an important part of it all, I am sure!" I suggest.

Arne agrees. My parents agree. The proceedings of the most important day of my life are settled.

It is also decided that we will continue to live in the house after marriage and while studying. No worries or time consuming household details of any kind. My large bedroom will be our bedroom, and our present guest suite will be our study. Until then it will be Arne's "residence". While on our honeymoon, it will be transformed to our wishes.

Then Mother invites Arne to see the house. Knowing Arne's desire for a library, I am waiting expectantly for his reaction to ours. It is healthy, but then he is hit again – our enormous music hall with two grand pianos, harpsichord, violoncello and violins. He looks at me with eyes wide open.

"Music is in the family and comes from Mother. At the present it is mostly Astrid, darling. One might call her a child prodigy, but we don't. We tell her that there is still much to be done and, there is. The more gifted one is, the more is expected," I explain. "She is just thirteen, but good – very, very good.

"Piano is Mother's and Astrid's profession. Violin, Astrid's love and hobby. She still has some growing to do, thus the violoncello… It, in fact, is mine, but just right for her at this age. We both play these stringed instruments as well… Dear, I am saying all of that only so that you know. Astrid is the master – I play only for my pleasure and the two of us cannot be compared," I say in a quiet voice out of respect for my sister and her artistry.

"Then, Arne, there's Mother…"

"Oh, Ingrid! Don't burden Arne with such details now!" Mother interjects humbly.

"I'll tell you about Mother some other time. Okay?" and I end my chattering.

After the tour of the house, I take Arne to our huge garden and he discovers that we own the properties adjoining our backyard: across, and on both sides. Ours is on a private dead-end drive.

Father has planned well ahead for his two daughters, so that we can live separately, and yet be together.

We have an excellent cook. When still young, she lost her husband in an accident, and was left with two small children. My Father heard about it and saved her out of her misery. She is royally paid and her children have completed their university degrees with Father paying all costs. Now her children are grown, but she wants to stay and continue to prepare our meals – supervise, in fact, for she has helpers. She goes shopping in a Cadillac with a chauffeur.

We all eat the same, the servants and us. Our cook remarried and her second husband is our full-time gardener and handyman. All the lawn mowing and snow removal is done by an outside contractor. In Household Science, she will be my tutor in matters pertaining to the kitchen.

There are three chauffeurs, so that one is available around the clock – not only for us, but also for all household needs. That's why there will be different drivers of the limousine.

I tell Arne all of that quietly, as we walk through the garden and show him where we will be married. I am sure it will not rain on that day.

"This garden is overwhelmingly beautiful! I could not have imagined how beautiful – and we are going to be married here! We will be one with nature," he whispers in amazement.

"Now, Arne, be frank, there's a lot to be desired in respect to our paintings. Do not deny it out of politeness. Isn't it so?" I stop and ask him, looking in his eyes.

"One does not discuss religion, politics and taste with friends, particularly taste in the opposite gender, and paintings are just about as fragile as the opposite sex. I took a bold step talking about my beliefs; but I did so only out of respect for you and your family. All of you had the right to know.

"As for the paintings, you yourself recognized something and asked me. Yes, improvements can be made and, in good time, they will come in a way that does not hurt the feelings of anybody.

"Each and every painting that you have may have its history in your family, and that is of paramount importance. No one has the right to evaluate them for their aesthetic beauty at this point in time only. We will start our own, in our own rooms. It may just open the door and our paintings may flow over the threshold to the rest of the house without dislodging the ones that your family already has."

"Thank you, Arne! I did not look at my own question closely enough, but I am right? There is room for improvement, isn't there?" I ask humbly.

"We will do it together. I will explain art to you and we will select our works together. Only together and only if both agree. A painting becomes an active member of the family and influences moods and actions everyday," Arne tells me so gently, so very, very gently that I cannot resist, but take his head in my hands and kiss him right here – in our rock garden – where we are going to be married.

"Arne! Are you an artist?" I exclaim, ashamed of my own one-sided story about music, not knowing anything about him.

"In music? I played the violin from age eight to sixteen and became a fiddler. Have not touched it since, and will not in the future. Please do not ask me to play! Save the embarrassment, I shall not play… Painting? Yes, I was best in the class. I know art, but I am not good enough.

"But there is something that I am not ashamed to admit. Ingrid, I am a gifted writer of poetry and prose, and a good one at that, for my age.

"I am also a baritone, singing second base. It is not a trained operatic voice, but natural choir voice. Have sung since I was a little kid. As a POW, I was the anchor of second base, selected from some 20,000 men. It was a highly trained choir, a well-tuned instrument. We rehearsed some six hours a day, seven days a week, and were invited to sing even outside our camp. It was the most famous male choir at that time," and with this Arne stops and looks in my eyes.

"Do not be afraid. No one will ask you to play. Remember, we do not do such things in our family.

"I'm still ashamed of what I did to you yesterday. I didn't intend it that way. It just turned out badly. Do you forgive me?" I plead.

"There is nothing to forgive, Ingrid! But if you wish, I forgive you; it costs your Father plenty! Now, let's switch to something positive…"

"Okay, dearest! You truly are one of this family! The writing? That's in Latvian only, isn't it?" I ask.

"Yes, Ingrid, in Latvian only, but I can attempt to translate some of it into English. Later on, in the years to come I shall…"

And with this we return to the house, have a snack, and our chauffeur takes us to Arne's place to collect the suitcases of books and what little else he has.

I help him settle in his temporary quarters. Our hands cross handling the books, and again our eyes meet in immense relief that we are as far as we are. Slowly we take each other in our arms and our kisses now are not full of passion, but loving care… Soft and gentle… Soft and gentle… I've overcome my weakness of last night…

Before supper, Astrid surprises us all. She has taken my mellow violin, her favourite, and plays Beethoven's *Violin Concerto*, transposed by her with non-violin parts in it as well. During some passages, she walks up to Arne and seemingly plays for him alone. The call for supper comes just after she finishes.

Supper in itself is an elevating experience as well. We have a new place set at the table beside me, and across from us I notice Astrid's looks at Arne, full of admiration. Perhaps Father is right, a brother image, but I shall find out much later that it is not…

Then, Astrid's after-supper concert takes Arne's breath away. She opens it with the majesty of Tchaikovsky's *Piano Concerto Nr.1* – just the beginning while 'warming-up', and then she lets us have it – from composer to composer; from one great work to another; from ppp to fff; and all of it seems to come so effortlessly from her heart – from her very heart, and memory.

Her face has a faraway expression, as if not of this world; angel-like – and now I see it too – it does appear as if light radiates from it, just as Arne said earlier.

At times, she attacks the piano, and then she looks up, as if in divine meditation. It is not theatrics. It is herself, immersed in the divinity of her true art.

She does not look at anyone, not even Arne – not a single glance. At this time Arne does not exist for her, I am sure; nobody exists, but the music…

At the end she sits for a while, quietly and motionless, with head lowered and hands in her lap… Then she closes the keyboard, raises her head, puts her hands together massaging them a bit, and goes over her face with her palms and fingers and then quickly over her hair a couple of times; she stands up, walks towards Arne, and on her approach Arne also stands up.

"Arne, the violin concerto was for you alone, welcoming you to this family. What I played just now was for both of you… I do not yet know what love is, but it must be singularly beautiful. Tonight's works were written by composers while in the ecstasy and pain of love. So it is recorded in history. The day will come when I shall write music like that – when I grow up," and she gives Arne a quick peck of a kiss, runs to me and falling beside me, puts her arms around my neck and buries her face in my hair, resting her head on my shoulder. I pat her gently and there is silence… Arne sits down and looks on…

Then comes Father, picks Astrid up in his arms, and carries her out of the music hall with Mother rushing to open doors… I am sure I saw a tear on Father's cheek… He took her to her bedroom, I suppose…

I join Arne in his arms with my head on his shoulder. There are no kisses, there are no words. For the first time, we are joined by touching each other and that is quite enough. Funny, isn't it? A kiss would be out of place now…

Our family has just been united in a once-in-a-lifetime experience: the beauty of music; the innocence of Astrid; and the love of Father. It is some time before we join Father and Mother in the living room.

Astrid is resting…

To say the least, she has accepted the new member of our family with such love and grace that even we are a bit surprised, although we are brought up that way. This is just another proof of the wisdom of our family traditions – open, honest, positive.

It has been quite a day and I suggest that we say goodnight to Father and Mother, but tears are in my eyes and all I can do is embrace and kiss them.

Then I take Arne by the hand and lead him to his new suite to tuck him in, so to speak. Arne reminds me of something I have not completely overlooked:

"Ingrid, we may have another bobby soxer situation here."

"Arne, let me tell you something about Astrid. She is just thirteen, but looks younger – a five-year age difference between us. At her tender age she has already fully graduated from the Royal Conservatory of Music, in keyboard instruments, as a performer on piano, harpsichord, and organ. Yes – even organ – considering how much she still has to grow. This fall, besides high school, she will start in the composition class and I think that she will do very well. She is a rare artist with an unlimited future if she continues as she has in the past.

"And here, Arne darling, I have a request. Everything is in her hands. Be observant and try to help her out of situations that may cause damage to her hands, her fingers. Look out for her. No insurance can give back a damaged limb, that is why we have none. Money-wise we can keep her in almost royal splendour for the rest of her life, but she wants an active, participating life in her profession.

"Watch out for such simple things as slamming car doors shut. Can you imagine what such a mishap can do to her fingers, to her life? Watch out for our dear Princess," I ask, taking Arne's hand in mine.

"Of course, that goes without saying, but I still cannot comprehend that today I was in the presence of such greatness! Now I understand the significance of her performances tonight. Now I understand how much more there is behind all of what we heard – and I am the first one who kissed her hand? Oh, how many more are to come when she starts performing!

"I quite well understand that here, perhaps, one does not kiss the hand of a thirteen-year-old, unless she is your sister and I happen to be around…"

"Ha, ha, ha!" I giggle.

"Have you noticed how beautifully her lips are formed – just like yours – wide, full, sensual—"

But I stop Arne: "Yes, and you are the first man to kiss them – or, rather, you are the first man she has kissed—"

"It was a kiss of a woman – not a sister, and I kissed back. I am not a brother image," Arne interrupts me.

"See, the family tradition is growing on you. Other men would try to do it on the sly, or hide from their sweethearts, wives or wives-to-be, but you admitted it openly and naturally. I'm not jealous, but proud of you, my Arne. Your eyes locked too, just like ours? Wasn't it so?"

"Yes, Ingrid, they did."

"I saw and trembled at the very thought, that Astrid has seen what I saw in you on Saturday, when our eyes locked. Yes, I trembled in immense pleasure... My kid sister, I, you – my family – are in tune with each other. Your arrival is not a cause for disturbance, but of yet deeper love and pleasure in all of us.

"The possibility of another bobby soxer is real, not imagined, but do not worry, dear Arne, this family will survive that too.

"We share everything openly. She is only a kid now, but as she grows, we shall continue to talk to each other about everything, just as in the past. Now we will have so much more to talk about. Remember, she will soon be a young lady and you wouldn't want her to grow up ignorant of 'things' that girls should know.

"If a bobby soxer situation develops, she'll tell me. Believe me, she'll not try to do anything behind my back, nor will she try to trap you... Wait and see..." and I kiss him goodnight. It is a longing kiss and assuring that everything will be well... but at the door I look back and add:

"It was her innocence and honesty that spoke when she said: 'We share everything – my sister and I.'"

Roses

I am slowly waking up – too lazy even to open my eyes… I feel that the window blinds have been opened… My windows face the garden and the morning sun… Funny… I sense the fragrance of roses… Do all newly engaged brides smell roses?

Newly engaged brides! I have to get up! There is so much to do today! With all of these thoughts hitting me at once – I pop my eyes open. I close and open them again. It is true! My room is full of red roses! And as I spring up, with feet over the edge of my bed, I notice that in a crystal vase right besides me, are white roses…

Not a petal has been bent… Not a mark on any of them! It's so difficult to handle white roses, but these are as pure and undamaged as can be… What fragrance! What aroma! And when I bend over them, I notice a small, white, plain envelope: "To Ingrid". There's a plain, white card inside with a white rose embossed on it… I open it: "With all my love! Arne."

This overpowers me completely, but it just couldn't be! He couldn't have done it! I jump up, grab my dressing gown and down the stairs I go! It's early! Would anyone be up?

I see Mother first and she just points to Father's study. Yes, there he is:

"Where's Arne?" my question comes out almost like a shout.

"Out in the garden, Ingrid, but wait, sit down for a bit," asks Father, and I do – just on the edge of the nearest chair.

"Arne could not have done it, as you well know," he continues, "in as much as you did not send roses to Arne, or did you?"

"No, Father!"

"But he received them, and a card: 'With all my love! Ingrid.' – smack in the middle of a bouquet of red roses, and right beside the red are two vases of white."

"So, you did it, Father! And I didn't think of it at all!"

"No, I didn't, Astrid did."

Father's answer stuns me.

"Yesterday afternoon, while we were busy with other things," Father continues:

"Her concert last night was so moving. It probably reflected all the love that she so lavishly expressed in making the arrangements with the florist, but we did not know that; the concert alone brought me to tears."

I sink in my chair and lean back. My dear, dear little Princess!

"Do you know what the roses mean to Arne?" he asks. "The red – 'With love', and the white ones – 'From two darling sisters!' Well, Astrid could not have done it alone; we helped her early this morning, but not yesterday. Yesterday we knew nothing about it."

"Father, my very heart has been touched so deeply that now I must tell you something that came to my mind in bed last night. Could I ask Mother to come in and then close the doors?"

"Of course, Kitten! Of course," and after we have settled down I begin:

"Last night in bed, I thought about yesterday and found something that I do not like at all.

"The white roses this morning and what you just told me reinforced it. I had not given any prior thought to the location of our honeymoon, as you may remember, and your help in securing P.E.I. for us is most appreciated. We shall go there. But that is not where, in just any bed, I would like to give myself away to the first and only man in my life. It's so far away and such a meaningless place.

"I am pleading with both of you, let us go to our summer home at the lake a week early and remain there until our wedding day. That place then would become sacred to both of us and be right within the family. Would you consent to that? It is important to me where I become a woman. Very important, particularly now, this morning – after the roses, the white roses. Arne does not know about this request. It's all on my own!"

"Ingrid! The greatest pride a daughter can give her father on her wedding day is the opportunity to give her away as a virgin. With your plan, and in spite of the beauty of your thoughts, it would still be destroyed. It would be a pretence to wear pure white, just as the white roses signify," thoughtfully and slowly speaks Father and then continues:

"However, considering the deep significance you feel about the place of your wedding night – there is a simple answer: you can get married one week early; go to the summer home: and then fly to P.E.I.! What do you say, Mother?"

"Larf, that is the thing to do. Otherwise, by the time they get to P.E.I., they would be exhausted and dead tired, not a recommended condition to be in on a wedding night. As a woman and her mother – yes – let the wedding take place one week earlier. It meant a lot to me, Larf... It meant a lot to me, and it was at the summer home... Remember?" asks Mother.

And I see Father looking in her eyes and, I'm sure, remembering where I was conceived.

"Let's hope that the minister is available. How about you, Ingrid? One week earlier?" asks Father.

I have both hands on my cheeks, and with wide-open eyes I nod my head in agreement in utter disbelief of what has happened just now! One week earlier I shall be his and he – mine! Without destroying the significance of the wedding itself! I thought about it, but did not dare to ask! Now I have it! We have it, my beloved Arne and me!

The phone call was brief and answer positive – it all will be one week earlier – on the weekend following this... I still sit speechless, sinking even deeper in my soft leather club chair...

"Mother, considering Ingrid's present condition, I will go and find Arne... Oh, that poor man in Ingrid's hands will have to learn to be flexible!" Father gets up and walks away briskly.

When he returns with Arne, I try to read Arne's eyes... No, he does not know yet...

First comes the explanation about the roses and Astrid, mentioning that Astrid should have made a note on both cards, "per Astrid". What she has done is most adorable, but nonetheless there is a pretence to it. This will be an example for her to remember in the future. Father will handle that tactfully and in private.

"Now, Arne! Your wedding will be one week earlier, if you agree with it. We, that's Mother and I, have given it our blessing and Ingrid will give you the reasons. But, being her father, knowing her – and now knowing her very valid reasons – all I can say is: 'Blessed is the man with such a woman as his wife'!"

Arne looks at me and it does appear that the roses and all of this has confused him even more. On top of that, he also sees me for the first time in my dressing gown, right out of bed, not "made-up" – not that I have much to do besides combing my hair well.

"Darling, there is a very good reason for the change. I'll tell you all. Come," I say, getting up and taking his hand.

"By the way, Father, could you arrange a private showing at Birks for us?" I ask.

"Shall do right now! Oh yes, I hope nobody has any objections to making Arne a director of the Company?" asks Father.

"Nobody!" answers Astrid loudly and happily right behind us, although she is too young to have a legal say in the matter.

I grab her, hold her dearly, and kiss all over her little, darling face. Arne tries too, but she is too busy for all of this fuss. Her question is straight:

"May I go with you two to Birks? Come, I'll tell you why," and she takes Arne and me to the library and slides the doors shut.

"I cleared all of this with Father. It is okay. Now, you both require the customary jewellery. My wedding presents to both of you shall also be jewellery, and as Father has said: '...once jewellery is in the family – it remains in the family...' So, it must be valuable. It must be of good taste and liked by all. Details I'll give you later – just take me along, please," pleads Astrid.

"Of course, Princess! After what you have done yesterday and this morning for us, I cannot deny you anything!"

The sliding door opens a little: "Would 3:00 p.m. tomorrow be okay?" asks Father, leaning out of his study. We nod our heads in agreement. "So be it! By the way, I shall be at the office again starting tomorrow, but available to all of you anytime," and Father slides the doors shut again.

"Astrid, can you make it?" I ask.

"Sure, I shall be there," she answers and leaves with a quick kiss for each of us.

"Astrid! Wait! The wedding will be one week earlier, the

weekend after this!" and that stops Astrid on the spot.

"What!" she exclaims.

"Princess, I'll explain it all to you some other time. Can you cope with the change?" I ask.

"Sure! I have not spoken to anyone yet, but now I must hurry! Remember, it's middle of the summer. Are you sure about the date now? July 24, this year, 1948?" she asks inquisitively.

"Quite sure now, Princess! Quite sure!"

"G-bye, you two confused kids!" and with this Astrid is gone.

"Arne, come to my room," and I take his hand and lead him to the unexpected glory of a roomful of roses and their fragrance. After closing the door – and with my back leaning against it – I say with seduction in my voice:

"It is not the custom of this family to trap anyone, let alone young men by naughty daughters, but now I have trapped you! The only escape is bed!" and I look at him mischievously.

"Oh no, no, no, my darling! I shall not harm you! Just kiss me for the first time today," and I run to him between the roses and my unmade bed.

I kiss him and he answers, caresses my hair and then looks in my eyes with his very being, with his soul:

"Ingrid, you are most beautiful this morning. Just as you are – fresh out of bed. That means – you take your beauty with you when you go to bed at night, and keep it there all night long. How many husbands can say that about their wives?" he asks most admiringly.

"Do you really like me like this?" I tease him.

"Oh yes! Yes! After I have seen you like this – here – the week and a half will be an eternity in itself. Oh, how I desire you! How I desire you now," whispers Arne in my ear and holds me tightly, very tightly.

"Well, then you are in the same spot I was Sunday night! Oh, my dear, dear Arne, I desire you too, but it seems to me that it is my turn now to keep us cool," and I wiggle myself free of his embrace.

"That's only part of the reason in the change of our wedding date – there is much, much more. Once you know it all – I'm sure you'll agree, but do not make me tell you now, in a rush.

We've a lot to do today, but first I have to take a shower and get dressed. I won't be long," and with this I let Arne go. This is the first time he has been in my bedroom.

I now realize how quite unintentionally and unknowingly I have tempted him this morning – as he tempted me on Sunday. If he desires me so much as I am now, I shall be a very happy and most grateful wife. As grateful as a satisfied wife can be, with the fruits of love in her arms and hands.

While undressing, I go from one bouquet of roses to the next and stay with the white ones. Yes, Father, I shall be in white when you give me to Arne at the end of next week... I shall be as white as these roses...

★

The day presents only one problem – Arne's academic record requires a notarized translation. While our firm of lawyers does that – we go to City Hall to get our marriage licence. I whisper in Arne's ear the nickname this licence has and he turns towards me with a broad grin.

He is accepted in the third year of the BA course, with a provision that within two years, that is, before graduating, he has to pass three extra exams: English, Canadian history, and Economics – at our high school level. We both enrol in the same course of Philosophy as well. That means that we'll both graduate in the spring of 1950, and then again in 1952, and then...? We'll see...

At our tailors, I discover that in spite of his broad shoulders and long arms, he has only a 28½-inch waist – a definite asset in my eyes and in the eyes of all the girls I know... We get casual things too, for the lake and at home. He didn't even have a dressing gown.

The necessities of today are behind us and I take Arne to the Queen's Park – "our park" – and tell him of the reason why the wedding date is advanced by one week. He takes my hand and pats it lightly.

"Ingrid, you have your heart in the right place. I was also concerned about the importance of the day, the rush, the long flight, etc., all of which, I am sure, would destroy our wedding night, or how it could have been.

"I also could not accept the thought of registering in a hotel right here, where we live. It would make a masquerade of something holy and sacred. If there would be no other choice, your bedroom would be better. I was going to talk to you about it, but now that problem has been solved by you alone – and with the most beautiful reason behind it all.

"You had some courage to ask your father for his, and your mother's approval and sanction, for what I did not even dare to dream about. I am very glad that you did it. This morning when I was told, I knew that the reason for the change must be a sound one. Let us think about it and make it really memorable and beautiful," and he kisses me for it.

"There is a lifetime ahead of us. There is a lifetime to remember that it is the one and only night a woman has as a wife. It means very much for me too, for you shall be my first – such as you are," says Arne slowly and very quietly.

Yes, I shall think about it... I know the place... I will have my surrender plans ready... My unconditional surrender to him... We get up and beckon to our chauffeur.

On the way home, Arne acknowledges the convenience and time saved by having a chauffeured limousine at our disposal.

Astrid is not home yet, and we decorate the house with my red roses. One bouquet of my reds, with one of Arne's whites, are placed by the piano Astrid played on last night. The florist arrives just in time, with a huge bouquet of the most beautiful pink roses for Astrid. He supervises their placement in her bedroom, and one solitary pink rose in a special crystal vase by her place setting on our dining room table.

We are somewhat tired, but with our minds at ease. We are on schedule and talk about the day with Father and Mother, when Astrid rushes by with just a "Hi folks!" and she is gone, but then she comes back slowly with kisses for everyone...

We all have succeeded. Astrid surprised us and we surprised her. Today is, again, one of those days that makes our family so strong – the mutual expression of love in the most tangible and unforgettable way.

Had we been poor, a single rose would have been just as important and meaningful.

It is the thought that matters...

Birks

"Sis, how come you aren't shopping for your wedding gown and things?" asks Astrid briskly.

"We have an appointment tomorrow, Mother and I."

"May I go too? What time?"

"Of course, Princess, of course! It's at 1:00 p.m.," I say, looking at my darling sister and smiling. I may want to ask her the same question when her day comes.

"What kind will it be?"

"A very, very simple dress and veil. I do not want the dress to outshine me."

"Will it have a train?"

"A small one, perhaps, nothing to speak of. Everything shall be very, very simple, but that does not mean 'cheap'," I answer thoughtfully.

"Sis, I want to talk to you about my wedding gifts. Do you have time now?" asks Astrid and sits down beside me. We are in my niche of our living room.

"Sure! We'll be at Birks this afternoon. Remember?" I remind her.

"Yes, I know. Look at this," and Astrid shows me a drawing.

"They're cufflinks for Arne. Each with two aquamarines.

"For you, this," and she shows me a couple of drawings of bracelets. "Aquamarines again. Metal for both of you shall be platinum and only as much as necessary to hold the stones securely. It's okay, I checked with Father," she adds.

"My dear, dear Princess! Thank you! Thank you! What else is going through your enormous mind?" I ask with genuine surprise.

"Much! Too much to talk about just now! Let's stick with this! What do you think? Is it any good?" asks Astrid.

"I think it's marvellous. Now, one at a time. I do not see how Arne could dislike this idea. Two stones set side by side. It would look exquisite. Aquamarines? Is it because Arne called your eyes 'aquamarines'?"

"Yes, Sis! I love that word!"

"Astrid, would you have any objections if I give Arne cufflinks too? Just like these, but with emeralds and in gold. He called my eyes 'emeralds'."

"No! Not at all! I'm flattered by the thought that from time to time he will wear your emeralds and my aquamarines."

"Princess, this is a secret! I may give him at Christmas or on his birthday, cufflinks with very dark rubies – for that is what he called my lips," and I look at Astrid seriously.

"Sure, Ingrid, sure! Could I give him pink sapphires? It's the same gem, but pink!"

"That would set him up with such cufflinks for life! He would use ours on festive occasions only, I'm sure. We'll clear with him only your design, emeralds and aquamarines. If he accepts that, we know that we can go ahead with the rubies and pink sapphires too. What metal for your pink ones?" I ask.

"The same, brushed platinum."

"So, mine will be in gold, and yours in platinum! Okay?" I ask and Astrid agrees.

"Well, now, the bracelets!"

"Ingrid, it's only one bracelet, but I have two drawings for it. One with two aquamarines only, and the other with aquamarines all around. It's also in brushed platinum with a minimum of metal and maximum in stones. Which one do you think you would like the best?"

"The one with the gems all around it, my dear, dear Princess, but let's ask Arne too, and the jeweller. The other design is very imaginative, but I predict a problem – gravity. The bracelet would have a habit of staying upside down all the time. Don't you think so?" I ask.

"Yes! True! That is my first design and I came to the same conclusion. That's why I designed this alternative as well."

"Astrid! Whenever I wear this 'alternative', I shall remember your beautiful design of the original, and our discussion about it right now, but let's show them both to Arne and the jeweller – if that is okay with you?" I ask.

"Sure! Father has left the purse strings wide open!"

"Astrid, money spent on good jewellery is wisely invested. Father told me what to do. You'll probably faint when we start the whole thing with diamonds for me," I smile, looking through my eyelashes.

"Could be, but don't forget the cufflinks are 'made-to-order' and will cost plenty," and I hear concern in Astrid's voice.

"Princess, this is the first time in your life when you are directly involved in spending as much as we shall, but the time will come when you'll receive as much and, perhaps more, for only a few of your performances."

"Do you really think so, Sis?" she asks with a faraway look on her face.

"Do we ever say what we do not think?" I counter her.

"True. My question really was not a question, I was daydreaming aloud."

"Do not dream! Continue practicing as you have in the past and the world shall be yours," I encourage her.

"The world shall be mine with my compositions, Ingrid! Performers die, composers don't. But that is not the true reason. How do I explain the storms that I have in my mind? Quite a bit has been written already, but you have heard very little of it yet...

"I do not work on them at home because every piece should come to you as a surprise – something new, fresh and unheard of. Do you like it or not? That is the true test. And I want to hear the verdict from you, the family. But remember, all of it has been written before formal studies. Phrases of music come suddenly and I must fix them on paper, otherwise they get lost in the jungle of other music that I hear."

"That means that you are a born composer. You have what it takes. The studies will only teach you theory and techniques."

"True, I can harmonize instantly, but I have a lot to learn about orchestration. Yet, I already know much by playing the organ, but that is not enough. There are so many instruments and each has its specific tonal shade, its character – in the context of the whole orchestra, and I do not know that yet, not each and every instrument and its place. Yet, there is no such a thing as a 'proper' place for any instrument. It varies from composition to composition and composers have various preferences of emphases. All of this has to melt in my mind. I know that what I just said might not make sense, but that is how I feel before studying the subject. I may be way off...

"The answers for me will come, but you can be sure, Ingrid, I shall not be an ordinary composer, because what I hear is not ordinary. Unexpectedly, I hear a single instrument stand out and play a phrase, as a lark in midair over its nest. I have an innovative approach and unheard of surprises, not cheap effects – and all within the realm of melodic, beautiful music. Each composition with its own unmistakable, distinct personality.

"For both of you I'll have something simple to start with... It will be piano, violin or violoncello, or a combination... While you are away, I shall start to work on my compositions at home.

"Starting this fall I'll have to do that anyway, but no one should ever interrupt me and ask what is it, or what it will be. I shall play a composition for your listening only when I am sure and completely satisfied with it myself," and Astrid stops.

I look at her and see that she is no longer with me here in our living room. She is alone with the giants of music. But then she is back.

"Arne's birthday is December 31, isn't it? And he will be twenty-five this New Year's Eve? I may have something for him then." Quiet and thoughtful is Astrid's voice as she continues: "I do not know when the inspiration will come for both of you... I just do not know..." and Astrid leaves.

Soon enough I hear her playing again. It's not the music of a thirteen-year-old child. It's a master at the height of perfection. Will she be able to hold it? I ask myself.

*

We are early at Birks, just looking around for ideas and waiting for Arne. He arrives on time and, after the formalities of introductions, we are led to a private showroom.

"Mr Johannsen called me today again and we have selected, for your viewing, the best diamonds that we have at the present," and the representative opens a hand-held showcase.

Arne reaches out and picks up a ring with a medium sized solitaire, smaller than some other rings in the case. Nothing outrageous, just a bit larger than average. He turns it in his hand and asks for more light. A narrow beam of light is switched on and I see enormous sparkles.

"That is a blue-white FL, with exceptional brilliance – the best we have. It is rather small for its price, but that is more than compensated for by the bolts of light it will throw at a distance," explains the white-haired representative.

We pass it around and I compare it with other rings, but Arne insists that it must be a solitaire. We had agreed on that before we came, but it doesn't hurt to compare.

"Mr Peterson, why did you pick out that particular ring?" asks the representative.

"From where I am sitting, it stood out in its brilliance, and I was looking for a solitaire."

"Well, as I said, it is exceptional. Why do we still have it? People who can afford such a gem, expect a rock – and go for a rock. We have them too, but this one costs much more," he mentions the price, and continues: "It is the most expensive ring in this display case."

I look up in disbelief and then the ring is in my vision again. I start to comprehend its uniqueness...

"Ingrid, do you remember last Sunday in our park? All the stores were closed. I could not give you anything at all. Remember?

"Well, darling, this is it – from me to you on that day. I could have given you only a small fraction of this, and only the run-of-the-mill quality."

"Arne, would this then be for everyday use as our engagement ring?" I ask humbly.

"Yes, Ingrid, but only if you like it. Only if you like it as much as I like you to have it."

"I like it best of all the ones here, but such a gem for everyday use? Isn't it too much?" I ask again.

"One can keep it in the vault and think about it while wearing an oversized poor or average quality rock at half the price," he answers.

I try it on… It fits perfectly… And at this very moment I know that it is my destiny to have this as my engagement ring from the man I love so.

"It is very securely held in place – we double-checked its mounting before you arrived. Miss Johannsen, the reputation of your family is well known and our firm gives you an unconditional warranty against loss due to dislodgment of it, under normal use," states the elderly gentleman with distinct pride.

"Do you? I did not expect that much!" I respond in bewilderment.

"You are reliable people and we are a reliable establishment," is his answer.

"I love it, Arne, but for festive occasions it may be a bit too small and that may reflect on you," I say doubtfully.

"Ingrid, every day for us will be a festive occasion – every day – and that is what counts. For other 'festive occasions' you may have a rock as well – to commemorate our official engagement this Monday with the blessing of your father and mother."

"Are you sure you would not mind?" I ask ashamedly.

"Of course not! A 'festive ring' for 'festive occasions'! Nothing wrong with that!" Arne replies in a jovial voice, and he smiles.

"Astrid! What do you say?" I ask Princess.

"Take this one and place a standing order for a large blue-white FL with equal brilliance," is her straight answer.

I look at the representative with a big question mark on my face…

"We would accept your standing order if you are prepared to wait for such a stone. It may take years."

"Please accept it. We have plenty of time," replies Arne, and I nod my head in approval.

"We will place a special order for it. The rest is up to time. Such gems are in great demand by a select few. Most never get to the open market. The one you are taking now is a rare exception indeed and its comparatively small size has preserved it for you, but its brilliance has no weight – it will outshine most, if not all, that you shall see in your lifetime," adds the representative.

"Take it, Sis! Don't let it go!" interjects Astrid.

I look at Arne, lean over and give him an appropriate kiss under the circumstances. He smiles his usual wholesome smile and with that the most important purchase has been made, but Arne does not let me put it on my finger now – nor would he do it. "Later tonight," he tells me...

Then Astrid and I fuss over the wedding bands. Arne told me that he will not interfere with that, as long as his is a simple gold band.

I select a pair that we both like and show them to Arne. He looks at them carefully and tells us that the design is elegant and very appropriate to my engagement ring. The truth is – they are from that very set. The representative tells us that now. He wanted to see us choose them independently. Had we not done so, he would have recommended it. A very, very expensive set of *three* rings. That also may have helped to preserve it for us. So far so good. We are fixed up at least for next Saturday.

Then Arne asks for pearls – the ones set aside for us. He had called Birks about them earlier today from a phone booth while having his first day of driving lessons.

"These are the ones we picked out for you, Sir, but there are more in the store," and the representative opens another showcase.

There's a large one – teardrop shaped – with a fine white gold chain and matching earrings. Arne puts the chain around my neck. The pearl sits in just the right place and its size fits in with my features. It also has a peculiarity, it seems to be in constant motion and the earrings are dancing a mysterious dance. Yes! That is beautiful! My wedding gown will have to fit the pearls!

"This is my wedding present to you to start with, and there will be more to come every year. That is, if you like it?" he asks.

I do and so does Astrid.

We surprise Arne with Astrid's designs for his cufflinks and my bracelet. He likes them and we place the orders, but at the end comes a surprise for us. He orders a necklace based on Astrid's original design for the bracelet, but with five aquamarines. It's a splendid idea we did not even think of. Final designs for our approval and price estimates will be ready by early September. The jewellery itself – by Christmas at the very earliest.

Now we all want to see some of these gems themselves. Soon enough, a tray is brought to us with samples of emeralds and aquamarines. Arne takes them one by one and compares with our eyes:

"I was right! Both of you are two colours of the same gem, emeralds and aquamarines!"

Ring

After a quick shower and change, I feel fresh and delighted. There's still plenty of time to supper. That time of day, between 6:00 p.m. and supper, is for adjustment to quiet relaxation.

Supper isn't a rushed affair. It's the opposite – enjoyment in a jovial atmosphere, free and casual. It is the same tonight, but I am full of expectations for later.

"Ingrid, would you take me up to your room? I shall behave," asks and promises Arne, after the meal.

"Sure, darling, but do not promise anything. I may want you to 'misbehave' a little and provoke you accordingly." I laugh heartily, take his hand and, side by side, we slowly walk up to my bedroom.

Throughout our home the roses are now at their full beauty, half-open, and so rich. My bedroom is the very essence of the fragrance of roses. I close the door and we sit down on my sofa, turning toward each other and our knees touch again. Arne looks up and we both smile. I shove my knees against his and we break out laughing. We remember "our park" and last Sunday…

"Ingrid, I must tell you something. Relax and listen patiently," starts Arne after we settle down. Then he continues slowly, quietly and most sincerely. No – I want to say – very lovingly:

"If I am to touch the subject of your gifted family, your philosophy, your wealth and position – there would be no end of it, because where I am, and what I am experiencing, has stunned me. Perhaps the time shall come when I may be able to do that, but not now.

"Tonight I want to talk about you, Ingrid! You alone!

"Last Saturday I lost myself in your eyes and your beauty. Believe me, even as you walked away to get dressed – I did not observe the most feminine and beautiful lines of your body, let alone undress it with my eyes as men sometimes do. And then, when you were coming back – my eyes were on your long curls of deep golden hair, swaying with your footsteps and the gentle breeze. Can you imagine?

"During the last few days I have tried to catch up with what I lost then. Seeing you in different dresses, I recognize the beauty of the whole of you – not just your eyes, face, hair…

"Last Sunday, when you came to the park you had a pleated dress. With your high heels and a gait like a coiled spring of an athlete: when you were walking – your whole body was walking; when you were sitting – you left the impression that you were not sitting at all – your sitting was a continued movement. Your pleated dress accentuated all of that – revealing, not hiding, the beauty of your body. But I did not fall in love with your body, I fell in love with your eyes, your soul… The beauty of your body is only a highly desirable bonus.

"Yesterday morning you stunned me again right here with your fresh-out-of-bed looks. With you beside that unmade bed, was a temptation only a man can understand. I apologize for trying to keep some distance between us. It is an unhealthy situation, for I may die of a heart attack before our wedding."

"Ha, ha, ha!" I start to laugh uncontrollably and ease up to him, embrace him and my body's tremors make him laugh as well.

"Arne, and you have tempted me in a way only another woman could understand. Do not be mistaken – I have tried to undress you with my eyes a number of times and I do not know which version is the real 'you'," I tell him quite seriously looking into his eyes. "I would have to tell you that when I see the real you, but why not now? Other girls would not admit their secret thoughts, but I do. Remember, truth is the strength of this family.

"Other girls would be joyous, but pretend to be insulted if a man would disrobe them with his eyes. I do not pretend. I see in you the embodiment of the very principles of this family and am full of joy. Our souls seek each other and so do our bodies. It is marvellous!"

"Ingrid, you do not know what you just did!"

"What did I do?"

"I will tell you, Ingrid! I will tell you, but let me first tie us together with this," and he takes out of his pocket the engagement ring case, opens it, takes out the ring and, looking in my eyes, slowly slips it on my finger saying:

"Ingrid, with this ring I give to you my soul, my heart, my thoughts, my deeds and my body – for life. Can you accept it in the same spirit? My dear, dear Ingrid – can you?"

"Yes... Yes... Yes..." I whisper, raising my hand to the back of his head and with my lips slightly open, I pull him towards me, embrace him and our lips meet in a sensuous kiss. He holds me gently... It's good that we are sitting... I turn my back towards him, leaning against him, and put my head on his shoulder... Our kiss gets interrupted and as he is caressing my hair, face and shoulders I take his hand and put it on my breast.

"Through the dress it is not petting," I say quietly.

"Ingrid! You do not have a bra on!" exclaims Arne.

"True... I don't have any... I don't wear a bra yet... Didn't you notice Sunday night? For you tonight I put on a special dress... Tell me now, what did I do?" I say in the same very, very quiet voice with my head thrown back in a wave of pleasure that is overtaking me...

"You laughed and admitted having desires like mine. That was a deadly combination of punches. Now, what a minute ago was so far beyond reach, is now in my very hand. You have knocked me out, dear Ingrid!"

"Arne, take both of them! Take them and kiss me softly and long," I whisper and he obliges... When my trembling is over we disengage our lips and I look in his eyes and I can read them!

"Oh, Arne, darling! What have I done to you?" and I caress his hair and face.

"Ingrid! How do you think we shall survive the next week and a half?" he asks.

"I don't know... Tonight you have to be the strong one... I can't..."

Arne lifts me up, stands up and pulls me on my feet as well. We go to the window and look at the rock garden. He stands behind me and slowly embraces my waist and then my breasts... I lean back and feel him...

"Ingrid, do you remember that Sunday evening? And my apology? I could not dream of touching your breasts intentionally, and felt 'empty-handed'. Now I do not apologize and – as for my hands – this close is beautiful and quite enough to pull us through. My desire for you is being satisfied, partially at least. Even if you ask me, I shall not go farther. Better be forewarned...

"Just a sec! Turn around! I have no objections to touching your inviting buttocks!" and with that we are face to face in a kiss, his hands are on my buttocks and he presses me against all of himself...

"I am sure of one thing, Ingrid. I will dream of you and, they may be wet dreams. It happens when a man has not been with a woman for some time. It is natural. Nothing wrong with that, but I would not want the maids to see it."

"Oh, my dear, dear man! If and when it happens, tell me first thing in the morning and I shall take care of the 'evidence'," I say maternally.

He just nods his head in agreement. I do not see it, I feel it. He pats my buttocks lightly and we part. This 'woman-made' storm is over. We somehow shall survive them all.

I do not know it yet, but nature will help us. Expecting my wedding, I'm mentally all worked up and way early with my period. I will whisper that in Arne's ear and we shall both smile, clear sailing weather after the wedding. Victory! I shall be "untouchable" before the wedding and "very touchable" after! A double victory!

*

We return downstairs and one and all look at my ring. Father is exceptionally happy:

"You all did the right thing. Size alone attracts attention of the criminal element. This one, with all its sparkle will be noticed, but the size will discourage as a not-worthwhile undertaking," and Father pats Arne on his shoulder, lifts Astrid's face up by her chin, plants a kiss on her forehead and continues:

"A standing order for a 'rock' is also good. I know, I had to wait for years myself. But now, kids, we are going to celebrate a little!"

Mother has a special order European-made cake and Father,

champagne and cognac. For the first time, Astrid also is permitted to wet her lips with both. About the champagne – she tells us that it is too sour; and about the cognac: "How could or would anyone want to drink that? The smell bites my nose off!" and we agree with her wholeheartedly.

Astrid plays again. This time, happy and jovial melodies with childish delight and utmost virtuosity. The menfolk, Father and Arne, are still warming, nursing and sipping cognac. I stick with champagne and almost continuously marvel about my ring, small enough for daily use – yet brilliant – so very brilliant!

At the time of retiring, Mother comes to me with a warm smile on her face and in her eyes:

"Ingrid, you should start to wear a bra…"

I put my arm around her shoulders and answer naughtily:

"I know, Mother, but not now! I'm already starting to undress!"

Wedding Day

The sun greets me in the morning as I am waking up on my wedding day... It's early. There's plenty of time...

I look at the white roses beside my bed. So close and yet, I feel that there is a distance between them and me. Is it the sad feeling of goodbye for ever to all that is pure? No! It could not be! There is so much purity in one's soul – and nobody can take that away nor destroy it, if one stands on guard for it! No! White roses will always be part of me, Arne and the family – for there is so much goodness in our souls... And yet, every petal of these roses do seem like saying goodbye...

Perhaps to my youth? The innocence of my body? My mind has lost it since nature woke up the woman in me. Tonight my body shall experience the ultimate offering that a woman can give to a man. The roses shall be red from then on – and a rainbow of other colours, but never shall there be a morning of pure white again. Never...

Much has happened during the last week and a half. The rush hit me with the wedding dress. Once that was decided upon, there were a thousand other things: for me, for the lake, for P.E.I., for Arne.

Oh, yes! Arne and Father will have cutaways. Father insisted, for Arne would then have it available at anytime, and give us something to look at and remember when we are old.

And my dear Arne! He passed the driving test on the first try. The company bought its new director a top model Oldsmobile with automatic transmission, the first manufacturer making one. It's waiting for us – serviced, delivered and tested. It was a rush order, but we were lucky.

Poor Arne, he needed everything new, but himself. I'm so happy! So very, very happy! And I constantly remind myself that I am also very, very lucky.

*

With satisfaction and awe, I'm looking at myself in the mirror. Myrtle and a pearl and diamond tiara. Conservative. Petite. In good taste. It's from Father and Mother. It has taken them years to plan for it and, I'm sure, there is one in the works for Astrid as well.

My dear, dear folks! Do you know what is in my heart now? I'm sure you do: how proud I'll be beside my Arne and wearing it on formal occasions and at dances.

Mother is with me, and Astrid too – both attending to my dress and everything. Yes, my dress – it is silk, with a small train, simple, and very complimentary to the pearls and myself... Arne has not seen it yet...

"Ingrid, I want to be Arne's Best Man! After I have led you and Father to him, I can just step over, stand beside him and give him your ring when the time comes! Please, Ingrid! May I?" Astrid suddenly pleads, all in one stretch.

That wakes me up from my thoughts. "That's a very good idea, Astrid! I'd be happy to have you as his Best Man, but you have to ask him!" and with that Astrid is gone and back:

"He gave me a kiss on the cheek and the fingers of both hands and said: 'Thank you, Astrid!' and gave me your ring! Here it is!" and Astrid shows it, her lovely face beaming all over.

*

Variety and beauty of flowers engulf us in the rock garden. When the minister comes to the most eagerly awaited questions, we turn to each other and receive the rings from each other – looking in each other's eyes, as we did two weeks ago.

And it's done! We're married!

*

It all seems like a dream. About the same time we met two weeks ago, we are married and on the way to our country home at the lake. Another chauffeur is driving in Arne's new car a few miles behind us.

We do not kiss, but sit close together holding hands. When I'm not looking in Arne's eyes, I'm marvelling about my rings. How much beauty and meaning there is in these rings – an entire lifetime for both of us is there in a bond of promises…

As if knowing my very thoughts, Arne lifts my hand, kisses it and the rings and then, knocks with his ring on mine. That is so meaningful that I respond likewise, and from now on, this little ritual shall become our reminder of today – a renewal of our bonds.

We look in each other's eyes long and deep. What do we see? The unexplored depths of our souls. A lifetime will pass and we shall not yet know everything about each other, but shall never tire of seeking the unattainable, our inner selves – us.

I put my head on Arne's shoulder. Mile after mile passes and we do not have to speak, our eyes do that more eloquently than any language could. We are madly in love and heading towards the fulfilment of our destinies…

*

Alone at last! Just us, and the Oldsmobile, of course. We are at the lake. The wedding was at 11:00 a.m. and now evening soon will be here. We had a splendid supper on the way in. That's where we shall have our main meals.

All the goodies have been unpacked and put away, and I'm busy sorting our things – his, mine, ours…

Arne is reclining in a comfortable chair and observing me quietly. Nothing stands between us anymore; nothing holds us apart – but the unknown.

With everything done I go to him, stretch out my arms and pull him up:

"Let's go outside, Arne!" I say quietly. "Come, I have a lot to show you."

He kisses me first – gently, gently and softly. Our embrace is tender in our first real kiss as husband and wife. I am glad he so patiently waited until my chores are done.

Taking him by the hand, I lead him out of the house, show

him around and then down the steps to the lake – dipping my hand in the water and slowly swishing it about.

"Arne, say 'How do you do!' to our lake. Wait! 'Dear Lake, I present to you Mr Arne Peterson!' – 'Arne, this is Lake!'"

Arne swishes his right hand in the water just as I did.

"By the way, Lake, I'm Mrs Arne Peterson, former Miss Ingrid Johannsen! Remember me?" and I laugh:

"Remember, dear, this is the very first time I have been introduced as Mrs Arne Peterson! Isn't it wonderful? And to our lake!

"It's our lake now, Arne! Our lake and it shall be even more so by the time night will cast her starry cape over us. Over both of us – tonight and for the rest of our lives.

"Look over there! Do you see that small island of sheer rock? In the cracks of the granite some grasses and wild flowers find foothold and survive the coldest winters and the hottest summers.

"The last ice age has polished it as smooth as silk and, at one place, almost level. The rest is cracked and with sharp edges. Below the water, it drops straight into the depths, just as steeply as above, excepting the west side. There's an underwater shelf – the only spot safe enough for a dip in the water or a short swim. Be careful around it.

"Darling, that is where I would like to give you my body. I shall be part of that rock as much as the rock is part of this Earth. Be my Sower and Rainmaker. I shall surrender there and submit to you – just as this Earth does to seed and rain.

"Our souls merged two weeks ago. Now's the time for our bodies to follow. Isn't it funny? We so desperately waited for this and now – we are hesitating!"

"Ingrid, what we are doing is enjoying the mystery of mastery over ourselves. We can grab each other now and devour in an outburst of a short-lived flame of passion, or savour ourselves later with love and care. With love and care, softly and tenderly… The flames of passion will come regardless, but out of love – not for brute satisfaction. And then we will be united in our bodies and souls, and both shall be satisfied…

"The satisfaction of the body alone is an empty shell. It's much more important to give our souls the satisfaction they crave for. When the soul is satisfied – so is the body, but if one fails to satisfy the soul – repeated satisfaction of the body will still leave the soul screaming for more! And more! And more! And there is no end to its screams!" Silence…

"I'm guilty of keeping the 'appetizers' at your disposal, by touch and sight. When I was putting our things away, you enjoyed watching me. Didn't you?" I ask boldly.

"In the car your embraces were feminine and enticing. Here you were outright seductive."

"That was the intent, my dear. I wanted you to have me at the very height of passion, and I shall respond accordingly. I know.

"It was dreadful even to think that the long and tiring day might make you nonchalant!"

"I know, Ingrid! There is a purpose in everything you do. You make your body and mind pursue your target. It was so two weeks ago – so it was and still is today and shall be in the future. I admire your persistence in reaching your goals in a way your whole being dictates.

"It was such a pleasure to sit back and watch you bending, reaching, shoving and pushing – with the surety of mind that tonight we shall not escape each other. It was a double pleasure to see how you are 'ripening' me to perfection – knowing that that was your very intent.

"Do you remember that we discussed the possibility of me having 'wet dreams' and that I would call for your assistance? Well, as you know, I did not have any.

"Do you realize that a woman can entice a man to a point where he does not care who she is as long as he gets his relief in her? He may be sorry after, but not at the time.

"You have accomplished your goal. I am wide-awake and ready at any time to have my wife the way she wants me. I am also struck with awe of the unknown – how will it be with my first and last virgin?

"Oh, I desire you, but also enjoy immensely the air of expectancy of the experience to come – to both of us – to both of us," Arne speaks calmly and quietly, whispering at the end.

"The sun has set. Two weeks ago you stood behind me with your arms around my waist and we looked out of your window.

Come, let's do that again and look at the lake," and I look up to Arne and we do just that, but after a little while he whispers:

"And now, Ingrid, the way we looked out of your bedroom window that evening. Remember?" and his palms slowly embrace my breasts.

I hang back my head and he kisses my open lips... It's a sensuous kiss, a kiss that I had hoped for – the fulfilment of my dreams.

I turn around, embrace him, kiss him anew and, with my golden curls hanging down my back, look in his eyes again. He is pleased and hungry! I can see!

"Arne, darling, come!" and I grab him by the hand and we run back to the house. Without saying a word I undo my blouse and let it slip off my back. As I start to take off my skirt, he follows suit until we are facing each other, as we are.

I try to ignore his obviously aroused masculinity, but as we embrace – it is very much in the way... And then I feel its hot, pulsating growth to a size and hardness I could not have foreseen in my wildest imagination.

A quick look scares me. I am caught completely off guard. What to say? What to do? I wish we were on the island now, but then again – perhaps it's better that the island is some ten minutes away. It'll give me time to recover and, maybe, Arne shall not come up so big again, but that is what I wanted at the peak of his desire, and now I'm scared!

I stretch out my arm and pass to him a dark softly green bathrobe and take a deep carmine red one for myself. I put mine on and almost have to laugh seeing Arne struggling to get all of himself in his, but this is not a laughing matter.

Oh, how I imagined it all when I was shopping for us, for tonight, for the island! I could not have dreamed that it would turn out like this!

I'm sure he noticed my fright. I only hope that I have not insulted him, and in my mind – on the way to the canoe and while paddling it to the island – I'm pleading:

"Forgive me, Arne! Forgive me also for enticing you so! For me it was a pleasurable play, but for you! Behind the very great physical change, there must be a tremendous change in your mind as well – in your very soul! You spoke about that!"

I promise to wear a bra from now on – just as soon as we get back to Toronto and have them made – and never to entice any man deliberately – and you, my darling, only at the proper times and in the marital bliss. Marital bliss? How can such a monstrosity fit into my small, tender lap? And be tender about it?

But he wouldn't have married me if it wouldn't be okay. He's been married before! And I suddenly realize that his first wife was not a virgin. And he's had other women too! It must be okay! Babies are born too! We may be tender there, but tough too! I shall be in his loving hands and I trust him. I trust him, and with these thoughts we arrive at the island, just as it is getting dark, just as I had planned all along.

Sun has heated up the rock; we feel it with our bare feet. I take his hand and lead him to the smooth and even part of it and open his bathrobe – and mine, but we do not take them off. I put my arms around his naked body and pull him to me.

"It has shrunk!" I exclaim without thinking.

"My dear, dear Ingrid! Do not be afraid as you were at the house. Everything will be well. And do not worry, it will all come back and eventually get even bigger and harder – if you were not worried, but disappointed!"

"Disappointed? Arne, darling, I was worried stiff!"

"Then trust me. I shall be very tender and careful."

"I trust you, Arne. That's why I am here."

"You will just have to get used to my 'alter ego'."

"Your what? 'Alter ego'? Oh no! Is that what you call it? Ha, ha, ha, ha, ha..." I explode and no matter how serious and sensitive is the situation – I just cannot stop laughing.

My unexpected outburst has an eerie, uncanny sound over the lake. If not at the house, I surely have insulted him now: is the very first thing I can think of, as the echoes of my voice bring me back to my senses.

"I'm sorry, Arne! You are full of surprises. Come to think of it, I can call it 'alter ego' in public and no one will know what I'm talking about!"

"Yes, Ingrid, that is what I call it."

"Darling, I'm sorry! The name you call 'it' came so

unexpectedly!"

"Would you like 'my sidekick' better?" Arne asks suddenly and I'm going to break out in laughter again, but he takes my breasts and that stops me.

"Ingrid, I shall be brief. Very, very brief," he whispers again.

"I submit to you, just as this Earth submits to seed and rain," and with that I cast off our robes and Arne takes me in his arms, embracing me with the left and caressing with the right. Now I know how it shall be. I shall sleep at Arne's left, so that his right hand is free. That's the last thing I consciously think – before drifting in the pleasure of the present – in the arms of my man.

Soon enough his hand reaches my lap, and with the first touch it is all lightning and thunder. A heavy wave of passion is growing within me and I get down on the rock and ask him to come and take me away.

He does, slowly but surely. Both arms are supporting his body over me. I'm between the same arms that held that board when I slid on it two weeks ago, but now – not even my swimming suit – only his "alter ego" is between us.

No! No longer between us – it is touching me and playing with me so intimately and pleasurably in my wet and slippery… ah, it can go on like this forever, but then I start to tremble and press against him repeatedly in a premature orgasm. It induces Arne to come as well – in my lap, all over my belly, and even over my head go the spurts of his massive ejaculation… And I still am a virgin!

When this storm is over, Arne whispers caution. I feel pressure building up and then – a sudden breakthrough and a small, quiet outcry from me.

"I am in, darling! I am all in! Hold still for a while… Hold still," whispers my husband…

The little pain was nothing in comparison to the immense pleasure of feeling all of Arne in me. All of it, in disbelief. That must be where the pleasure is. And if that is not enough – with my pleasure mounting in rhythmic spasms my pelvic muscles are gripping Arne's alter ego even tighter. I lift my lap against him as much as I can. Now he is even deeper – all the way he can go, and I start to move in a way I never thought possible. It all comes so naturally and is so pleasurable that I whine with every thrust he makes. I start to feel faint and with tears of joy I have my husband for the first time in a way quite unimaginable and indescribable...

And then comes my climax with a loud cry of pleasure! And it lasts! And it lasts! And then I feel how Arne grows in me even more, as he said it would, and his thrusts become stronger and stronger and with every one I whimper, moan, groan and cry out uncontrollably. Then comes his orgasm. I feel every spurt of it – and I cry out for even more...

I start to slow down – the storm is receding, and I do not whimper any more, but turn my face from side to side in silence – still in the grip of passion.

His breath is heavy and deep. We are locked motionless and as tight as can be.

"Ingrid... you should rest now... for a couple of days... a wound is a wound... and it must have time to heal..." he tells me quietly with bated breath.

"I feel no pain, darling... None at all," I whisper back and notice that my voice has gained something – a deeper undertone over my sonority.

He puts his hands and arms between me and the rock, embracing me, kissing me all the way to my soul... Now I know what he meant when he said: "Satisfy the soul and the body shall be satisfied". I kiss back tenderly and caress his hair, his face, his whole body – as far as I can reach, and then I put my arms around him and hold him close to me – hold him close to me...

And so we remain locked together, not by eyesight alone, but now by our bodies as well, with my husband over me...

"Ingrid, darling! Now you are my wife – truly and for ever, and ever, and ever..."

I see stars twinkling above... Has one fallen in my arms? I am sure it has!

Honeymoon – Our Lake – Passion

It's morning. Late. I awake refreshed and feel the warmth of Arne's body behind me. We've slept spoon-like. I do not want to stir or to wake him, but he asks whispering:

"Ingrid, did you just wake up?"

"Yes, dear, how did you know?"

"I noticed it in your body and breathing."

"Have you been awake long?"

"No darling! No, – some five minutes or ten."

I turn around, embrace him sleepily and press my whole body against his. It feels so wholesome and wonderful. And we lay so quietly for a while – not caressing, just feeling each other.

Then a thought hits me and being me, as I am – and as my family is in general – I lift up our covers and look at Arne:

"Yes! This morning it's your 'sidekick'," and I lift it, have a good look and let it drop back down. "Now it's a nice and tidy bundle," and I look in Arne's eyes:

"You're none of the versions I imagined!"

"Do you like it now?" he asks.

"Immensely! And all my own!"

"Not entirely! I have to use it too," and as he gets up – he whispers: "I guess you know where I am going now!"

"Me too! Me too! Wait for me!" and so we go hand in hand, and part where we have to: I head for the little house with a heart on it; and he – with the new moon.

Then we have a hearty swim and go back to the house. While we dry ourselves, I notice Arne. His "configuration" has shrunk to a 'dinky-toy' miniature – just as I have seen on ancient Greek sculptures – neither here, nor there. It's the opposite with me, I crave for him.

"Arne! This is our first morning as husband and wife," and I walk up to him, embrace him and put my hand over his very tiny masculinity. It's very cold too!

"We both are cool and calm, but I would like to pet you and – shall it come to that – have my husband and be your wife in the comfort of a soft bed. I do not know that yet! Remember the hard rock? Then I will wait for the two days you asked me to."

"Ingrid, dear! This is when…" but I put my finger on his lips.

"Arne! It's important for me," and with that the conversation is taken over by our bodies…

★

We wake up from the light sleep that engulfs lovers after their bodies have received their dues and souls are at peace. We are in each other's arms lovingly curled up. I kiss him lightly and he opens his eyes. I look in them.

"My dear, dear Arne! Now I know what it means to be a woman and a wife. And all that treasure is ours for the rest of our lives."

"There is more to come. Much, much more. We cannot see that yet, but it shall come."

"More! How could there be more?" I ask in disbelief.

"It cannot be explained nor described. Put your mind at rest. This is the one thing that you cannot speed up, or slow down. Wait. It shall come in time and show itself inescapably and unmistakably – if one seeks it."

"And we shall never get tired of seeking. That's what I thought yesterday while our limousine was taking us here. Never get tired of seeking," I answer very slowly. Then there is silence again…

"Darling, I've an important phone call to make. That's my very first obligation as your wife. Don't ask me and let's not discuss it ahead of time. It's my private obligation, but for both of us. You'll see. Pick up the extension here. I shall call from the living room!" I ask the operator for my father's private line.

"Hello!"

"Hi, Father!"

"Hi, Kitten!"

"No! I'm not a 'Kitten' any more, Father. I'm a 'she-cat' with fully grown nails. You should see Arne's back this morning!"

"Oh?"

"Yes, Father, that's why I'm calling on your private line and as early as I can. By the way, I asked Arne to listen in so that he is fully informed, but, again, Father – he knows nothing – I'm the one! Do you want to say anything to him?" I ask.

"Hi, son! How are you?"

"Barely alive! Barely alive!" and I start to snicker.

"Ha, ha, ha! The news must be good!" laughs Father.

"Marvellously good, Father," I cut in, "but a bit of an extra worry for you. Well, I have spoiled your vacation this summer anyway…"

"Anything for you two! Anything!" assures Father.

"Now, here it goes. Father, I didn't know it, but now I do. I made sure of it this morning as well.

"I'm very passionate and make all kinds of loud noises that I can't control and Arne is just the right man to bring the whimpering, moaning and groaning out of me. I'm very sexy, Father, and, at times, I can't control my vocal expressions. Do we live somewhere else? Or what? It would make me very self-conscious about you two, but it's a 'no-no' for Astrid.

"Father, I must remain uninhibited. We must be free to do as we please – in our privacy! A Sword of Damocles over us may, in time, destroy everything! Remember, it's only now that he hears my plight and it's only now that I know our predicament!" and I stop.

"Ingrid! You are one of few blessed women! How about Arne?"

"We fit together as if made for each other. We both could go on all night, but he won't. I must heal first, he says."

"Does he have a pet name for you?"

"Just a sec! Arne, darling, do you have a pet name for me?" I ask over the phone.

"'Body Beautiful' – or 'BB' for short – if that is okay with you?" I hear Arne's voice,

"It's very complimentary, darling! Are you sure?" I ask.

"I'm as sure as one can be, at the present! Unless you do not like it or want something better?" he asks.

"Did you hear that, Father?"

"Yes!"

"You did? And so did I! I had no idea of it!"

"Don't worry! We all can use BB anywhere and at any time. Do you have objections? Not that it is any of my business," says Father.

"No! Just surprised! Very pleasantly surprised! Now 'BB' has a 'Pet'! Ha, ha, ha – a 'built-in Pet' – so to speak!" and we all laugh.

"Ingrid!" I hear Father's voice: "You are just as I predicted and Mother agreed.

"We already have two plans. As you know – our mansion at one time shall be Astrid's, because of the music hall.

"The first plan: we can get the larger mansion ready for you, but I think that that it is too early yet, while you both attend university.

"The second: we can drastically enlarge and completely soundproof your present bedroom. All you would have to do is, keep the windows and the door shut. How does that sound?" asks Father.

"The second, Father! What do you say Arne, Yes?" I answer Father and ask Arne.

"A 'Pet' belongs to his master and goes where the master goes, my Body Beautiful!" answers Arne teasingly.

"Darling, be serious! Did you also mean that the second plan is better for now?" I plead.

"You know me, Ingrid, and yourself! You know that it is 'Yes'," answers Arne, and I instantly know what he means: all the changes I have made during the past two weeks! Everything!

"Ha, ha, ha!" laughs Father, "I told him to learn to be flexible with you around!" and then continues:

"Ingrid, I know you, but despite that, I observed you both very carefully during the past two weeks and my mind is at peace – the Company shall be in good hands.

"So, do we proceed with the second plan?" asks Father.

"Yes, Father!"

"Do you give me a free hand?"

"Of course, Father! Of course! How else? And thank you. I called today to give you maximum time. We are faced with an unpredicted impediment."

"Not entirely unpredicted, but 'impediment'? No, Kitten –

joy! Every man is entitled to a sexy wife, but only a few are fortunate to marry one! It sounds to me that you both are blessed with the greatest treasure and pleasure there is. Enjoy it now – while young. Age will diminish it and even take it away at the end."

"We are, Father! We most certainly are! And thank you for the advice – we shall heed it!"

"From us both," comes Arne's voice quietly.

"Will you have enough time?" I ask.

"Yes, Ingrid, by letting us know today, I shall have the drawings ready by tonight. Five weeks is enough. I'll have it done in four, with enough spare time for a 'test-run'."

"Thank you, Father!"

"And I have a free hand? You are sure of that?"

"Absolutely! Are Mother and Astrid home?"

"Yes, they are."

"I would like to say hello to Mother and then Astrid. And, Father, I know that I have spoiled your vacation this summer, but thank you, thank you very much, once more!"

"You're welcome. Very welcome. For whom would I do it if not for you, Arne and Astrid? Now, here is Mother."

"Hello!"

"Hello, Mother! It's me!"

"Ingrid, dear, how are you?"

"I couldn't be better, Mother. I'm all set for marital life and all that it means. Father will fill you in on some of the details."

"I'm glad, Ingrid! I'm very, very glad!"

"Take care and don't worry about me, nor us! Is Astrid around?"

"She is right here awaiting her turn!"

"Hi, Sis!" comes Astrid's sweet voice, fresh as spring.

"Hi, Princess! How are you?"

"How am I? That's what I wanted to ask you! How are you?"

"Very well; very happy; very, very much in love."

"How was it?"

"I'll tell you all some other time!"

"Just give me a hint – in a nutshell – just a bit!"

"I was the Earth and he – the Sower and the Rainmaker. Is

that enough for now?" I ask.

"Oh, yes, Ingrid! Oh, yes! Beautiful! Beautiful! Beautiful! And did it happen that way?"

"Yes, Princess! Very much so. Much more than I could have ever expected."

"Sis, you do not know what you just did! I hear the music! I must rush now to fix it on paper! G-bye!" and Astrid is gone.

"Hello!" comes Father's voice again.

"Father, dear, that is all at this end!"

"Arne! My congratulations!"

"Thank you, Father! Thank you, for such a daughter and everything else – and best regards to Mother too!" and my dear Arne has just called my parents: "Father" and "Mother".

"Thank you, son! Thank you – for becoming our son!" and the line goes dead.

Arne called my parents "Father and Mother"! No longer "Mr Johannsen" and "Mrs Johannsen". We're now one big, undivided family. Arne has not forgotten his own parents and his nanny-stepmother! Oh, no! Not at all – only recognized mine. What a big step and through me! Love did it! Love, and his big heart.

I return from the living room, embrace him and hold him, kissing his forehead, eyes, neck and lips. I shall be worthy of this man – be his pride, joy and life itself.

"I have much to learn from you and your family. Such openness and honesty about everything, even the most intimate details!

"I hope that in time I can justify your trust in me and your love. I do feel that I have new parents, through you. I shall do the best I can to be a son worthy of what you all have bestowed upon me. The best that this man knows how."

"With the first day at university I shall start to wear a bra and it shall be part of my wardrobe thereafter. Now I know who I am and what I am. Enough of me is showing through my personality without flaunting my breasts around," I promise.

"A bra shall preserve their form, but cannot improve them!"

"Yes, I know, darling, but under control they must be! Don't worry! They will be custom made and not rob you of me, but protect your 'property' from the eyes of strangers. They're for your eyes only, darling! For you alone.

"I'm doing this out of respect for you, and the promises I made to myself in the canoe on the way to the island last night!" and I look at him.

"Is that how scared you were? Dear Ingrid! My dear, dear BB! You did not know that you are producing all the lubrication required! Did you know that?" he asks.

"No, I didn't! I've been wet there before when sexually excited and had a vague idea, but I didn't know, and in such a quantity?" I answer, ask, and kiss him gently.

"Of course! How could you?" and he caresses my hair with long, loving strokes to my bare back.

"Arne, dear, we're not dressed yet!"

"Ingrid! Walk away from me as you are – barefooted and then come back, please!" asks Arne and sits down on a low wicker chair.

I do as asked wearing a big smile.

"Now, put your high heels on and do the same!" he asks, and I do.

"Barefoot – you are a beautiful woman and, with good fortune, within reach. On high heels you are a goddess – unattainable!"

"But you have it!" I tease.

"Yes, dear, and for the rest of our lives."

"Somewhere there must be an answer for both of us. When we came back from the swim, you were a Greek god to me – and even without high heels," and I laugh, walking right up to him teasingly – right up to the tip of his nose.

"Do we dress now?" I continue to tease.

"Oh! Yes! We'd better!" and he embraces my buttocks, gives my belly a quick kiss, gets up and starts to dress.

I freeze in surprise. This man is everything to me and I'm sure now – I'm everything to him.

We dress and have breakfast.

Then I show him how to handle a canoe and we set out for the island in two canoes side by side. Arne learns fast, but I warn him not to be overconfident, only in time and with practice he may become a safe canoeist.

At the island, we stand hand in hand before the evidence of last night. Let it be just as it is. Nature shall take care of it all in its own way.

"Ingrid! After P.E.I., I would like to come back here. I would like to bring wild red poppy seeds and sow them in the cracks of this rock. They may or may not bloom, but I would like to try and see. And try again. There is enough thick moss, and some grasses have grown covering the cracks. It may just work!"

"It would be a wonder if they take root and blossom. And it would be beautiful. I'm glad you thought of it.

"Everything that we have is here: our hearts, our minds, our souls and our bodies. Only the next ice age may destroy this rock and, even then – not all. Some of it shall remain somewhere, and we both with it, but for the rest of our lives – this shall be our temple," and I put my head to his shoulder and lean against him a little.

"You have no idea how scared I was last night. It most certainly is not recommended for girls to see it aroused before the 'job' is done – before they know that it is okay and the pleasure it brings."

Arne is silent. He only caresses my head and my hair and then kisses me tenderly.

After we return from the island, we settle in a shady corner and Arne looks at me:

"Ingrid! Let me tell you how I see you! Your golden hair! The sun has made it multicoloured by bleaching it, with light shining gold on top and various darker layers of glowing gold underneath. Together, combined as they are, in long curls, they are beauty in itself, but for you – it only forms the framework of your lovely face."

"My hair is very thick. Constant brushing since childhood has stimulated my scalp, made it blood-rich, and thus its thickness. My beauty salon assists it with a little extra washing and curling, but otherwise, just daily thorough brushing is all that I need."

"Ingrid, could you let it grow a little longer? To the waist?"

"To the waist isn't a little longer"! That's a lot longer, but it can be done. It's below my shoulders now. It would take two to three years at the very least.

"With my hair at that length I would become a spectacle – I'd have to fight off admirers regardless of my married status! I had it that long once, and all the trouble – even at that age, or maybe because of it. I just had to have it shorter. But now I am a lot safer – older and married.

"You won't be jealous of all the looks I shall receive?" I tease Arne.

"No! I shall be proud, because you are mine alone."

"It is said and done, we just have to wait."

"I shall wait patiently. Can you think of me, and you, and all that hair? Ingrid! Can you?" asks Arne and now I realize the possibilities.

"Oh, my dear, dear Pet! You want a pet too? Isn't it so? And you shall have it.

"Come to think of it, I'll surely enjoy my long hair as well, to tease you with and feel your hands through those curls," I say quietly looking in his eyes again and thinking of the nights to come.

"Thank you, BB! That is the only thing that my mind can improve on your beauty," whispers Arne.

"I have very strong fingernails too and my manicurist is very happy with what she has done with them. It would be a shame to have them cut off, she would be in tears."

"No need for that! I shall buy you a pair of boxing gloves for my protection," he laughs and I laugh and it seems to us, the whole world laughs with us – at least our lake does.

"The nails shall remain. I shall be careful, now that I know what I can do with them. They are handy weapons as well, if need be," and we agree on that.

"To continue on the subject of you: your emerald green eyes are a subject in itself. There is a beginning of that story – Saturday, two weeks ago, but there shall never be an end.

"Now, your lips. Your natural light-red lips can grow quite dark when you are aroused, excited and kissing. They are muscular and very much the extension of your mouth – wide, well formed and just plain sexy – full of passion.

"One can look *in* the soul through one's eyes, but one can look at it in one's face. Your carefully cultured intelligence reflects in the face. It cannot be hidden – it is there. Faces may be dull and empty, rich and overflowing, or all the gradations in-between – and ash grey for smokers.

"What I saw in your soul through your eyes, is one thing; your face was a confirmation of that, and held me captive then, and now – even more. In the future, I may drown in them.

"Your nose takes an important part in your classic profile. Head on, it is neutral and does not detract from your eyes, your mouth and your determined, intelligent face.

"This morning, after the swim, I followed you and had my first good look at your body in daylight. Slender hips with a very feminine, continuing curve. Straight, beautiful legs with proportionate knees. Slender arms with long fingers. Your breasts cannot be improved on and you are very, very blond all over.

"I am a lucky man. Two weeks ago, about this time, I thought that I was very fortunate to have at least one date with you. I could not hope for more. And then you encouraged me to make a formal proposal of marriage. I could not believe my ears and eyes when you accepted.

"I did not know what to expect, maybe you already had twins at home and needed a breadwinner! All of that did not matter, if you truly loved me. Even if not as much as I loved you – at least you would know what difficulties are and we should both overcome them all, and in time, you would love me more than I thought you did then.

"I was concerned for both of us while looking at the mineral exhibits in that great hall of the Royal Ontario Museum.

"And then came your unbelievable story about your family and yourself, the early supper and direct disclosure of your innocence in respect to men. What you said in the park could be understood in a number of ways, but what you told me in my room was unmistakable.

"You said that you were scared stiff last night? Well, I was not scared, but concerned two weeks ago today, while waiting for my first date in this land – not knowing whether you would come or not. Even then, after you arrived, and in spite of your quick kiss and expressed wish to be my wife, I was doubtful whether I should be fortunate enough to have another date with you. I had nothing to offer but myself..."

"That's all I wanted. That's all I needed, but you, of course, at that time did not know that.

"Sorry, Arne, but I had to make sure of your love before you knew of my financial independence. When you proposed, I was in heaven, because you accepted me as I am: a girl, a woman, and nothing more. And you needed one."

"Yes, I did, but, if we failed, I doubt that I would have made another date with a Canadian girl. I would not want to be hurt again. You were someone very special and I risked being rejected.

"Yes, Ingrid, you are right. It seems to me now that so far my life has been a continuous preparation for that moment in the water, when I met the angel sent to me and for me. I hope that I have earned you and that I can compensate your family adequately," and with these words he puts his head on my lap and I caress his hair with my head bent and my curls hanging over him.

Silence... Long, long silence...

After a while I take one of my curls and, stretching it, tickle the tip of his nose. He turns his head up and I look in his eyes.

"Would fate have sent you help in the form of an angel as sexy as me?" I ask with a smile.

"Perhaps to punish me?" he asks.

"No, Arne! Food to a hungry dog is not punishment – in as much as a sexy angel is not a punishment for 'hungry' and well deserving you."

"Then you forgive me for doubting your motives at the outset?" he asks.

"Arne, darling, I have nothing to forgive. Remember, Saturday, two weeks ago, at your place? We were engaged, but, as you said, we had a lot of talking to do. We did not know each other.

"We're just two human beings out of the crowd of people around us. We were two strangers attracted to each other by our eyes, our looks and our desires to hold on to something that each of us thought he or she had found and was not to be lost in that crowd.

"Even if I would have lived to be an old maid – I could not

have hoped to cross the path of a better man than you, but that is besides the point.

"I love you, Arne, even if you would turn out to be the worst man in the world. It would have been too late to correct, because I love you, Arne!" and I continue to look in his eyes.

"I love you!" I repeat.

He raises his head and kisses me gently and slowly. There is no embrace – just our lips touch and I immerse myself in all that this one simple thing can do – in our kiss.

"I forgot to tell you about the most beautiful mouth full of bright and white teeth you have! You just bit me a little!" suddenly Arne says with a smile and we both laugh…

"What time is it?" I ask and then realize that we both have left our watches in the bedroom.

"Ingrid, I value your wedding present too much to use it here – outside. After all, it is an eighteen-carat expensive make."

"Wait a minute! I have forgotten something! Wait here, I'll be right back," and I run back to the house. When I return, I have a small package for him.

"This is for you as a part of my present!" and I give the small box to Arne.

He opens it carefully. It is a special watch for outdoor life and even moderate diving. Not too clumsy or large, just right for him, I hope.

"Thank you, Ingrid! It's just the kind I was thinking about, but did not have time to look for. Thank you! Does it show the correct time?" he asks.

"Yes, darling, it does! What time is it?"

"As of two weeks ago – we were feeding our 'kids' – the squirrels."

"Two weeks ago! The blessed two weeks ago," I murmur quietly. "What would have happened with us and our lives had we not met?"

"Think more about yourself – had I not survived the war!" he whispers: "I would no longer exist! That was the greatest possibility. Only a few survived in our unit.

"And then, think of the permutations of probabilities! The exact time and place our paths crossed! It is beyond human understanding!"

Silence... We both are thinking of that impossibility... Yes! The very thought that we could not have met is an impossibility for me to comprehend, although, in my subconscious mind, I know too well that our meeting each other is more than we can understand with a rational mind. It must be providence and even more than that. It may well be an act of God.

After a while I take Arne by the chin:

"Now, sit back and I'll tell you how I see you!" I say with a victorious smile:

"Your high, square forehead, very square, masculine jaws, forceful nose and mouth are only the forerunners of your eyes. The eyes are everything.

"Then, of course, your very sexy voice with a delicious accent and your slender body with very narrow waist, but broad shoulders and long arms are things that every girl wishes for! And your etiquette! But your eyes and face set you apart."

"Etiquette?" asks Arne, "I do not speak French!"

I do not answer, just smile and pat his head a little. French? It will come.

"Now I'll say something that I have not touched upon yet. Your face reflects all the intelligence others may wish to have, but can never obtain. But you have a very fragile soul. You have a very, very fragile soul.

"I shall do all I can to protect it from anything that may hurt. I shall place myself between the worst of this world and you. I much rather be hurt myself than to see you suffer. I shall be your guardian 'angel' as you just called me," and I embrace him around the neck and kiss him repeatedly, turning my nose from side to side in order not to collide.

I put my cheek on his chest and hear his heart pounding. He caresses me and we stand as we have become used to, with his right leg slightly between mine and it feels so good and reassuring.

Married, and with my husband I love so much.

So very, very much...

Honeymoon – Our Lake – Family

I take Arne on a canoe trip today.

It is early morning. A thin mist rises from the lake, but soon dissipates. Our lake is spring-fed and clear – very unusual for Ontario lakes.

The surface is calm as a mirror. I alone paddle along the shore and with the sun. We do not talk, just enjoy the sights and sounds of nature. There's also the beauty of a song – a duet – my paddle and the water. It is quiet, hardly discernible, but it sends waves of pleasure through my body. I know this song well and love it so much.

As our canoe slices the surface of the absolutely still water, we are joined by a school of very large black bass – all about the same size, somewhere between a foot and a foot and a half long, and that is large for bass, and so many! Fifteen? Twenty?

The fish are just below the surface and not the least bit disturbed by my paddle breaking the water – even those just out of reach, give a quick flip of their tails to gain some extra six inches, or so, that is all.

They're on both sides of the prow of our canoe. I continue at the same rate and with all my skill – no splashes of any kind. It is a sight to behold.

They look so slender that Arne mistakes them for trout, but he's behind me and cannot see them as well. Besides that, this is the very first time he sees bass – large or small mouth – and I quietly explain and point out the unmistakable features: they are like giant perch; the spots on the back; the second dorsal fin in particular; and the translucent tail with an almost black, straight, vertical line at the tip of it. Once out of water, the black line seems to disappear and no longer do they seem slender, they are fat.

"The bass are escorting us, just like dolphins escort ships," Arne whispers, "but of course, dolphins jump."

"It's beautiful! Isn't it?" I ask quietly. "I have not seen anything like it so far! Even the fish have come to greet you, Arne! Even the fish! I have grown up here, but this is the very first time I see such a spectacle!"

And so we continue until suddenly we are alone – the fish are gone! Ahead of us is a small bay. I let the inertia of the canoe carry us into the bay, stop gently and we are surrounded by its beauty.

I turn around to look at Arne, but all I see is sunlight on golden water and in the centre of it the dark outline of Arne amidst all this interplay of light. It seems as if he is crowned by the sun.

I know that I'm looking back, but do I see the future? Do I see my life with this man in glorious light and beauty? Everything points to that, but for it to happen, I must do my best and earn it, along with him. We both must do our best and then, perhaps, it shall happen – our lives become a beacon of light, if not for others, at least for our children. For our children.

I turn the canoe to follow the shoreline and stop – after all – I want to see my brand new husband. When I look back now, I see Arne admiring a water lily. He lifts it out of the water, looks closely and then puts it back in gently.

"What were you thinking about, Arne?" I ask.

"You, Ingrid! You! This water lily cannot be improved on, nor can you, darling. Nor can you, with that one single exception," and he looks at me and smiles.

"This white water lily is about the same as those in Latvia. Here, some stand a bit out of water, as lotuses do, but ours all float, just like this one," he continues.

A little further on, but still in the bay – we look straight down, and against the background of an almost white rock we see a school of small bass – some tiny; some a few inches long.

I throw something edible in the water and as it sinks only the smaller ones come to get it at first. A bigger chunk is too large for the small fry and, with them dancing all around it, it sinks deeper and the larger fingerlings get it. And so it goes over and over again until the larger ones forget caution and come closer to the surface to fight for any size and kind of food, until we tire of this game and continue our journey.

Soon enough there's a breeze and the surface shimmers in silver and now Arne is also paddling in time with me.

I guide our canoe and beach it at the foot of a hill. I shall take Arne up that hill, but first we have a hearty breakfast – we are hungry.

The hill is in a mostly white oak forest, but there are red oaks too and Arne tells me that the white water lily is his flower and white oak is his tree – the only type he remembers ever seeing in Latvia.

"And what else?" I ask.

"And you are my favourite wife, that's all," he laughs.

I lean over, topple him on his back and fall on him, kissing him madly. We embrace. Just kisses! What a store of treasures are kisses! Kisses given and taken in love.

We climb the hill and the tall forest fire observation tower. From here we can see the whole neighbourhood, but not our home.

The lake is not too large, but forests, forests, forests all around it. I show Arne the general area where our home is. Further on – a clear, small creek flows out of the lake in the direction of a muskeg swamp some distance away, and then brownish, to the nearest river.

"We have no aspen trees there, and therefore in the creek there are no beavers – never have been. It is entirely different below the swamp – plenty of aspen, beaver lodges, ponds.

"Now I'll tell you how all this began. Shall we sit down and be comfortable?" and we do.

"My grandfather bought this land in the 1930s. Times were bad and he did an extraordinary thing for that day – and I would say – for any day.

"He paid all the surrounding farmers twice the asking price and let them keep the farms and all arable land for ninety-nine years free of any charge or obligation. Only the lake and the forests he started to use as his exclusive property.

"Of course, all the farms belong to Father now, and we pay all the taxes and other assessments for all of them. So, the farmers got double the cash and kept their farms. Out of gratefulness they all got together and offered Grandfather their moral obligation to look out for forest fires and keep out strangers. Farmers do not fish much – they are too busy tending their farms, and fishing, in their eyes at least, is a waste of time.

"They may hunt for rabbits, grouse, pheasants, deer in season, on their fields, and may follow a wounded animal in the forest to retrieve it. There are no ducks on our lake. We can see and appreciate plenty of them in the swampy marsh and the creek below it. I'll show you all of that tomorrow.

"That ninety-nine-year provision runs out during the 2030s, and even then, the descendants of the original farmers, including all who married into these farm families, may keep the land in perpetuity, as long as they work it.

"There's another provision. If a farmer quits farming, the other farmers have the right to split the farming of that land between them, with the neighbours on either side having first choice on an equal basis. As long as there is one family left farming all the land, it is theirs to farm. What, eventually, is not farmed, reverts to us.

"They may not touch the forests without permission and such permission is granted only to take out dead underbrush. Dead trees may not be taken out because they are a part of nature, providing for woodpeckers and other wildlife that depend on dead trees. Even fallen dead trees must remain and rot away.

"There isn't a single public road leading to the forest. As you noticed, we entered through the courtyard of a farm with two strong gates. That farmer receives $10,000 a year for his 'trouble'. They are very grateful and, as you have seen – open the gates if any of them happen to see our car coming. Only the back gate is always closed. It is our moral obligation not to enter or leave our place during the night, unless it is an emergency.

"We also use their farm road to the fields, which imperceptibly blend in the forest, and then we follow a natural forest road under the branches of the trees, skilfully laid out by Grandfather and maintained as such by Father. We use it very seldom and it has remained almost invisible.

"In all of these years there has not been a single case of fire – large or small, or any kind of vandalism.

"The house was built by Grandfather and depicts the heavy

log construction so prominent in Sweden and Northern Europe in general. It's old-fashioned for today, but solid. The steep unusual roofs are built to avoid heavy accumulation of snow on them. The attic is used for storage of this and that.

"We have some internal rules as well. Canoes and row boats only, no motorboats. Father is entertaining the thought of electric boat motors – sometime in the future, but not now – we are still young and can row.

"No laundry is done here and washing is kept to the minimum, and even then, only with biodegradable soap. No chemicals of any kind are brought in: 'If one cannot stand the forest as it is, get out of it!' is our motto inherited from Grandfather.

"By the way! The same applies to our outhouses. There is more to them than may seem. A geological drainage profile has been made and the 'facilities' are situated so that none of their content may drain into the lake even after a heavy rainstorm or snowmelt. If it did, it would be right in front of our house and that just would not do. That is why they are so far – on the other side of the 'drainage divide'.

"Father wants to build a sauna and modernize everything, but he's still studying the drainage and other long term problems of pollution.

"He's still a young man, only thirty-eight. We have plenty of time for studies and apprenticeship under him. I meant 'we', because should anything happen to either of us, the remaining party can continue.

"Arne, dear! The family has been lucky so far. Anders Johannsen, my great-grandfather, who came to Canada and started the company, was an only child. He went back to Sweden in 1883 and married Matilda Ibsen, an only daughter. On my father's side, there are no relations in Sweden or anywhere else.

"We should have more kids to take over in time," and I look at him not knowing what his reaction will be.

"I do not mind having kids at all. That is if it is okay with you, dear?" He smiles and continues, "Remember yesterday? We were discussing the constant search for beauty, for fulfilment, for new venues in our souls! Having children will open the door to motherhood and you shall bloom in new blossoms, in new fragrances, in eternity itself. Seeking the unknown."

Silence... Long silence... We both contemplate parenthood and all that comes with it... He need not say it; I can read it in his eyes...

"Arne! How about another look around and then let's head for home and go out for a steak! I shall introduce you to the family of farmers 'guarding' our gate.

"I hope I conceived on the rock! Oh, how I hope I did! I'm in a very fertile period! There is a product of female hygiene that I can now use as germicide. Mother gave it to me. You cautioned me about my wound, and I inserted it after we returned from the island. I do not know how long it would be effective, but as long as it is, it destroys your seed as well.

"We should know before we return from P.E.I." I whisper and our lips meet again in a kiss of soft care and deep love.

★

After dinner we go back to our shady corner of yesterday and I tell Arne about Mother.

"Mother's is an exceptional and sad story. As you have noticed, she is a very young and beautiful woman – still only thirty-five, but very, very quiet.

"Her maiden name was Miss Gunilla Andersen. At the age of sixteen, she was already on an around-the-world concert tour as a professional pianist. She travelled with her rich father and mother, leisurely giving a number of concerts in a city and staying there to get to know the place before going on to her next concerts. Everything was carefully planned well ahead of time.

"She was in Toronto during the month of October 1929. That's when the Stock Market collapsed and the world economy with it, at least, the industrial world. Her father had to return to Sweden and there he had a heart attack. Her mother followed to take care of her father. After the concerts in Toronto they all were supposed to go south for the winter – New York, South America, and Australia, but events of the day changed everything.

"After the first concert there was a formal reception with a ball. Gentlemen in tails, etc., the works. That's where she met Father and a bond between them developed on that evening. Father was nineteen. That was at the very beginning of October.

"Father was on her card for a waltz. The entry had taken place during a momentary inattention of her parents and when the time came – Father presented himself gracefully and she went quickly, leaving her parents with open mouths.

"While they danced, and unknown to Father, but suspected by Mother, some activity took place, the result of which was my grandfather's and grandmother's introduction to the Andersens.

"My grandfather was a tall, imposing man and with the 'Order of the North Star – Grand Cross'; and the 'Order of Vasa – First Class' clearly in sight. The Andersens were surprised, impressed and mollified. Their daughter, after all, was not dancing with any Tom, Dick or Harry, but the son of this gentleman. Of course, they did not know that Grandfather had a lot in his head and very plenty in his pocket, having very recently sold all his investments, but in comparison to the Andersens, he was very poor indeed. With the Andersens it was the other way around.

"After returning Gunilla to her place and thanking her properly, Father was also introduced to the Andersens. Then, of course, Grandfather was introduced to Mother and Mother to Grandmother, and so on.

"After the introductions were over, Mother did the unthinkable: she asked Grandfather, Grandmother and Father to join them at her table. After those fateful words were spoken, Mr and Mrs Andersen had to keep quiet – after all, their daughter was the centre of attention, the cause of the celebration – 'the star of the show'! On top of that, Mother arranged that Father would sit at her left as her escort, isolating him from the elder Andersens. It was, after all, her table!

"That's how it all started, but Andersens would not hear of any talk of marriage to this 'nineteen-year-old boy' – no matter how tall and handsome he was. The Johannsens were nothing to the Andersens – nobodies.

"After the Stock Market crash the Andersens were wiped out. Grandfather offered every conceivable assistance, but the Andersens would not accept any – even after Mr Andersen died, early in 1930, Mrs Andersen still said 'No'.

"Finally, Mother accepted Father's request for her hand in marriage, in spite of Mrs Andersen's continuous non-acceptance of Father. Mrs Andersen died. We have no relations there either.

"Father and Mother were married on March 1, 1930, and I was born on December 15 of the same year. After me, there was a miscarriage of a son, and then, after some rest, they risked it again and Astrid was born. After Astrid, Mother could not have any more children.

"Mother did not return to the concert stage, but has given me, and Astrid in particular, our inheritance and all the music we needed to grow up with. She has not played since you came, but she will start again and then watch out, but Astrid is still the best by far.

"Perhaps now you'll better understand the two grand pianos! Do you?" I ask.

Arne only nods his head in silence.

"They were only nineteen and sixteen," I continue, "we are almost twenty-five and eighteen. That helped a lot. They did not want to impose on us what they suffered. They also fell in love in one single evening, but were married more than five months after that. What were those five months like for them? I do not know. Certainly it is something they did not want us to have in our memories."

Silence… And then Arne starts slowly:

"You all have entrusted me with unimaginable wealth: a wife; family; education; money; and a future in your company—"

"Pardon me for interrupting, Arne – *our* company – *our!* You're already a director of it! Remember! Hey! The Oldsmobile should remind you of it!" and I laugh.

"Okay, Ingrid! Okay! Now, the only way I know how to thank for it all is through hard studies and work. I know that I have a philosophy of life harmonious to yours, but I lack knowledge of a profession and experience in depth. In ten years I should have the knowledge and your father will be forty-eight. Give me ten more years under him, and I shall be ready to take the reins at forty-five and your father, then a respectable fifty-eight, at just about retirement age.

"My effort will be concentrated on basic facts, philosophies and issues, in those areas your company needs me as an integral part of the society and state."

"What you just said were the very reasons the King of Sweden used when decorating Grandfather so highly!"

"Well then, the King of the Swedes and I understand each other! Isn't it so, Ingrid? It is so!" he jokes.

"Yes! The Company; The Society; The State; Ingrid, shall be my all-encompassing considerations in my quest – for one cannot exist without the other two and it is far better for all three to prosper in harmony, rather than whither in strife.

"The Company... The Society... The State..."

Honeymoon – Our Lake – Adoption

I wake up very early and with eyes closed stretch out my arm to find Arne. He is not in bed. Oh! I wait, but he does not return. Where could he be?

I get up and tiptoe through the house. He is writing something at the dining room table and does not see me. That's good – I have not disturbed him, and tiptoe back to bed.

I wake up again much later. Arne is beside me on his back, with legs and arms stretched out and all covers off. My dear, dear husband, in all his resting glory and I feel a very deep attachment. Here he is – all of it – and mine for life. Oh, how I love this man!

I get up and bend over him to have a good look at his masculinity. This is my very first opportunity to do so in detail. Should he wake up now? So what! I am paying homage to something that has an important place in my life – his as well, I'm sure.

When I'm good and ready I want to lie down beside him again, but notice a sheet of paper on my night table, propped up against the night lamp.

I don't have to touch it to recognize the looks of a poem, and I take it with great care and expectation. As I begin to comprehend the title and the first verse, I hold my breath and my other hand covers my lips. My eyes are flying over the lines and at the last verse it touches my very soul.

I walk slowly away from the bed, sit down at my dressing table and start to read it again – very slowly and absorbingly – holding it in both hands now:

> To My Mother
>
> Mother, dear, you do not know it,
> But I am already near;
> There is nothing yet to show it,

But I know that I am here!

Soon I shall be in your care –
Small and tiny little me;
I will grow up year by year
And how proud of me you'll be!

Teach me all you know of life –
Teach me all you can to live;
Let me have your worldly wisdom –
Let me have your depth of soul.

I shall learn to know it all:
Not to stumble, not to fall;
But when I do – and I shall –
I'll get up and be well.

Time will come when I'm a father
Passing your gifts to my "kids";
We shall all be bound together...
Mother, dear! – My dear, dear mom!

Your Yet Unborn Son.

Tuesday,
July 27, 1948
At the lake

I let my hand with the poem rest on my knees and with a faraway look, gaze at the sky through the window and then turn my sights to the human being in bed. How similar are these two eternities! The universe around us and the soul of this man! And I join this man – my husband – in our marriage bed – slowly and quietly and with piety.

Arne is changing position, but he's still asleep yet, his hand reaches out for me and, taking my breast, goes into a deep sleep again. It feels so good in the heart and the breast! It shall feed our son some day, but now it gives his father something to hold on to.

So be it, there's a proper time for everything – and with these thoughts I put my arm over him and slowly fall asleep as well – and see a most beautiful dream: about our son at age five – here, at the lake, suntanned and very, very blond.

Now we are both awake and I roll over to him and kiss him softly and gently and long.

"Would this be it?" he asks.

"No, darling. No. Let our souls enjoy today as it began – with your poem. Who gave you that insight and those beautiful words to express it?"

"Poets are prophets. The feelings come from a divine spark in the soul, just like Astrid's music. The words follow. The words flow from the subconscious mind."

"Thank you, Arne! Thank you a thousand times. A thousand times – and even that is not enough. How can I give you something to strike you with awe? Just as much as you have struck me!"

"Give us a healthy baby, Ingrid! Give us a baby from the rock," he answers very, very quietly.

"Gender does not matter. Do not set your mind on a son or a daughter. That would be the wrong thing to do for the baby and us. Should it be a daughter – you would not want her to grow up as a 'disappointment', for sooner or later she would know – particularly in our family. A son or a daughter will be the will of God."

"I shall do my best. From this day on whatever I do, eat or drink – it shall be with that in mind.

"I didn't know that your poetry is so good!"

"It came too easy. Much, much too easy. I am concerned about plagiarism. Have I not read a similar theme somewhere? Not the style, the theme – the idea? I am thinking about Rudyard Kipling as a possibility. Isn't it a limerick?

"Well, it is a shadow only of what it could have been in my native tongue, but it is for my dearest 'favourite wife' now, and ever."

And I cast a shadow over him and this kiss is for a poet. All his life he will carry this wealth in his soul for himself, me, and the family. How fortunate I am to be his wife! When, where and how did I earn such a blessing?

I put my head on his chest and hear his heartbeat and the rush of his blood. Isn't this also awesome? Every second of every minute and throughout our lives we both are being kept alive by this miracle. All we have to do is live worthwhile lives to produce more than we consume; create beauty, love, goodwill, friendship; and leave behind us values of a permanent nature – values that can be enjoyed by next generations, as we are now enjoying those left by our ancestors.

"Ingrid! You have some plans for today. Let's carry them out. That will make it three days, instead of only two: a record – wouldn't you say so? Could we have believed that on Saturday or Sunday? But do not worry – once we start to celebrate our honeymoon in earnest, we will not have much strength for anything else," and he laughs in his quiet, wholesome way.

"Yes, dear! Today we shall see the creek, the swamp and the rest of it, right down to the river. We have to cover a lot of ground. So, let's get up!" but Arne holds me back.

"Ingrid, there is something very important that I have to discuss with you and we can do that in bed, safely.

"Your mother had a miscarriage of a son."

"Yes, Arne."

"Now, hear me out. What I have to say will surprise you no end, but it does make sense to me.

"I could be adopted by your parents retroactively and thus become a Johannsen. The minister may still be able to amend the records accordingly. By the time we return I will be a Johannsen, you will be a Johannsen again and our son will be a Johannsen. The social announcements will be those of the new Johannsen dynasty.

"I know that I can change my name at the time of obtaining Canadian citizenship, or by a court order, but that would take years and be too late for you and our son or sons.

"You willingly gave up the name of 'Johannsen' for mine. I surely can do the same for you!

"The very notion of imposing any conditions on you is repulsive to me: to have children or not; nor their genders; nor anything else, but, should we be blessed with a son – the Johannsen name could live on.

"The poem, my wish and this, are all tied up together in one – to continue the noble traditions and the name of your ancestors.

"Could you call your father and set the wheels in motion? If you agree and, of course, if your parents agree!

"The date of adoption could be, Monday, July 12, 1948, the very day your parents took me in.

"What do you say? Ingrid!"

"I am speechless, Arne!"

Silence...

"Take your time, Ingrid."

"And all of this for the sake of our family name?"

"Yes, Ingrid! Now that I know something about your family – it is a name worth preserving, and if we have sons, as I predict our first one shall be, they shall carry the torch of the future."

"Arne! You have become a giant in my eyes this very morning. You, undoubtedly, were a giant all your life, and now I know what I saw in your eyes on that fateful Saturday, but still did not recognize it fully. What other unselfish treasures do you carry in your soul? What other?" I ask.

"I do not know. Time will show – and that applies also to your, yet to be discovered, treasures. Only the passage of time shall disclose that. Continue seeking for them all your life, but one shall never find them all," answers Arne slowly and thoughtfully.

"Did you have a 'nickname' at high school, Arne?"

"Genius."

"That confirms everything I and my parents have seen in you. That confirms everything. Both boys and girls?"

"Yes, all."

"Oh, Arne, Arne! I can't put in words what this morning means to me. I noticed you were missing. I saw you writing. When you were prostrate on your back – I examined all of you in detail, only with my eyes, of course—"

"We will do more than that, Ingrid! I am sure," he interrupts.

I smile, take his hand and continue. "And then, in sleep, your hand was searching for me. Your palm took my breast and you continued your peaceful sleep. I'm sure your subconscious mind knew – I am here, all is well, I can sleep. That was after I had read your poem and returned to bed with it.

"You have made me fall in love with you all over again. Is there no end, no limit of how much someone can be loved?" I ask myself, but Arne answers:

"No, Ingrid! No limit!" and I kiss him as I have never kissed him before and then jump up:

"No! I'll lose control! Later, this evening – okay?" I ask.

"Okay!"

"Now I have to call Father! Relax! Stay in bed, you have earned it, after giving birth to all of this! You have done your share today! I'll be right here with you! I want to look at you while I talk to Father! Okay?"

I find Father at the office. He is as surprised as could well be expected, and more. He will call the minister first and then us. The social notices shall be held for later.

The phone rings! It's okay! This is only Tuesday morning and the minister has done nothing with our marriage papers yet. Everything will now be in the hands of lawyers, the minister, the witnesses and a judge.

While we are dressing the phone rings again. The lawyers see no problem and, peculiarly, just because it is midsummer – they may have everything in order by the end of August.

Mother is so emotional about Arne taking the place of her miscarried son, at least to the degree of preserving the name of the family, that she cannot come to the phone. She cannot speak – she is crying. Astrid is not home.

I turn to Arne and we cannot stop kissing and caressing each other.

"His name will be Johann Johannsen!" announces Arne.

It's just what I had hoped.

*

We're at the spot where our trout stream flows out of the lake, like over the lip of an overflowing crock.

It's narrow and small, bubbling over stones, in between rocks, and then resting in small pools. Other springs join it here and there. Soon enough there are deep shady pools under the branches of tall trees.

That's where the good fishing starts for speckled and brown trout. And then there are places where the creek has a very wide bed – lots of gravel, shallow water, and the beauties are there too, in the rippling stream, invisible, but there – nonetheless.

"Do you like fishing, Arne?" I ask.

"I am an ardent one, Ingrid! An ardent one!" he answers.

"Well, you'll have to forego fishing on this trip. I'm not sure of open seasons and licences. We have all kinds of gear. Father will surely enjoy showing you all he can and have your company. He will introduce you to these waters. Your time will come. Besides, now I want you to 'fish' for me!"

"But Ingrid! You are already 'in the bag'! The most beautiful trout I could have hoped for, the child of nature, you.

"It still does not seem real to me how similar we are, particularly in the forest, lake or stream. It seems as if we have grown up right here. Yet, one look at you and I know that underneath this goddess of the forests is my very sexy wife."

"Hey! Don't say that, or I'll have you right here and now! Remember, this is the third day and I am starved!" I tell him seriously with a smile.

"So am I, Ingrid! So am I! I would enjoy having you here in the open – as you are. Your jeans are very tight and have been advertising your very feminine lines and other features. I have been trying hard to ignore the most obvious temptations."

I walk up to Arne, take his hand, and stop, looking in his eyes:

"If you wish to have me – here I am – and shall always be – all my life, you do not have to wish for nor ask – just take me, Arne. Just take me," I say very quietly.

He kisses me gently and our embrace would have ended, and in the future shall end, in a passionate intercourse, but not today. Not today.

"Ingrid! Remember our talk on Saturday about the mystery of mastery over ourselves? Let us wait till evening today. Okay with you?"

"Sure, darling, sure. I just wanted you to know in no uncertain terms that you do not have to wish or think twice about it. I am yours anytime."

"The same goes for me, Ingrid! Just come and 'collect' your dues as a wife, whenever it strikes your fancy. Do you promise that?"

"Effective now?"

"Yes, now!"

"No! Not now! I do not want to spoil our plans for tonight. It's effective tomorrow! Okay with you?"

"Okay, Ingrid, effective tomorrow for you."

And we continue the enjoyment of our trout stream, the forest, wildlife – the sights and sounds of nature.

We reach the swamp and see our creek disperse in many small branches and disappear in the muskeg. I lead Arne by the most direct route around the swamp and an entirely different world opens before our eyes.

To start with, there's a huge beaver pond, and only the stream over its dam is the first recognizable sight of the rebirth of our creek, now a small river. Arne sees his first beaver, tail and all. It was in the open and gave a good splash after returning to the water. And so it goes from pond to pond. We see many ducks of all kinds. I tell Arne their various names.

Our creek has become a string of ponds that empty into the nearest river. I tell Arne that in this river one can catch rainbow trout, pickerel and pike.

This lower part of our creek runs through the property of one of the farms Grandfather bought. This farmer knows us well, mostly because of my father's fishing expeditions. We shall return through that farm, but first – lunch and a bit of rest.

On the way back we cover different ground, a huge forest, and at one spot Arne stops and looks up.

"Ingrid, we are in a cathedral!"

That's the way I have always felt about this place. Tall pine trunks with branches at the very top only. Practically no undergrowth due to lack of sunlight. The colour of the trunks changes from dark at the bottom, to reddish higher up, and then almost red. It's a sight to behold. That's why I took Arne here. Yes! He responds as I expected. He also is a child of nature – just like me! It feels so good to have a kindred spirit as a mate for life.

How many women are blessed as I am?

How many? Rich or poor?

Honeymoon – Our Lake – Explosion

The western sky and the still water of our lake is glowing in various tones of gold – separated by a black, jagged outline of the forest and its reflection. It darkens slowly and the colours change to orange and red.

The sun has just set and we are watching its blaze of light reflected in a myriad of colours. Wherever there is just a suggestion of a cloud, the hues are even more striking – red, green, blue, violet. The higher the cloud, the more dramatic is the reflection and interplay of light. What a display of beauty for every one of us – rich or poor! One only has to wait, watch out for, and appreciate it.

With the sunset, the moon takes a more and more prominent place in the sky. It has already risen and is full, low and large. In time it shall be almost too bright to look at.

Shine over us, dear goddess of the sky. Shine over and bless us tonight. Here are two of your subordinates on this planet Earth trying to find themselves in the well of pleasure. Help our bodies to find the ultimate fulfilment that only true love creates and satisfies.

I've had only a taste of it by the grace of my man. Give me a full chalice tonight.

*

The light of dawn finds us spent – after Aphrodite and Eros paid us a visit – so patiently waited for and desperately wanted…

And only then we are at peace…

Only then…

Honeymoon – P.E.I. – Night

The maid leads us, unlocks the door, and switches on the lights and a radio.

"Hey! Ingrid! Are you sure we are in Summerside, P.E.I.?" Arne exclaims.

"Why?"

"Listen to the radio!

Love somebody!
Yes I do;
Love somebody,
But I won't say who…

"There is no end of it in Toronto, as I remember! Is there no escape?" he complains.

"True, dear. Would you shut off the radio, please?" I ask the maid, and she does it quickly.

We order supper – boiled lobster for both of us with champagne and 7-up. Plenty of oysters as well.

"Until further notice, I would like a boiled lobster side dish with every meal," orders Arne.

"Yes! For me too! Whole, small and hot! No coffee nor tea for either of us ever!" I add.

"Is there a fridge here?"

"Yes, ma'am!"

"We would like milk and buttermilk in it at all times, various canned fruit juices and 7-up. Of course, freshly squeezed orange juice as well. We'll look at the menu and call in for tomorrow," I add.

"Arne, we are going to eat here alone, aren't we?"

"Of course, Ingrid! Of course," he agrees.

Arne tips the maid and porters and takes the key. The maid gives him another set of keys, "It's your car for the duration, just outside – the Cadillac," she mentions with a quiet charm.

We are finally at our honeymoon cottage in Summerside, and I run around examining the place.

"There are two full bathrooms, Arne! With a double-size tub in mine!" I announce excitedly. "That's what we want – a hot bath! Oh, my goodness! From the lake we went directly to the airport and then here."

Arne is sitting in a corner of an elegant chesterfield. I join him, tilt his head back and look in his eyes.

"Ingrid, we could not have experienced our first week here as fully as we did at the lake – thanks to you, dear BB. We shall never forget that, shall we?"

"No, Arne. Besides, I got you one week earlier, not so?"

"Me too! Me too!" Arne jokes back.

Yes! It is so! That golden week at the lake. Memories for the rest of our lives.

Now that we have gotten the first onslaught of bodily passion over and behind us – our real, more mature honeymoon will start here, but first we must take a bath, and we do. We'll "play" in mine in the days to come. After that, in night attire and dressing gowns, we sit quietly chatting about this and that.

The phone rings. Would it be all right to serve our supper now? Yes, it would, and soon enough we toast champagne and enjoy P.E.I. lobster in season. Delicious! I've only a little bit of champagne – the rest is 7-up. Have to think of our son.

Arne enjoys it instead, and for the first time I see him somewhat light-headed. Well, the best thing to do now is bed and we are in it with nothing on – it has become our custom.

Arne starts to kiss me all over. When he kisses my nipples it feels so tantalizingly good that I hold him there longer. There, where our son some day will have his daily bread. I just put my hand on his head and hold him tenderly and he kisses one, and then the other... It's heavenly...

I caress his hair with velvet fingers – the same fingers that at other times, like springs of steel, are holding him captive. Is it an animal instinct still left over from our ancestors for the female to hang on until satisfied? I couldn't have imagined that. It came by itself.

"Ingrid! I could kiss you like this all over – with the exception of that small orifice that we all have at the tail end," he whispers.

"Ha! Ha! Ha! Ha! You couldn't have put it better! 'That small orifice…' ha, ha, ha!" and I can hardly stop.

"Arne, there's something that I've desired all week at the lake, but I wasn't ready for it – it was too early, I couldn't. Now I can – I think. It would also be a memory of P.E.I. for both of us.

"What is it, Ingrid?"

"Could you introduce me to your 'bundle' and show me all there is to know?" I say shyly, sipping 7-up and looking at him through my eyelashes.

"Of course, dear, but right now I am somewhat aroused having kissed you so ardently," he replies.

"Could we do it properly, from a cold start? From that very-next-to-nothing-little-bit?" I ask again, with a naughty smile.

"Sure thing! A cold shower should do it!" and he jumps out of the bed and is gone.

★

"I love you, darling, and your masculinity. Even after a bath, it has a most peculiar fragrance. I noticed that at the very start – the whole 'package' and the musky air about it. It's a sure knockout for me. I love both of you – you and your 'alter-ego' with its 'travelling bag' – the proximity, feel, sensuality and aroma. You are not jealous of it, are you?" I whisper with a smile.

"My dear, dear Ingrid! What would we have done had we not met?"

"I do not know. I just do not know," I reply and jump out of bed, grab our glasses and come back, pouring for both of us.

"Now, my dear, dear husband – let us toast to ourselves," and we empty the glasses. I too. All of it at once! I kiss him, then pour a new glass for him and go to get 7-up for myself.

"Hey! Arne! There are twelve more bottles of champagne in the fridge, with an envelope: 'To Mr & Mrs Arne Johannsen'." I open it – there's a telegram to both of us. I open that too:

…CONGRATULATIONSSTOPWEHAVEDONEITSTOP
ONLYYOURPRESENCEANDSIGNATURESREQUIRED
STOPFATHER…

"Hurrah! Arne! You have done it!" and I jump and spill the last of the supper champagne.

"That calls for a fresh one!" and I go to get it.

Arne pops it open and pours. It's pink! He samples it, looks at the label and shakes his head:

"Where did he get it, and of all places, here?" he asks to himself.

We toast and empty the glasses – sampling it.

With the glasses empty and safely out of our hands, I put down the bottle, topple Arne over and kiss him; and kiss him; and kiss him. He's on his back and I on my belly beside him. He's somewhat tipsy even in this position, and I am a bit dizzy – I have had two full glasses of champagne by now.

We both are still novices in our marriage and immensely happy with each other. It makes me dizzy just to think that we still have a whole lifetime ahead of us – together.

"Arne, we can both enjoy ourselves with what we have. We can play and fool around, but that does not mean we should misuse what God has given us so freely to enjoy. Let's enjoy it all, but remain pure in our hearts.

"I love you, Arne, and would do anything for you – as I know you would give me all you have, and then some. I love you, my darling husband. Let's enjoy all that is good. Let's play with 'open hands' in the game of life, such as it is, in and around all of us!"

"I wonder where is the boundary of acceptable moral and ethical standards in love?" he asks.

"Who is to draw the borderlines for us, but ourselves? No one else has the insight in our souls, our hearts and the all-encompassing love. No one has the right to interfere.

"True! From the viewpoint of the community and society 'as such', we may have already overstepped some boundaries, but what we do, or choose not to do, in our sexual lives is not the standard of the community and society – it is ours alone… If our minds are at peace with it, we have done nothing wrong.

"With our marriage we have given our bodies something new to experience and know. We do not have to make excuses or justifications to anyone but ourselves, and that we have done.

"Our bodies have experienced pleasure and our minds are at

121

peace. We are at peace and that is what counts.

"'Beauty is in the eye of the beholder' – and so is ugliness," I remind Arne.

"Are we at peace with each other, Ingrid? Are we?" he asks.

"In my very soul I'm glad about this evening. We are becoming more like a normal husband and wife. I'm at peace and securely in your hands, my dear, dear incorruptible husband!" I exclaim and nudge myself over him kissing, and kissing, and kissing – but then I stop and look in his eyes:

"Arne! Let's toast again to everything that has so far happened in our marriage! Without the physical, there would have been no need for the mental exercises reconciling our inner selves, and the latter was the most important aspect of all – the foundations for a lifetime.

"All of that has strengthened our bonds, not weakened them! We have learned and grown tonight internally, at least I have," I say, resting on my elbows, and he raises his glass to my 7-up.

"We could, quite easily, expose ourselves to perversion and profanity, but have chosen not to. Your soul is pure, Ingrid, and that is what counts," says Arne, before lifting the glass to his lips.

"Arne! Let's look at the entire picture in the light of an academic discussion. You kiss my body: ear lobes, neck, shoulders, breasts, nipples, etc. – are they to be kissed? Is kissing them okay?

"Now, take our very lips. Have they been created for kissing? We have discovered the pleasure of kissing and that is what we do with our lips and call it 'kissing', but are they created for that purpose, besides eating, drinking, speaking and keeping our mouths shut?

"How about other races and cultures? Upon meeting, Canadian Eskimos rub their noses together, we don't. Do they kiss? Or just rub noses? I don't know. There are people on this planet who do not know such a thing as 'kissing'. I have seen pictures of some people with intentionally and grossly disfigured lips stretched out as horizontal rings. They can't kiss.

"But let's return to ourselves. So far we have not seen anything wrong in behaving as we have. What do you say, Arne? Have we done anything wrong?" I ask.

"No! You have given a healthy perspective to it all, Ingrid."

"Arne, dear, when I was beginning to feel that I was slowly becoming a woman, I read a lot. It was professional material. I prepared myself for life and made my decisions," I reply very quietly and then explode:

"But, in the meantime, you are my brother now, Arne!"

"Oh! That makes it even worse! We are living in sin! Do you realize that?" he jokes.

"Oh, well! We can't have everything! Let's now pour and toast to our husband-wife-brother-sister relationship! Skol, Arne!" and I lift my glass of 7-up.

"Skol, Ingrid! Skol!" he replies, we touch the glasses and they sing in reply.

We look in each other's eyes... Now I feel as if the 7-up alone makes me dizzy. Yes, no more alcohol for me. Got to think of the baby, if it is on the way.

"Ingrid, fill mine again for the night. Should I get thirsty, I would not have to get up."

"Oh, you'll get up all right, dear – after all that champagne!" I pour the glass and tease him.

Then I put the rest of the bottle in the fridge, turn off the night lights, embrace him, kiss him again, and again, and we commit ourselves to the waves of love.

I've become tamer and feel like a sponge, a blotter. I want to absorb him, soak him up. All of him. Yes! The honeymoon is a good custom.

Arne whispers:

"Sleep well, darling. Sleep well. You are right – 'Beauty and ugliness is in the mind of the beholder!'"

Honeymoon – P.E.I. – The Sea

Yes! We are by the sea! From dawn to dusk, seagulls loudly announce their presence everywhere. We drive around and end up at a beach on the north shore.

There's a breeze from the north. It's so refreshing to let it caress our bodies. We stand hand in hand on the top of a grassy dune and look north across the sea – the Gulf of St. Lawrence, in fact. The water is very shallow here – people are wading in far before there is enough depth to swim.

We change quickly. I have the same very pale brown swimsuit on – the one that I was wearing when we met.

"Hey! I know you! Aren't you Miss Ingrid Johannsen – the one I met on that fateful Saturday?" Arne asks.

"No! I'm not! I do not know who I might be, but it's Mrs for sure, not Miss!" I laugh.

"Yes, Ingrid! I do remember now the colour of your swimming suit and that it was a two-piece. I was eagerly waiting to see you in it again. Now, here you are, BB. What does that prove?"

"The opposite of what you said later! You were undressing me even then – after all! That's why you saw my body and not what covered it," I say looking in his eyes.

"Could it be so? Could that be it? Did my subconscious mind do that?" he asks quietly and then continues. "On our wedding night, I was sure that you had been wearing only two-piece swimsuits, but could not think of this particular colour."

"Perhaps it matched my tan?" I ask.

"That could be it! I distinctly remember how tightly it fitted you. You are not a 'dyed-in-the-wool' blonde – that is why you can tan, not burn."

"Yes, Arne, I tan very well, but Astrid and Mother burn."

"I can well imagine how Astrid's lovely white skin would turn pink and never tan, and it is so with your mother too?

"Let's hope that our kids are blond, but can tan – like you, darling," and he pulls me by the hand and kisses me quickly and lightly.

"Let's hope! Do we go swimming now?" I ask and we run down the dune, cross the beach and wet our feet. The water at the very edge is hot and the minuscule waves are boiling with the ever-present sand.

It takes some wading before we are knee-deep and the water is still swirling tiny particles of brilliantly shining sand around us. When we are up to the waist, the shore is far, far behind us and the water still warm. It's the northerly breeze, having blown the warm surface water to this shallow beach.

We wade, and wade, and wade until I'm up to my armpits and then we start to swim back toward our distant shore. At this depth there are waves, but my hair is okay under a bathing cap. We wade and swim, wade and swim.

Arne enjoys it immensely and is very surprised about the distance of the shallow water and its warmth. Well, he shall experience cold water too, after the wind changes.

After the swim we sunbathe. We are lazy and do not talk.

Seagulls fly over us and their cries sound like lonesome complaints and arguments. I would like to be able to interpret them as positive sounds, but I can't. No wonder, the existence of a seagull is not easy. They live here. We come and go as we please.

We will be gone? What has the future in store for us? What wonders? What surprises? What joys? What pains?

I turn my head toward Arne and open my eyes just a little bit. He is on his back just like me, but his right forearm is over his eyes, as if guarding them from sunlight, although we face the north.

Here he is – my husband in the swimming trunks I bought for him. Here he is – and for the rest of my life.

I took along the other trunks as well, those that he had on when we met, but, obviously, he didn't know my plans for today and didn't want to hurt me by not wearing these that I bought for him. Considerate gentleman at all times.

What does he carry within him from his childhood and his youth? Aside from the little he has told me so far? What is it that makes him as he is? Deep down? In details?

"Arne!" I whisper, not to wake him if he's asleep.

"Yes, Ingrid?" he murmurs.

"You told me that you know all about war and women, several of them.

"I do not ever want to know anything about your women, but could you tell me about the first girl who had satisfaction in your arms? The very first time you knew that it had happened?"

Arne slowly turns towards me and looks into my eyes for a while.

"Ingrid, it is a very, very dear memory – from the second year at high school.

"We were permitted to attend balls held by the school only, in its great hall, with extremely elaborate and beautiful ornaments on its very high doors, the ceiling, etc.

"It was a special high school, preparing future public school teachers – a six-year program and very tough. The regular five-year high school is equivalent to the first two years of university here, as we know now. The music was always melodic, classical and most beautiful.

"On one such occasion, I danced with a classmate of mine, a very slender girl, almost as tall as myself. It was a 'foxtrot' and we danced fairly close together. We just fitted that way, in a natural position, my right leg between her legs.

"After a while I noticed her breathing heavily, and her legs closed together, trapping mine between them. We made some five or more steps like that. The friction between her legs was very pronounced – as hard as it could be – and she trembled.

"What was happening was most obvious and I helped her by holding her firmly. After it was over I noticed that she had closed the gap between our chests – embracing me and her chin was on my left shoulder. We had danced too close. That was strictly forbidden, but it did take place. Only later I realized that girls mature much earlier than boys.

"Then we continued to dance as if nothing had happened and I did not in any way indicate that I had noticed anything. At the end I escorted her back to her place, thanked her, turned and walked away. We were not allowed to have more than one dance with the same partner during any given ball.

"We continued our school work as if nothing had happened. I did not approach her in any way. I did not want to jeopardize her reputation and the rest of her life – in case a teacher had noticed us during that ball and was keeping an eye on us.

"At the end of that school year, I left that school and city. It was spring 1940 and, on June 17, the Russians marched in our land.

"Later I was told of the beauty she grew up to be. She and my other classmates were the graduating class of 1944.

"I have her photograph, but will never reveal her name to anyone. Is that what you wanted, Ingrid?"

"Yes! Arne, yes! Beautiful! And you were a perfect gentleman!

"Do you know that I have had such experiences caused by your presence and touch alone?" I ask.

"Yes, Ingrid, I have, starting with that Sunday."

"No, Saturday, in the darkness of the cinema."

"I remember! You bent your head down too. I thought that you were suppressing a laugh!" and he turns on his belly, lifts himself on his elbows and looks at me seriously.

"Ingrid, have I struck you so deep?"

"You have, Arne! You most certainly have!"

"I did not realize you knew yourself that you are so hot – let alone tell your father! BB! Your 'Pet' is at your service, as you well know by now."

"Shhh... Let's not talk about it. Let's just do as we please! Okay?" I ask.

Arne just nods his head in agreement.

We go for a swim again, to cool off. It takes some time to wade in so far, against the resistance of water, but only further ahead is the water cool enough for us. Not many people have come this far. Most are with their kids and stick close to the shore.

Here we are – alone and I put my arms around Arne's neck and kiss him. It is a wet, somewhat salty kiss and we end up licking each other's lips and tongues.

It is a "soul" kiss and carries us to our paradise...

Honeymoon – P.E.I. – Travel

"Arne, I would like to show you this part of Canada," I say after supper one evening. "Here, I have a map. Let's see," and I spread it out on the table.

"There's a three-day 'Lobster Festival' in Shediac, starting tomorrow. We can leave on any of the two following mornings and still catch it. If we leave tomorrow morning, we can divide the time between Shediac and Moncton. At Moncton, I can show you the tidal bore coming in.

"Then we could go to Halifax and Peggy's Cove! That's here," and I show it to him. "You should see it at high tide as well as low.

"After that – north, along the Atlantic coast and then around Cape Breton. It's a most scenic drive. That's here," and I trace the route with my finger.

"The westside heads north and the eastside returns south again. That way we would travel the land, rather than the seaside lane of the highway. It's a small safety margin. The sun also will be behind us during the most beautiful part of that trip going north.

"That would take more than a week, but, believe me, it's worth it. I would be driving all the way, so that you can enjoy the scenery.

"What do you say, dear?" I ask at the end.

"Yes, but don't do it because of this isolated place. I like it here. I like to be with you and grow more and more accustomed to you – more and more appreciative of my good fortune to have you for the rest of my life. With you, I shall never be lonesome – although we may do nothing else but sit side by side and look out to the seemingly endless sea. Just to know that you are beside me is quite enough. Holding hands or embracing, even more so."

"Darling, I have enjoyed the last few days with you here, just as you described for yourself, just as much in love with you and just being near you.

"Shall we not make the trip then? We'd still have nearly a couple of weeks here after that," I ask.

"I would like to see this part of Canada, but only if you would enjoy showing it just as much as I would seeing it."

"Oh, I would! That's the whole purpose! It'll be part of our memories of the honeymoon.

"We shall be in different places and in different motels or hotels every night. Then we shall return here again – to recover from the constantly changing scenery, to the grandeur of this solitude."

"Let's start that trip tomorrow!" Arne agrees.

"Then we have to hit the sack early! Tomorrow will be a long day!" and we go to bed, after I inform the office of our plans.

★

The ferry ride is remarkable in itself – for me too. It has been a few years since I was here last. At Shediac, we have supper – our fill of freshly boiled lobster.

Shediac is a small place, but charming in its own way. We spend some time there the next day and after a lobster lunch – taking some along for a snack later – we head for Moncton.

Arne is very impressed with the sights at low tide and then the tidal bore coming in with such speed, size and force. After the bore we drive out into the country and watch it slowly flood. At high tide we seem to be in a different world altogether…

Halifax has its own wonders. We spend a day in Halifax and Dartmouth. Arne tells me that after leaving the port of Genoa, Italy, he couldn't wait to see the harbour of Halifax. After the ship stopped, he inquired as to when they would enter the harbour itself, and was told that they had already gone through it. Only then did he realize how small everything is in Canada, excepting the land itself.

The weather is beautiful, and Peggy's Cove is calm and at peace when we arrive at low tide. Below the high tide mark, all the rocks are covered with seaweed, full of snails in small shells. We would like to walk down to the edge of the water, but with every footstep, we crush to death a hundred or more of these small crustaceans. Arne stops and invites me to turn back – in our previous few footsteps. There's no need for so many to die – just because of our capricious wish to wet our fingers in the water. We'll get that at full tide.

We look out to the ocean, hand in hand; walk slowly over the smooth, water-polished rocks; kiss to our heart's content; and we do not talk – but now and then look in each other's eyes; embrace and let our eyes do the talking. There's peace all around us. The distant sound of waves lapping at the seaweed-covered rocks is soothing. The gulls? We hardly notice them now – they and we are part of it all.

Oh! What a glory it is to be alive and so much in love!

Peggy's Cove at full tide! In the harbour itself, fish have come in with the tide and are swimming in small schools, even just below the wharf.

The weather is just as good, but the water is full of movement now. The waves, small as they are, seem large and demanding.

We take off our sandals and let the water lap at our feet. It's refreshing! I see Arne's lips moving. He is obviously saying something, but I can't hear what. Although the sea is calm, the roar of the waves is still too loud.

"What?" I shout.

"We are one with the nature now!" he shouts back.

I just nod my head and remember our walk along the trout stream at the lake. Yes, we are two kids of nature – and always will be.

When we kiss now, our kisses are stronger, not mellow as they were at low tide. The presence of the ocean at our very feet intensifies everything. Arne is holding me with more strength, as if the waves could sweep me away.

And then, there is another grandeur for our sights to behold – sea, mountains and the winding Cabot Trail on the western slope of Cape Breton.

This is a very silent grandeur, absorbed by our senses and souls in a much different way. It quietly settles in one's mind and subconsciousness permanently. Once seen, experienced and appreciated – it never leaves – it forms a part of us, our feelings, our thoughts, and our deeds.

★

After our return – we doubly enjoy the peace and quiet of our cottage at Summerside – including our dear friends, the seagulls. We have become accustomed to their cries. Now our days and evenings are spent in already familiar surroundings.

After a couple of days of good weather with swimming and sunbathing – a storm arrives and we let the wind chill our bodies and the first drops of rain pelt them until we're almost numb.

We run in then, get out of our swimsuits and jump into my large bathtub – filled with warm water ahead of time. Soon enough the numbness is gone and we play around.

Arne took a dip in the Atlantic on the way to Cape Breton and told me that he couldn't feel his legs up to his knees. That's how numb they were. I had to massage life back into them again. Oh, it was cold, but Arne wanted to know that he had swum in the open Atlantic. So there! He's done it and we remember that in the warmth of my bathtub.

There's no one to tell us now, that in the years to come, he will swim in the Pacific Ocean at Long Beach on the west coast of Vancouver Island on a cold, cold day. No one else dared, but he did it. Even a car stopped to watch the unbelievable.

"What fragrance do you like?" I ask.

"Jasmine!"

I push around various containers of bath salts and yes! We have some!

"Eureka!"

"Good," replies Arne lazily and I pour enough in the tub.

"The whole cottage will smell of jasmine now!" I laugh.

"Good! We too! Not so?"

"Ha, ha, ha… ha… ha…"

I lean back in the water and slowly embrace him. He puts his hand on my breast and it feels wonderful…

What a glory it is to be alive and so much in love!

Honeymoon – P.E.I. – Russians

The next day is still under the influence of the cold front. It's windy. We drive out to the north shore and now Arne finds the water cold, even at the very edge. The sea is angry. We take a walk and decide to return to our nest. Arne is going to tell me about the war.

We settle down facing each other, closely and comfortably, with glasses of 7-up handy.

First I look in his eyes and kiss him lightly. I'm ready.

*

Silence... And then Arne starts:

"I was fourteen when, in 1938, Russia demanded and received military bases in Latvia. Our government gave them the bases against its will and the will of the people, but we were reminded of what happened to Finland who said: 'No...'

"Upon arrival and depending on the location, Russian officers and their wives were assigned as 'guests' to Latvian families with suitable homes, the best in the community. It was unbelievable to see these Russian women, the wives of officers, unpack small bags of dried rye bread. They had been warned way ahead of time that there is terrible hunger in Latvia and to be prepared for that. They did as they knew how and with what they had – black bread. Whatever they had brought was to sustain them for a while until Latvia is 'liberated'.

"Then the Russians woke up to the truth. A splendour, such as ours they had not seen – nor could have imagined in their wildest dreams. They just could not believe that such prosperity could even exist. They bought everything in sight and sent it to their relatives in Russia.

"Russian officers' wives bought nightgowns mistaking them for formal gowns and attended formal balls in them. When fish was served with two forks, Russian officers demanded knives too.

"Another example of a similar rush of parcels out of Latvia took place earlier, when sailors of visiting German warships sent large parcels of butter and bacon back to Germany.

"I was not quite sixteen when Germany and Russia attacked Poland. That was 1939. By mid-June next year, 1940: while the whole world was looking with horror at the surrender of France and the German occupation of Paris; while the attention of the world was somewhere else, Russians just drove long columns of their tanks through the Baltic States – Estonia, Latvia and Lithuania – thus occupying our lands.

"That was done in accordance with the Molotov-Ribbentrop Pact, with Bessarabia of Rumania thrown in for good measure and the Russians keeping their part of Poland, along the so-called 'Curzon Line'.

"Such was the German–Russian agreement – *on the basis of which Germany and Russia started WW II as allies.*

"That was the end of our freedom. Russians ignored all peace and other treaties – they just marched in. With that starts my sad story of occupation, war, and horror.

"I was visiting some relatives in Cesis when, on June 17, 1940, Russian tanks rolled through the main streets of that city – all in south-westerly direction toward the Baltic Sea and our capital city, Riga. There was seemingly no end to them, nor their rattle.

"Their tanks were small (that is why they rattled, not rumbled, as I learned later tanks do). They were dark, unkempt and dirty. So were the Russian soldiers, in baggy pants, wooden-soled boots, and with a 'plug' on top of their odd hats. After seeing their empty faces and ignorance, they earned the nickname: '...above a plug – below a fool...' (in Latvian it rhymes).

"Our land was a land of milk and honey, although we had only twenty years of freedom and peace. The last six years were the most prosperous. We grew in affluence by leaps and bounds. We were rich in everything, except imported and restricted wartime commodities such as gas and oil, etc. The war created that. All consumer goods were just waiting to be sold and our stores were emptied in a few days by the Russians – having come from a land of slavery, starvation, and just plain deprivation.

"Our President was forced to resign. He was promised freedom, but died in Russia under arrest. The first workers' government was set up by the Russians. There were only some four or five communists in it at the beginning.

"All jails were opened immediately and all political prisoners, including a great number of criminals, were released. They, criminals included, soon found themselves in very high positions indeed, such as police chiefs, etc. The chief justice was a criminal, a public school dropout.

"At the start, Russian political commissars said that all the nearby stores had been intentionally stocked with goods to demoralize the 'simple' Russian soldier. What they meant to say was: 'poor and just plain hungry soldier'.

"When they saw that all stores throughout the land were full and warehouses too – they changed their story and pointed out that all this affluence is for the rich bourgeois class – at the expense of the simple working man, but, alas, they could not find the 'poor working class'.

"When a communist political agitator, in a forced meeting at a factory said that the working men and women were starving – they did not see bread – a working man replied: 'That's true! We couldn't see bread for it was covered with butter and sausage!' That 'poor working man' disappeared and was never seen again.

"Railroad freight cars carried away the wealth of the nation to Russia. The springs under the cars were a dead give-away – compressed on the way to Russia, relieved on the way back.

"I was in the country during the summer as usual, at my grandfather's farm in that beautiful part of Latvia I already told you about. My elders were my only sources of information of what was happening.

"Elections were to be held. Everybody eligible to vote had to vote and have their passport stamped at the time of voting. Whoever was later found without such a stamp in their passport would be called 'An enemy of the State', arrested, imprisoned, tortured, and murdered. An NKVD man stood by and watched to make sure that everyone voted 'correctly'.

"The results of the 'election', with some 99.7% or 94.7% having voted *for* the new 'government', were announced by the

BBC in London *before the polls closed!* Somebody goofed in Moscow by releasing the predetermined results a full day early. That was and still is proof of Russian lies.

"Just as soon as this new 'government' convened, under Russian dictate it voted unanimously (as it was the only acceptable way to do things), in the name of the people of Latvia, to request Russia to accept Latvia as one of their 'Republics' – which, of course, Moscow did, giving Latvia the sequential number '15'. In other words – the Republic of Latvia became the '15th Soviet Socialist Republic' of the U.S.S.R.

"From then on all hell broke loose. The 'appointed government' – set up by the Russians upon invading our land – was dissolved, having served its purpose. Now the 'elected government' was a puppet in the hands of the Russians just as much as the first one had been, and terror became the new standard of life: people disappearing regularly, never to show up again – unless dug up from mass graves after the arrival of the Germans.

"A classmate of mine (he sat right behind me during the 1940/41 school year) – was found horribly tortured: tongue and eyes out; ears and nose off; teeth smashed in; genitals mutilated and torn off; and on top of all that – his arms and legs cut off and piled with his body as cord wood. Just some moss was scraped on top of his remains.

"How innocently did this all start – and tragically end!

"He and two of his friends had swum to a sand bar in the local river Gauja and were sunbathing. A car stopped on the road by the bridge. A number of NKVD officers stepped out and went through their clothing. The boys shouted and swam back to the shore. They were told to dress and were taken to the Militia building in Cesis, where they were transferred to a covered truck. NKVD soldiers with bayoneted rifles guarded them. Some spades and shovels were also thrown in as well.

"They knew what was coming and, in one way or another agreed that, just as soon as they were told to jump out – they would run in different directions. This they did when the truck stopped on a small and isolated forest road, across from the same area of the river and bridge where they were swimming and sunbathing only an hour ago and taken into custody for no reason at all.

"One of them was shot dead. My classmate was wounded in the bone of his leg and could not run. The third one received a wound and escaped. He was cared for and hidden by a local farmer. After the Germans arrived, he came out of hiding and led the people to the place in the forest. That is when it was discovered that one was shot dead, and my classmate suffered most unbelievable and horrifying torture, as he was slowly murdered.

"A girl from our high school was tortured at the prison in Cesis. Both her hands and feet had been dipped in boiling water and finger and toenails pulled out. Before that, splinters had been forced under her nails. Eventually she was stuck on top of a sharpened post dug in the ground. She was impaled on the post through her sex organs. I understand that it takes some three to four hours to die, with the post digging deeper and deeper into the abdomen.

"Just think of it, Ingrid! Just think of it! Was the post stuck in her while she was held down on the ground? Was she then lifted up with the post, while the post was put in the hole? Was she forced on that pole by her torturers, lifting her up and then pulling her down? Or was she given a rope to hang on to above the post – in spite of peeling skin and flesh and without fingernails – impaling herself and in the 'right place' – as assisted and guided by her torturers when the strength in her arms gave out?

"Can you imagine the struggle, between fading strength in her arms with the sharp end of the post just below her, touching her? And the commands of the brain to pull up again, if only a little, to delay the horror of excruciating pain! The end is inevitable, but the nerves command!

"Can you imagine the internal struggle? Did she lose consciousness? If so, at what point? I hope she did, and died with less pain than the torturers had planned for her... What pain did she suffer in her mind seeing and realizing what was going to be done to her body? Or had she lost her mind already, due to previous torture?

"These questions are always burning in my mind and there can be no answers, Ingrid! The possibilities are infinite and her suffering unimaginable.

"Why? What had she done to suffer so terribly? Here is the answer to that.

"She was born in the same year and in the same house as another girl of a Jewish family (in future I will refer to her only as 'The Bitch'). They were friends. They played together, went through public school together, sitting side by side on the same bench, and the same at high school. I should mention that we did not have individual benches for each pupil, but double ones, for two.

"One day on the way home the Latvian girl asked: 'Why do you carry the red rug?' Here, again, an explanation is in order. The uniform of the Communist Youth was a dark blue skirt; white blouse with a left breast pocket; and a bright red handkerchief in that pocket or around the neck.

"The Bitch was the leader of the 'Young Communists' in our school. The next day the Latvian girl was arrested and, after the arrival of German troops, found tortured to death as I just described.

"I knew her, but did not see her in death. Instead, I saw another girl murdered by similar torture in another city. She was lying on the ground with other victims.

"I was sent to a city called Valmiera to look for a relative, but did not find him. What I did find was the image of a sixteen-year-old girl's white inner thighs and legs covered with blood, right down to her toes. Her white thighs I see this very moment. But obviously, the torturers had not spent as much time with her as with my co-ed. There were no splinters pushed under her fingernails; her hands and feet had not been put in boiling water; and her finger and toenails were not pulled out. All she suffered was the post, but isn't that even more terrible?

"Having not suffered other methods of torture before and with a fresh mind, the sharpened post in her genitals must have been even more terrifying! And what about her fright, seeing and realizing what was going to be done to her! What a horrible sight! It is still burning in my memory...

"With the arrival of the Russians, all power over life or death was in the hands of Jews – from the very top in Moscow – to the executioners in Latvia at all levels. Our first high school commissar was one as well.

"They, including some women, seemed to enjoy torturing others just for the sake of it – to be in a continuous orgasm in an orgy of torture – as was the specific case of Mozus Citrons, a torturer at the prison in Daugavpils. In some places the NKVD were called just simply 'The Jews'. I cannot understand such bankruptcy of the soul in almost all of them!

"Then came the day of infamy – the greatest day of sorrow in our history – June 14, 1941 – when some 60,000 Latvians were arrested during the night (June 13/14) and sent to Siberia: men; women, even pregnant ones and those with small, still breastfed babies; children regardless of age; the very old; and youths. This took place simultaneously in all three Baltic States.

"Men were separated from women and children. All suffered horribly in railway freight cars. Even the small windows near the roof were closed with barbed wire. No food – no drink – under the hot summer sun. In Russia they were allowed to throw the dead out of the cars – and mothers, with breaking hearts, had to throw their babies from moving trains in the middle of nowhere. It was impossible to escape.

"Some men were not at home when the NKVD came to arrest them, so the NKVD took their families. Once the husband is on the list, the families were usually taken as well, but the people did not know that and the husbands went to the NKVD themselves – hoping that that would free their wives and children. Who knows where their wives and children were by the time the husbands showed up and were arrested with pleasure, of course – customary courtesy of the NKVD.

"My uncle, a Latvian artillery officer, was also taken to Siberia, along with some sixty other officers of his regiment. His wife and two small children were quickly relocated to my grandfather's farm.

"The Summer Solstice of 1941 was without a light, without a song, but I had an extrasensory contact with my uncle and godfather.

"I was looking east – over our potato field at my feet and over our forest in the distance. My soul was calling out for him and patiently waiting. I was at the peak of intensity and did not let it drop. The answer came! Yes, he is still alive! I was absolutely sure of it. I went into the house where all were sitting in darkness and deadly silence. We had been out for a walk and upon return we found that all three of our clocks had stopped at 11:15 p.m. That is what gave me the power to concentrate and call through distance and space.

"I asked Father to come out, whispering in his ear. He came and we stood as I had stood and then told him what I had done and the answer I received – his brother was still alive.

"Father put his hand on my shoulder and, swallowing tears, said in a trembling voice: 'Let us hope, son...'

I told him repeatedly that I knew. He just lifted his hand, and hiding tears, went back in the house.

"I had no doubts in my mind. I knew that he was alive.

"My calls for my stepmother's brother were not as intense and went unanswered. All I felt was a chillness in the air, although it was a warm night. Perhaps the chillness was the answer.

"He was taken from Latvia's largest airfield at Riga. He was a rare man and Russians needed highly skilled motor mechanics and technicians. We know only this: the retreating Russians did not know how to drive a truck, and ordered him to do the driving.

"He must have tried to escape back to his wife and small child, but failed. I hope that he was shot dead outright. If not, I hope that they did not have time to torture him right there and then – they were in too big a rush to escape the advancing German army – but only seconds or minutes of torture by our watches may well be more than a lifetime to the sufferer.

"The sheer horror of it all makes my soul scream!

"I should go back a little. On May 1, 1941, we, the entire school, were forced to march in the 'Mayday' parade and shout prescribed slogans in honour of Stalin, Russia and communism.

"We, in our class, all secretly agreed not to respond in any way. When the moment came, we did not turn our heads, did not open our mouths. With grim expressions we just marched ahead in deadly silence. Some previous classes had done the same. On top of that, someone wrote 'DEATH TO ALL TRAITORS' on a wall at the school.

"You should have heard our little Commissar Jenkins, exploding in the great hall of the school the next day, first thing in the morning, but obviously he did not have the power to arrest everyone, and our behaviour on the day before proved his worthlessness as commissar. He had to get lost because he felt that we might kill him. He was a Latvian Jew who had lived all the years of our freedom in Russia and returned with them now again. His language was terrible – a mixture of Russian, Yiddish and Latvian.

"In time we learned that he was responsible for the arrests and virtual deaths of sixty farm families – 200 to 300 people or even more in one neighbourhood alone – the one he was in charge of after he fled our school.

"His replacement was a rather petite and quiet, non-assuming young lady. I have good reasons to believe that her sympathies were with us.

"During a meeting of the school executive of the student body, The Bitch proposed that the play we were going to perform in the near future be advertised as organized and 'done' by her group of Young Communists.

"I jumped up and said: 'Absolutely NO! You earn your laurels by your own work – not as bourgeoisie, stealing from others, exploiting others for your profit and gain! You get it if you work for it!' – which is, of course, communist doctrine, but I had opposed the most powerful force, The Bitch.

"Someone sitting beside me gave me a signal to shut up and sit down. After I had done so, he whispered through the corner of his mouth that the lady commissar was sitting at the back of the classroom, just behind us to the right.

"After a little while I looked back and our eyes met – mine and the commissar's. I felt that I was not in trouble, but could not be sure. At the end, on the way out I saw a woman in her eyes. I saw a cool desire – not a commissar.

"Among the students, I was the top authority in the school in matters pertaining to theatre and literature. This, the commissar knew only too well and I may have had her sympathies long before that meeting.

"She saved me from that savage girl. The Bitch could not take up arms against me, because the commissar was present and if the commissar did not do anything, The Bitch just couldn't. Besides, I was right. What The Bitch wanted was exploitation and parasitism – just what the communists pretended to stamp out. Of course, at that time nobody knew what The Bitch had done to her best friend and that she was responsible for her horrible death.

"Russia was an ally of Germany from the very beginning of WW II in 1939 to June 1941, when Germany attacked Russia. Since Germany was at war and Russia its ally – we had no hope. Absolutely none whatsoever.

"The sudden German attack on Russia only a week after that terrible night of June 13/14 gave us hope and our partisans hastened Russian retreat. We all hid in forests with our livestock.

"One morning, on reconnaissance duty, I saw the flag of Latvia at the top of the tall mast of my grandfather's farm. I leaned back against a telephone pole, listened to its familiar hum, my heart jumped with joy, and my muscles and mind relaxed.

"Free! We are free again! I investigated as to whether it was not a trick... No! It's true! The Germans have arrived!

"We are free!

"But the German foot soldier was followed by the Nazi 'Golden Pheasants' and they enslaved us again. We were treated as Russians and our land as Russia, and according to the master plan, we were to become a part of Germany, but we did not quite know yet the extent of the plans Germany had for us. To this, I shall return later.

"I shall backtrack a little now. I told you about one personal experience with The Bitch and the lady commissar. Now I shall tell you a bit more about my other personal experiences under the Russians.

"It should be mentioned that high school in Latvia was not free – it was a very expensive privilege, with few exceptions and few scholarships.

"I was very active in the social life of our high school at Cesis.

It was my nature and dedication. Ability, of course, had to be there to start with. The student body is very selective and merciless in these matters. I think that you asked me and I told you that my nickname was 'Genius'. I earned scholarships every year, quite unintentionally.

"What did I do? I sang in double-quartet, men's choir and mixed choir. Besides that, I organized and led our theatre troupe and created and led a literary group – transferring its leadership to someone else as was pre-arranged. I had to start it to attract more participants.

"I played leading or supporting roles in our school theatre as well as in the Theatre of the City of Cesis. Consequently, I was well known by everyone in the school. My literary works were read by teachers to other classes as examples of good writing.

"There was an instance when, while I was writing, someone was sitting beside me, reading as I wrote. I did not know that and was greatly surprised when I finished and got up to go. He told me what he had done, praised me and asked how come everything came so interestingly, fluently, and quickly off my pencil.

"During the German occupation, I won a special prize in a competition sponsored by the Mayor of the City of Cesis. The theme was: 'The Importance of Unity in the Life of a Nation' – in support of our nationalism and yearning for freedom again.

"Now, during Russian occupation, prior to a double-quartet concert, a secret NKVD agent in the student body (about whom we learned the terrible truth only after the arrival of the Germans) told me that he wanted us to sing Russian songs only. I replied that we would sing Latvian folk songs only. He got mad, jumped up and down, got red in the face, and asked me if I knew to whom I was talking. I replied that I knew precisely to whom I was speaking, but, of course, I did not know that he was a member of the dreaded NKVD as well.

"He may have interpreted that as having blown his cover and put NKVD on my trail to get rid of me, but he did not quite know with whom he was dealing and, as you shall see, unwittingly, I gave them all an unexpected surprise.

"By the way, he was responsible for many deaths at our school. After the arrival of the Germans, he was hidden by the church minister and our teacher, but when it became known who he really was, he was surrendered to the authorities and, after a proper trial, sentenced to death and executed.

"Well, where were we? Yes, the concert. In both parts we sang only Latvian folk songs, to great applause. We gave only one encore at the very end – a Georgian folk song from Stalin's birthplace, 'Sulikov'. Practically no applause, although it is a beautiful melody, but that was our Anti-Russian stance. The will of the people could be silenced only in the chambers of torture and that too individually.

"Volunteers were required for 'census' taking and payment was offered for it. Volunteers? That means only one thing, under communism all must 'volunteer', but I went because I was going to demand the payment offered.

"When it was done, all were asked to donate the work to the 'Party'. I was the only one in the whole school who demanded and received the promised payment. Others were afraid to ask.

"In view of what we discovered after the arrival of the German forces – the huge mass graves and unbelievable tortures so many had suffered: disfigured faces in pain and/or mutilation; nails in skulls; cut throats; sticks in rectums or stuck through abdomens; etc., – I must have been out of my mind provoking the NKVD so, but that's me, Ingrid. What others can't, I must. That's me, and so it was also later at the front. Compulsive behaviour, perhaps.

"The most beautiful girl in the entire school asked me for a date. Most unusual, but she was aware of her beauty and sure of my friendship. There was mutual attraction – to say the least. She revealed that the NKVD was after me – I was to be careful. A security leak had sprung and she acted immediately to save me.

"During a late afternoon soon after, when all students are supposed to be home having lunch – a friend ran to the school and told me that NKVD officers arrived and entered my residence. I was living with relatives that winter, from where I saw Russian tanks enter our land the previous summer. Not finding me home, they turned my room upside down. One of them was a known local Jew and my friend knew where he lived.

"We went to his apartment and from behind heavily chained doors his wife told us that he was in the 'Militia'. What surprised me was the heavy animal or even industrial chain with which the door was secured.

"We both went to the 'Militia'. I was told that the man I was looking for was not in at that time, but would be in later on, and we sat down to wait. It was a very large room – a quarter of which, or even more, was set aside as the waiting room with benches along the wall. There was a counter, and behind that, NKVD men worked at desks, some ten to fifteen of them.

"After about three hours of waiting and numerous enquiries about that policeman, my brave friend departed. He was hungry and concerned about his parents worrying about him. So was I and it was long since dark, but I continued to wait.

"After about one more hour of waiting, suddenly a NKVD officer came to the counter and asked what I was waiting for. I gave him the name. He said that he was the man. I could hardly believe him, because this man had been coming in and out of the front office quite frequently after my friend had left. Now I had to accept his word that he was the man my friend told me about.

"I stated the reason why I was there, so patiently waiting. He and others had paid me a visit and searched my room. I wanted to help them. If there was anything that they wanted, I told them they should just ask me and I would give it to them if I had it.

"He said that he would come back shortly and he did – apologizing for the inconvenience and consternation needlessly caused. There had been a mistake. I was not the one they were looking for. He apologized again and told me to go home and continue to live in peace as if nothing had happened. No harm would come to me. I knew instinctively and immediately that the opposite was true, that I must be very careful.

"Obviously, they felt that a guilty man would run, but I stepped right into the lion's den, patiently waited for four hours in order to help them find what they were looking for.

"The NKVD did not have to have a reason to arrest, torture and kill a man, but I knew that I did not have anything incriminating at home. They could not have found anything. And being me – I could not passively sit back and let this go on without reaction. So, I reacted in a manner they did not expect – I did not run – I confronted them and won.

"The next time came in about two weeks. Again, I was at the school and my friend ran to tell me that this time there was a car and a covered truck. NKVD soldiers with bayoneted rifles encircled my home and then the officers entered.

"Well, this was it! There was no way out but the forest, and I left the school as I was, and headed for the forests and marshes near my grandfather's farm.

"My father and grandfather taught me how and where to hide. At the same time, they did not stay at the farm during the night either, only my grandmother did and even then – not in the house, not in her bed, but in different places every night.

"And now we are back to where I told you how I came out of the forest and saw the flag of Latvia flying again in the high mast of my grandfather's farm.

"Freedom!

"The 'Terrible Year' had ended!

"Germans are here!

"We are free!"

★

Silence… Long, long silence…

In the years to come Arne wrote this poem:

JUNE 14, 1941

In memory of those, who died a thousand deaths –
Their blood, and tears, and agonizing screams.
In memory of them…

In memory of those, who did endure torture –
The kind of torture that man can do to man.
In memory of them…

In memory of men: our fathers, brothers, husbands –
Who went to death – so we may yet be free.
In memory of them…

In memory of women: our mothers, sisters, wives –
The violence – which I do not dare to say.
In memory of them…

In memory of children, and infants only born –
With faces peaceful – or in utmost horror.
In memory of them...

In memory of those, who lived a thousand lives –
Their blood, and tears, and liberating deaths.
In memory of them...

In memory of all of them...

Honeymoon – P.E.I. – Germans – War

"Girls greeted the liberating German soldiers with flowers and kisses. We wanted to join the German army to help fight communism, but they did not take us. Only later did we find out why. Germans wanted to win the war by themselves so that there would be no moral obligation to share the spoils of war. All we wanted was our freedom, but that is not what the Germans had in mind for us, and anything less would make us their enemies.

"First of all, there was a general round up of those who had not escaped to Russia: communists, soldiers of the Red Army, and Jews. All commissars were executed on the spot. Captured soldiers were sent to POW camps and Jews to ghettos.

"Latvian partisans who had fought the retreating Russians and thus hastened the German advance and our liberation were disarmed and disbanded. This surprised and puzzled us. The answer came with the arrival of the 'Golden Pheasants' – the Nazi Masters.

"The Russians had nationalized everything – all state and private property. I already told you that we were treated as Russians and our land as Russia. This continued for a long time.

"Instead of liberators, the Germans turned out to be just another form of an oppressing, occupying force. Well, at that time, we did not know of Germany's secret deal with Russia – the Molotov-Ribbentrop Pact: Russia gets her part of Poland, all of Estonia, Latvia and Lithuania, and Bessarabia of Rumania, with Germany taking the rest. It was easy for Germany to give away these lands, because it fully intended to take them all back as part of conquered Russia. Here lies the answer to why we were treated as Russians and Latvia as Russia.

"Some ordinary police units were formed and dressed in Latvian army uniforms without the customary rank insignias. This was done, presumably, to use up the supply of these uniforms and to mark the wearers as non-Germans. Some such units became battle police battalions against communist partisans, customarily called bandits.

"At school everything returned to normal. There were no more arrests, nor victims of torture. As far as I was concerned, having just survived one year of Russian occupation, the German occupation was as humane as could be expected under the circumstances. We were no longer under uneducated and hateful, barbaric savages.

"There were rumours of Jews being shot in a forest near Riga. Latvians were used as guards – the triggers were pulled by Germans only. Latvians were not trusted, as we might aid the Jews in escape. There was no reason not to believe such rumours.

"There was an educated and national Latvian civil administration. We trusted them. Better Latvian than German – just like in occupied France – better French than German only. It most certainly applied to us. Our civil administration fought tooth and nail with the Germans – protecting us and providing for us as much as was possible.

"In the face of the 1942/43 winter tragedy at Stalingrad, Germans woke up and wanted to mobilize us, wanted our help, the same help that we so freely offered in 1941, but they had refused it then. It is illegal to mobilize in occupied lands, but Germans did not care about the legality.

"In return for our 'volunteers', our civil administration asked for:

1. Guaranty that Latvians shall fight for a certain political goal – free and independent Latvia;
2. Immediate stop to persecutions and arrests of Latvian nationalists and to free those jailed;
3. Return to rightful owners all properties nationalized by Russians;
4. Treat Latvians as equals in the availability of food, pay, consumer goods, and rights.

"In spite of their predicament the Germans refused all four requests and forced the mobilization anyway. Later on, when things were going very badly, partial return of private property to their rightful owners was made.

"I did not know all the details then. I just wanted to join the battle against communism, but my father would not let me: '…it's war. If you do not finish your high school now, you may never have a chance again…' He was right and I obeyed until that goal was achieved. Then I went to Riga three times to volunteer for the forthcoming Latvian forces, but every time I was turned back by the guards on the steps of Latvian Legion HQ building. I must wait, they said.

"Meanwhile, German General Jeckeln had concocted a devilish plan. Two trainloads of the very first draftees – one from northern, and the other from western Latvia – high school graduates and university students only, were to be sent to Bolderaja, a place near Riga, for basic training in Latvian police battalions and then – eventually – to be offered up for slaughter during the winter of 1943/44. That was another way of getting rid of the emerging generation of Latvian 'intelligentsia'.

"Some of us had connections in high places, but nothing could help us to get out of the police units and be transferred to Latvian divisions. Even if anyone managed to get into the Latvian divisions during a furlough, if caught, they would be shot for desertion. The only diversion was an opportunity to volunteer for police cavalry.

"There was a chronic shortage of NCOs and officers in Latvian divisions, but we had to remain in the police. Only during October 1944 – after being at the front and numerous hospitals and other healing institutions, and while I was being released from another hospital – I was told that my regiment was 'closed' and I was sent to our 15th division.

"At the division, I was immediately sent to a special German officers' school. I graduated as first and received a twenty-two-day furlough. I told you that, didn't I?

"I became an officer as of March 31, 1945 – the so-called 'Regimental Standard-bearer', equivalent to an Ensign in the U.S. Navy, or a Pilot Officer in RAE, I believe, but of a much more distinct and honourable standing in the German forces. That is documented.

"Then, a lieutenant as of April 28, 1945, but I think that the necessary documentation was never done in the panic of those days – nonetheless the order is there and I have a copy of it. I did not know any of this and went through the POW year as an NCO.

"But now – 'The War and the Warrior' – from the beginning."

★

"The date was April 16, 1943. Girls sent us off from the train station at Cesis in the morning with flowers and we arrived at Bolderaja in the afternoon. When the other trainload arrived, from Courland, I met my classmates of the teachers' college I had previously attended. Remember the ball, the foxtrot and the girl?

"We received strange uniforms: black breeches with putties and boots; and dark blue tunics with field service caps. And, can you imagine! We wore Latvian army infantry EM collar rank insignias and the Latvian sun on our field service caps! We felt that we were the very beginning of a new Army of Latvia! The Germans had given in and recognized our insignias!

"No such luck. The strange uniforms were to be 'used up' in basic training and exchanged for German police uniforms at the end, but still retaining Latvian insignias. Much later – during October 1943 – the order came to replace Latvian insignias with German police insignias. So much for our hopes.

"I served on the Latvian–Russian border and attended a special 'Anti-partisan' NCO course in direct contact with active communist bandits. There, on July 10, 1943, in close combat, I killed the first enemy and saved the life of a senior sergeant. The bandit turned out to be a brigadier – the highest-ranking bandit behind enemy lines – the commander of a vast area.

"He, and those whom he led that day, had ambushed and killed our captain. After some two to three hours of hot pursuit, we caught up with them, and I was lucky enough to get him. We were facing each other; I, an EM in the NCO course with a rifle; he, a very experienced soldier with a Russian hand machine gun. I had only one chance, but I was faster and, as it turned out later, the best marksman in our company in a combined rifle and light machine gun competition.

"A bit later, when I had time, I led the senior sergeant to the place and saw him dead at my feet. I had two successive thoughts: since I killed him in this way (my tracer bullet had entered his left cheek bone) – I would die in retribution and in the same way; but then another thought took the upper hand: since he died this way, he probably deserved it and I was only an innocent instrument of fate.

"I had forgotten all about it when, suddenly – six weeks later – I received a citation in the regimental order of the day and later the commander came and thanked me personally.

"By the first week of November 1943, we were in Russia, trying to reach defendable positions and dig in to stop a Russian breakthrough just west of Newel. The Russians reached us and attacked on November 7, 1943, but we held and the breakthrough was contained.

"The next Russian breakthrough came during the second week of January, 1944, just north of us and we were sent in to stop that one too – which we did, but in an inexcusable manner and at an inexcusable cost of lives. It was a wanton slaughter of Latvians by a new and inept commander of the regiment – receiving high decorations in return. It was blood money. We had already stopped the Russians. There was no need to attack their positions in two different locations on two successive mornings.

"There, Ingrid, we were dressed as lightly as possible for mobility, and armed very poorly – with Russian rifles and light and heavy machine guns only. Hand machine guns we had to get from Russian casualties.

"Russian hand machine guns were famous. Germans sat on them in storage. None were issued to us. It is pretty difficult to fight an enemy with rifles only when the enemy is armed with hand machine guns as well. On the border with Russia we had mixed machine guns – Russian and British WW I weapons. It was done so, perhaps, to ensure our destruction, but in spite of it all we were victorious, but only a few survived – and that was General Jeckeln's goal.

"Those were fateful days, Ingrid. We did not know it at that time, but, had we not stopped both Russian breakthroughs, they would have reached the Gulf of Riga in the winter of 1943/44 – trapping the German Army Group North in Estonia, thus eliminating any chance for the eventual development of 'Festung Kurland', which held to the end of the war; and trapping Latvians in their homes – eliminating any possibility of 'Latvians in Exile', as we know it now.

"Later on our regiment received a unit citation awarding us a cuff title: 'Lett. Freiw. Pol. Rgt. Riga'. During the whole of WW II, only two units in the armed forces of Germany received such distinction: Rommel's 'Afrikakorps', and our regiment. These were the only two *unit battle award cuff titles.*

"We were on our feet in a forced march, or locked in combat, for some seventy hours at a stretch with minimum or no food at all, but there was always snow to throw in the mouth. It tasted like wet newspaper, but that is where and how we got the liquid for normal functions of the body.

"We were dead tired, sleeping while walking, exhausted, desperate and short of ammunition.

"That is when only sixteen EM and two NCOs of our company survived and continued to hold our lines in a swamp, standing up in snow and water day and night, with light machine guns hung shoulder-high in branches of bushes.

"We were there for five days and nights until I received a concussion during the night of January 20/21, 1944. I lost consciousness and lay on my right side in ice-cold water for some two to three hours.

"I commanded the left flank of our company and my men thought that I had been killed. After the battle, they found me and dragged me to the 'dead' pile, but I woke up.

"From then on, Ingrid, I spent the rest of the war in hospitals and healing institutions. Many – seven of them. Two more as a POW. After that – in a number of them and a number of times in each…

"Slowly, from time to time, I shall tell you the grizzly details of death – if you want to know. What I have said so far should be sufficient to imagine war – to see a friend die, screaming in agony, his belly shot out with a burst of an automatic weapon fire.

"I was once gripped with horror and a number of times with varying degrees of concern, but the worst is that I was truly demoralized by the needless slaughter of so many for nothing, absolutely nothing.

"I do feel the existence of two forces around and about me: my mother's arms and hands; and the prayer of a simple Latvian peasant whom I had never seen before – nor shall ever see again. With his hat in hands on his chest and tears running down his cheeks, he prayed to the Almighty to stand by and guard me wherever I would go. It was on a road when we were parting – having walked together alone for about a mile. It touched me deeply and I feel it even today.

"There was a moment of weakness in me. I was calm and free of any notion of fright or concern – just weakness – the first and only time in my life. It was on the final leg of a 'suicide mission' that I had just led successfully and just about completed. The impossible was just about done.

"I bit into a rancid little piece of frozen butter – the only edible thing I had. Even now, I can see the cut my upper front teeth made in it. It started to melt with that terrible rancid taste. I looked at that parchment paper the butter was wrapped in and realized that I could not write on it and I did not have any other paper. I could not even leave a few last words to my parents before I died – for we would all die there. That was my only concern – only that.

"I knew that we all would die there in that swamp. It was only a matter of minutes, perhaps hours – two, three at the most. Even one day seemed an impossibly long time.

"I spoke to God and made myself ready for death. I said goodbye to my father, stepmother, and all others – to my unlived life. A couple of tears ran down my cheeks. I took off my helmet and wiped them off – making sure that no one had noticed them.

"Then I was ready. I felt that I was standing straight and tall with full knowledge of the inevitable and ready for it. I led my men to the full and successful completion of that mission, and then for five more days and nights – until I was disabled and unconscious.

"Prior to that, I had one more instance when I talked to God. It was during my basic training, in May 1943, on a weekend. I visited my maternal grandmother in Riga and the heel of my boot fell off. I nailed it back to the boot with one substantial nail, so that I could get back to the camp. After receiving a new pair of good boots, I took a walk along the lonely streets of Bolderaja.

"It was mid-afternoon on a Sunday. The small place was asleep. There was no one on the streets – just me. I thought of war and what was to come. I had eagerly reported for duty and never gave even a thought about death – it just did not exist, or my mind did not permit it to exist.

"I told God of the two wishes I had.

"First, I would like to survive the very first real battle and experience the calm that comes after, looking in the eyes of other survivors and thinking about those who fell. After that I am ready to die at any time. That was a very selfish wish.

"Second, I would like to know a woman as a woman – in full – before I die…

★

"I cannot speak for others – only myself and those who were with me. As POW's we were treated most inhumanely by the British, and some of us were shot dead or wounded just for the fun of it. I know it sounds unbelievable, but it is true. After the war, during the summer 1945 at Neuengamme.

"Just think of it, Ingrid! After surviving every day of that terrible war – some were killed as POW's, and at the hands of the noble 'West'!

"Just for the fun of it…"

Honeymoon – P.E.I. – German Plans

"What the Germans had in mind for us was disclosed in an editorial column of a newspaper. It was put on sale in Riga, but immediately withdrawn again – ordering all sold copies to be returned and providing harsh penalties for keeping or talking about it.

"Here it is, Ingrid! I brought it along just in case we got rained in, as we are. We shall be very busy when we return. Perhaps now is the best time for me to do a bit of explaining about the war and the side I, we Latvians, fought on. You have the right to know.

"Besides the atrocities under the Russians and my war experiences here is a sarcastic insult.

"It is a newspaper called *Das Schwarze Korps* (The Black Corps), the official organ of the NSDAP (Nazi Party) and therefore – very, very official – the law for all Germans. This issue is dated, Berlin, 20 August 1942, and the editorial is called 'Germanisieren?' (To Germanize?)

"It's written in a very high-handed manner and drives home a point of how the simplest of things can be expressed in the most complex sentences. It is the apex of arrogance, but I have to admit that the unnamed writer knew how to write in German and impress his masters. The German language in itself is very complex and here it is compounded by equally complex sentences – not all of them, but enough. Yet, some are so beautiful. They command the admiration of the reader and that, most likely, was the aim, besides the contents. Thus, the contents and the manner in which it is expressed are both important.

"Some parts I shall try to translate to give you the general gist of the article. Some I shall abbreviate, and skip others completely, because to understand them in full – one has to know European history intimately and in depth.

"It is interesting to note that the two most famous and frequently used words: '*Grossdeutchland*' (Great-Germany) and

'*Lebensraum*' (Living-space) are completely absent – yet, the ideas of them are kept constantly present in the mind of the reader as if spelled out in bold letters.

"Now, here it goes, dear:

Das Schwarze Korps
Berlin, 20 August 1942

Germanisieren?

Reichsführer SS (Heinrich Himmler) in a publication 'Deutches Arbeit' (German Work), dedicated to the colonization of the East, has given the following introduction:

Our duty is not to Germanize the Eastern areas in the same manner and meaning as before – to teach the people living there German language and German laws, but to make sure that in the future the people living in the East would be people with true German blood.

To reject the idea of Germanization is at least as old Nationalsocialismus, but when it comes from the Reichsführer SS, who, at the same time, is a Reichscommissar responsible for the security of the German nation. It becomes an order. That is the true meaning of these words.

THE SWORD AND THE PLOUGH

It is not a promulgated opinion besides which there could exist other opinions; it is a declaration of a program and it is done by a man who, at the same time, fulfils the will of the Führer.

The will of the Führer has been manifested in his book *Mein Kampf* (My Struggle). One is always emotionally moved by reading how this still lonesome WW I 'Gefreiter' (corporal), understood only by a few, has known to foresee in a sheer clairvoyance the decisive fate of the Germans.

Thus, in a certain place, he talks about: '*the bustling work of the German plough, where the duty of the sword is to provide land for it.'*

This very thought is being fulfilled by the German sword today, when the – as a state impotent – colossus of Bolshevism has decided to exist on the ruins of Europe receives its crowning glory in that sentence of the *'Political Testament of the German Nation'*, as the leading motive that stands on all of our flags of victory.

Do not ever consider the State as secure, if it cannot provide its citizens with ownership of ground and land for generations to come. Do not ever forget that in this world the most sacred right is the right to land that one wants to work on; and the most sacred sacrifice is blood that has been spilled for such land!

Therefore, victory in the East is only a prerequisite of securing our future, and the very guarantee shall take place only if the land obtained by the holy sacrifices of blood shall become German: German in respect to people that shall live in and build on it; and German with *'the bustling work of the German plough'*.

In the past, a superficial alpha and omega of a State was: whoever babbled in French was a Frenchman and those who could understand each other in German were Germans.

The statesmen of France were not even ashamed to bastardize their own blood with those of the Negroes, if it served France and if with such acts there was an increase in the number of citizens.

Thus, in the same manner in the East, Poles and Jews became *'Germans'* – something that never served well the German people, but satisfied those who thought that this kind of Germanization was the most expedient way to increase the number of Germans in multinational border areas and even to assimilate Jews.

Such superficial efforts to Germanize and the negligence of those responsible has preserved the wholesomeness of the German people. This carelessness has, in fact, been their greatest contribution in the positive preservation of what truly is German.

People, families and kin, who for a hundred years or more had lived in a Germanizing influence, had obtained German education and had enjoyed all, so called, German advantages – suddenly, overnight, became Poles again (1918) and it is not important whether it was done out of convictions or opportunism. The German nation did not lose values of national interest, but gained experience that serves us well in our time now.

This experience teaches, and at the same time confirms a natural, biological fact: foreigners cannot be turned into Germans; just as it has proven itself that isolated Germans in some other states could not be made members of the nations where they lived.

A nation is the result of racial selection, and supplemented by common culture, history, and a way of life for hundreds of years under common conditions and experiences of togetherness. It cannot be changed by force nor forged – and if tried – it hurts those who have been estranged from their own people and even more; our own people who expected to augment our numbers from foreign cradles.

THE FATE OF THE GERMANS

Because the future of the German nation can be guaranteed only by the establishment of a Germany that *'for hundreds of years ahead of time can guarantee ownership of land to each member of future generations'* – the newly acquired lands must be filled with German blood and German life – not Germanized people.

The old kind of Germanization, that we have learned from history, would have brought death to our nation. It was a blessing that it did not happen. (Germans have remained Germans).

The expansion of the State in the East must become a bulwark of European culture.

Our fate rests in the East not only today, but for hundreds of years to come – therefore it cannot be entrusted to Non-Germans.

Because of that, it is the duty of the Reichsführer SS (Himmler) to see that only people with true German blood live there.

This, of course, should be understood within reason and what is humanly possible. In the East, Germans shall be the leaders and we have to understand clearly that racial segregation must be well established and maintained. What in the East is and shall be German – must, in fact, be truly German – of German blood.

THE BLESSED EARTH

It is our sacred duty to do what we can to secure it for our future generations. Our children will have plenty to do for themselves in their time. We must secure the land itself for them.

It is the responsibility of the State to provide the hundreds of thousands and the millions of our soldiers with their own land and help them to establish themselves on that land. It shall then depend on them and their wives to secure for themselves for ever what they have fought for and have won on the field of battle.

We are National-Socialists and not Imperialists. We shall not increase our population by 'questionable Germans'. Quality comes first.

Where tomorrow is one true German, after a hundred years shall be a hundred true Germans. Where tomorrow is a 'questionable' German, after a hundred years a hundred 'questionable' Germans will live. That would be bad and hard to correct.

The greater is the number of 'questionable' Germans – the greater becomes the risk of losing leadership.

We can trust the future of the land and our security in the hands of those men who today win victory after victory against the Bolshevismus and thus obtain the land for the German plough. Therefore, it is one of the most beautiful duties to turn our soldiers of today into colonizers tomorrow.

It is difficult to accept the casualties of this war, but we must use the historic opportunity offered to us now, while our enemies are dazed.

Everyone who falls in combat, secures and blesses the land his comrade will someday plough and a hundred cradles shall stand on.

In the immense reaches of this new land, the nation shall live in prosperity and German mothers shall bring forth many children full of happy laughter over and above the graves of those who died. That gives it all the greatest of meanings and reasons for the blood that has been spilled.

They have fallen so that Germany can live. If it is possible to justify anything after a war – this is the justification of their sacrifices.

★

"That is the end, Ingrid, and I am tired. Very tired. Think about it all, how do you understand it? I shall rest for a while."

I run up to him, make him comfortable and kiss him lightly on his forehead and lips. He puts his bent arms behind his head and then lifts his right forearm over his eyes.

After a while he starts to speak again, very slowly and quietly: "Our reasons for fighting with them were simple:

1. The atrocities of Russians just witnessed;
2. The need to get Latvians armed under our own officers;
3. We would be ready to free Latvia at the end;
4. We simply had to fight – under penalty of death to us and ours.

"The article was published during 1942 – their heyday – although somewhat frostbitten by the preceding winter at Moscow. The occupied area was immense. But they got badly beaten during the winter of 1942/43 at Stalingrad and were in retreat.

"That is when we were called upon to form our own Legion (Army). It was widely thought that, when Germany would start to crumble, we would be ready to free Latvia, just as it happened during our 1918–1920 Freedom War.

"We could not possibly conceive that the West would sell us

repeatedly to Stalin (at Teheran, Yalta and Potsdam) – just as Hitler did – before he and Stalin attacked Poland as allies to divide it between them, with us thrown in for good measure. Do not forget that at the outset of WW II, Germany and the Soviet Union were allies.

"After Germany attacked Russia in June 1941, Russia turned to the West (until then the enemy) for help.

"Be that as it may, one thing we did accomplish. Women – even pregnant women and those with small babies – as well as our children and elders, people unable to contribute to the life and death struggle for survival (not victory any more), just for the survival of what they had brought upon themselves, people who, in fact, were liabilities in the bombed out Germany – requiring shelter and food – scarcities at the time, were not left in Russian hands.

"All who really wanted to escape the Russians were taken to Germany and provided for. Russian submarines sank many ships and Russian fighters shot down even Red Cross transport planes even after the armistice of May 8/9, 1945.

"Nonetheless, that is how my parents got out, just to be killed in Dresden for no reason at all. An atrocity in itself.

"After the war we learned about the details of what Germany had in store for us, after their victory, of course. Estonia, Latvia and Lithuania would not exist any more. All that area would be expanded toward the East as far as our ethnic boundaries once were, and all this area would be called Dünaland – named after the major river in the centre of it, Daugava, that, at Riga, empties into the Gulf of Riga.

"In twenty-five years from the time that article was written, by 1967, there would be no Latvians in that part of Dünaland where Latvia once was. None.

"But now I shall try to sleep a little if I can."

I bring over and cover him with a soft, light blanket.

"Think of it all – how do you understand it?" he asked...

★

I sit by the window watching the storm-torn clouds and try to recover from all that I have heard. I was speechless while he spoke and tried hard to comprehend it all. This man is a living witness. He has gone through hell.

I had only a few questions, but I have a lifetime to ask them and he has a lifetime to answer.

We had supper just before he started the translation. It is getting dark when Arne stirs and looks at me:

"I did fall asleep."

"Yes, dear, for about an hour," and I go slowly to him and sit beside his warm and rested body. I caress his shoulders, chest and then his hair and face.

"Rest some more," I say quietly.

"No, Ingrid, I feel rested. I do not look forward to returning to this subject again. Perhaps when our children have grown up to the age of some maturity, I shall tell them the basics, in as much as they may want to know.

"How about you? Do you have any questions?" he asks.

"Yes, darling, some. Do you want me to ask them now? After all this exhaustion?"

"Yes, dear, now! All at the same time and then let us turn to something else, more pleasant and productive! We have so much to talk about – our future, our lives."

"Well, Arne, just a few. Besides your concussion, were there other times when you were so close to death?" I ask.

"Ingrid, dear, a soldier never knows how many times and where bullets or shrapnel has passed him by – particularly in the heat of battle, but I have memories of some clear instances.

"Do you remember July 10, 1943? Streams of hand machine gun bullets passed my head so closely that I became dizzy and did not realize what had happened. It was my Kyrilian aura that had been badly disturbed. That was my first day of combat.

"On November 7, 1943, a mortar shell landed just inches outside my knee-deep dugout. I was violently thrown aside, but it was behind me – not on my face or lungs.

"On January 14, 1944, a bullet shredded the fabric of my glove on top of my middle finger of the right hand – just as I was loading my rifle. I am sure that it was intended for my head, but while loading, I had to lean to the left.

"After that, on the same day, streams of bullets from an automatic weapon hit the snow a number of times just below my head and belly as I was lying in the snow and firing. My face and head was blasted with snow and covered, and I heard the bullets below me rushing through the snow with a funny, sort of gurgling sound. More bursts came, but again too low and then, I remained motionless for a few seconds.

"That is when, in my squad, only two survived. The entire squad to my left was killed.

"Later on that day I discovered a machine gun frozen piece of bread – having first penetrated the bag on my belt and the drinking cup in it.

"One particular incident was reported by commander to the battalion and incorporated in the Order-of-the-Day of my regiment.

"I was then commanding the left flank of our company. We were preparing to withdraw from a certain area at midnight. My company commander was one step ahead of me when I was hit by three stray bullets coming from the left.

"First I heard something in the branches of a tall pine tree. I had just managed to turn my head and look up when I was hit in the area of my knees as if by a water-soaked terry bath towel.

"The company commander asked what had happened. My men answered that I was hit, but I was only testing my legs for pain, blood and 'operational status'. 'No, I am not injured!' – I answered.

"The next day my company commander sent his runner for me. I had to undress and we found that two bullets had penetrated my uniform and heavy underwear of both legs in front of me; and one bullet behind me – also on both legs. Right over the kneecap of my right leg, the fleece or lint of the threads was shot off. It was threadbare there, in the direction of the bullet. We were wearing very fine underwear that was clinging to the body – similar to the tights that ballet dancers use. It was to protect us from the heavy and harsh wool underwear.

"While dressing, a bullet was found on the floor. It was the bullet that had gone through the pants behind my legs and got stuck in the heavy leather near the right heel of my boot.

"I also have a couple of fragments of exploded shells that struck the dugout behind me – having just missed me.

"I could go on and remember some other such incidents, but who knows the majority that passed me by, unnoticed? Well, I did notice the concussion though, that is, after I had the 'misfortune' of waking up," Arne concludes with smile.

"And God granted both of your wishes," I smile back.

"Yes, Ingrid, and if no one else, but there are – as you know – you are the final proof of that."

"Were you ever afraid! Really afraid?"

"Not in the face of danger, like the helpless lying in the snow in front of Russian positions and with no cover at all. Strangely enough, not then. It may not seem normal, but I was not afraid. Come to think about it – I probably did not have time for that.

"A squad commander, or 'leader' as you may call him, has the greatest number of direct subordinates – nine. A platoon commander has four squads. A company commander has four platoons. A battalion commander has four companies. The commander of a regiment has four battalions, and so on. Well, when I commanded the left flank of the company, I had about twenty men – including reinforcements received.

"I just was not afraid. But I do know fright, terror and panic. Oh – do I ever know panic! It lasted a few seconds – terrifying seconds, and saved my life.

"During the battle of January 14, 1944, my assistant and I had just about reached the Russian bunker and were safe from their fire. I had already tried to crawl up the steep slope, but had to slide back to rearrange the position of my rifle. All I needed were about ten more feet before I could stuff my grenades in it. I was ready to crawl again, but the order came: 'Retreat!'

"Well, then I felt the futility of the situation. We had sacrificed so many lives to get the two of us where we were, and now to retreat over the same ground – under Russian fire – just the two of us! With just the two of us for all the Russians to shoot at! All this effort for nothing! My assistant was hit, but only his belt was cut in two. What happened there was a miracle.

"This is one instance when and where I was engulfed by a superior force. As I was running back, it made me jump one step to the left and back again. It was a command against which I was helpless. I was literally thrown to the left and back again and felt the direct presence of my mother – her will – her protecting arms and hands.

"Because I had jumped to the side, a bullet aimed at my back hit my assistant, who was running ahead of me. He was thrown in the air and let go of the light machine gun that he had taken from our dead machine gunners. Both fell to the ground. I was so tired that I could not stop on the spot – inertia carried me – and I jumped over him.

"I was sure that he had been killed, but I stopped to help him, if I could, and looked back, but he was already getting up, grabbing his belt in one hand and the machine gun in the other. There was so much killing around us that day, but he was not hurt – only his belt was cut in two.

"There were some other instances when I knew ahead of time what was going to happen, and it did happen. Those were unexplained premonitions or extrasensory perceptions…

"Later that day I was asked three times to take command of our company while the captain was lost – hiding in a German bunker, in fact. I took the command – for a few hours – until the captain showed up. Half of the company was lost and ammunition gone. No reserves – not even ammunition! I pulled the company back without further losses and saved our wounded platoon commander, but he died in the sleigh on the way to the first aid station.

"It is the greatest honour any soldier can ever receive from his battle-hardened comrades, to be selected by them to lead them.

"I was concerned, but not afraid, only deeply critical over the whole darn thing – the stupid order even to attack this hill in that manner over a featureless field of snow when we could have advanced under cover.

"Now, the next day was different. I was gripped by terror when I could not get up a slope of a very deep drift of snow; so deep that it was over my head and my feet could not find the bottom of it yet. I tried, and tried, and tried, and then, once more, with the last bit of energy – knowing full well that this was it – now or never. This was where I felt panic; it gave me a shot of adrenaline and I made it.

"Something gave way and I got up that slope. I realized only much later that what was holding me back was my helmet, hung on the belt behind hand grenade heads. This deadly combination was acting as a plough under my belly. The helmet and the grenades remained in that snowdrift without me knowing it at the time.

"I did not want to die like that – defenceless – just because I could not get up a slope! It was panic that saved me.

"A number of things preconditioned me for it, I presume.

"I had a strange weapon in my hands – a strange rifle. The night before someone had taken mine. That demoralized me no end, and there was nothing that I could do about it. I shall return to that later.

"A strange soldier two feet to the left of me was wounded in his lower abdomen by machine gun fire. He pulled out his pistol and killed himself, to avoid being captured alive by the Russians. He knew that it was impossible to save him.

"Our heavy platoon was completely destroyed – all men and weapons lost. I saw them being killed, one death in particular is etched in my mind. He was hit while running and fell, but struggled to get up and continued to run, but a new burst of machine gun fire hit him again. He fell again and did not move any more. He, probably, was dead before his body hit the snow. And so was the whole platoon – some thirty men.

"The cook's helper of our company was a frail, short man. Even the shortest overcoat was too long for him. He had fallen somewhat behind the others and a Russian was trying to take him prisoner. With my own rifle I could have picked off the Russian, but with the strange one in my hands, I did not dare risk it. The small man killed the Russian with the butt of his rifle.

"We had encountered a battalion of Russian fusiliers on skis who were armed with hand machine guns. That is where I got mine. It was wrapped in white gauze as camouflage – heavily saturated with blood.

"All of this, probably, ripened me for panic, although it lasted only for a few seconds, but I felt its effect long after, I was not so sure of myself anymore – something had been broken within me by sheer force; but whatever it was I regained it all, and then some, on the return leg of the suicide mission I told you about. And then I realized I had become a man – a quiet fighting man – reconciled with the imminent inevitability of death. I had left the years of my youth behind me.

"Ingrid, I was never afraid of the enemy nor of combat. As a matter of fact, I enjoyed the sound of battle and being a part of it. What terrified and demoralized me most was the loss of my bride, my rifle. During a very short rest after a forced all-night march, while I was asleep standing up, dead tired, and leaning against a wall, someone had taken my rifle, substituting it with his. I was no longer surrounded by my old squad. And I am still asking myself, how could anyone have done it in complete darkness and jam-packed with soldiers?

"Oh, Ingrid, did that hurt! I was the best marksman in the company. With a strange weapon in my hands I felt naked. It happened at night and in the most excruciating circumstances. Perhaps, it was not intentional.

"There is a silver lining to it all. After getting the hand machine gun – how could I have said goodbye to my rifle? Perhaps leave it with the company command for sniping purposes?

"After that morning our company consisted of two squads. We had been continuously awake in forced marches or in battle for some seventy hours, but we had stopped the Russians…"

Silence…

"What was that suicide mission your company commander entrusted you with?" I dare to ask quietly.

"A whole battalion was missing. My task was to enter Russian occupied area and find that battalion – wherever it was – and lead them to our left flank so that a continuous front line would be re-established. I found them decimated and hiding in a forest, and led them to our left flank. I was in command of the left flank of our known front line then.

"I selected the best men for this mission. We succeeded.

"More questions?" he asks.

"Just one. You gave a lot. What did you receive in return?"

"Well, the customary battle decorations, under the

circumstances. Above all, the honour of being selected by my comrades of all ranks, as their commander in battle, and, the recognition by my superiors.

"That suicide mission demanded a sharp mind, resolute action and luck. My company commander knew and trusted me. It was not a voluntary undertaking. He selected me for it – the same as previously, for other most dangerous and difficult tasks. I do not think that I was Uriah, the husband of Bathsheba, to be repeatedly sent into battle and surely get killed.

"It was more important to get the job done – if humanly possible – and in his book I was the one who could do it. I was known to be able to do what others could not. My men knew that too and considered it an honour to be selected by me for any action.

"Proximity to me did not mean safety – I was just lucky as a person and have never sent anyone into death. That was known too – I went where they went, always leading up front.

"The day before, having commanded, 'on invitation', what was left of our company, I had earned a battlefield commission with plenty to spare, but nobody knew anything about it outside the company, and our company commander could not report it without incriminating himself. By next day most were dead and I did not talk.

"I did not receive any worldly laurels, but the greatest: I am in peace with my conscience, and alive.

"What I have done, and with what was in my mind and my heart, is before God for Him to judge and He has given me life.

"I arrived at the front fearless and, through fear, terror, panic and successes, returned from it a warrior.

"Horrible memories of war is the price a soldier pays for surviving it, Ingrid… The price for life is high…"

And Arne has ended his story of war…

*

"My dear, dear man – never, ever, a question again. What I've heard today is burdening my soul. Millions and millions of innocent people lost their lives or were tormented, just like you – in the most indescribable ways – because of two tyrants and our gullibility," I whisper quietly.

It is late and after a light snack of lobster, we go to bed. Our embrace is tender, so tender – and for the first time we feel that that's quite enough for tonight. It feels so wonderful to have Arne's warm body so close against mine and to know that we can have everything, yet decide to have nothing. Our minds are tired and far away, back in history. We are not preoccupied with ourselves; we are with those who died and those who suffered – and my own Arne is one of them.

How wonderful is the very thought that the chalice is there, but shall not be touched tonight. The thought came uninvited – from our hearts, as if we could read each other's minds, and that is important. Let the chalice be tonight. It is so full for both of us and the rest of our lives. This is the very first such night in our yet short marriage...

"The mystery of mastery over ourselves," Arne had said at the lake. How impatient and full of expectations I was then! And how beautiful is the experience now, with myself taking an active part in it! I have grown up a lot since then and shall never be the same again.

Arne is long since asleep. I gaze in the semi-darkness of our bedroom. My dear, dear husband. Has he been saved for me?

No! That couldn't be! I'm not that important. He probably has a goal to fulfil in life, but he does not even know it yet. There must be something he has been spared for. There must be a purpose.

Perhaps his experiences have moulded him as he is – with features of determination in his face; yet tender is his soul and it shows not only in his face, but in his eyes in particular.

Those deep, deep eyes. And the way he walks! I didn't realize that that's the reflection of the military in him. All of that is what made him stand out as a giant that fateful Saturday, that most beautiful Saturday afternoon!

He carries wounds in his body and his soul... I shall do my very best to try to heal them – if it is humanly possible. I shall try with all my heart...

In the years to come he will return to his memories of war and tell me the most dramatic story of where and how he woke up from that concussion and what followed – and all those hospitals…

Why was he spared?

What is his purpose of life? And in life?

★

"Horrible memories of war is the price a soldier pays for surviving it… The price of life is high…"

Home Again

"Mother! Dear, dear Mother!" I exclaim as I embrace her at the door. "We're finally home! All of us! All three of us!"

"All three?" asks Mother, as she gently pushes me back to look into my eyes.

"All three! Or maybe four!" I laugh back and Mother kisses my cheeks as Arne looks on and smiles knowingly.

"Sis! Are you expecting?" asks Astrid, trying to get her head in between Mother and Father.

"No, Princess! I am not expecting – I am very sure!" I tease back.

"Glorious! Simply glorious! Do you know where?" Astrid is beside herself.

"Yes, Princess! On the rock."

Father leans back and enjoys the family union with a wide, wide smile all across his face and I grab him around the shoulders and kiss his cheeks and he, without saying a word, kisses my forehead. Yes, my dear, dear father can't speak right now.

Arne first kisses Mother's hand and then embraces her whispering, "Mother! Do you accept me as your son?"

"More than that, Arne! Much, much more than that!" and Mother reaches her arm out to Father and all three embrace together.

"Welcome home, son! Welcome home!" says Father with tears in his eyes – and so they remain for a short while with Astrid and me looking on.

Just as soon as the embrace loosens, Astrid jumps in, "Hello, brother!" and now there are four in the embrace. Since I have nothing better to do, I embrace them all.

We're all together – a complete family – and so we shall remain for the rest of our days on this earth.

Both sides of our front door are open and that's where we all still are, just inside the threshold.

"Now, let's go in, kids! Let's go in!" invites Father and we all end up in the living room, like a swarm of bees looking for a place to settle down.

Everybody was waiting for us. The chauffeur had called just as our plane was landing.

"Father! What's all that stuff in front of our house?" I ask. "It looks like a regular construction zone!"

"Yes, Ingrid! Upstairs is done, but the music hall is not finished yet."

"The music hall?"

"Yes! We are doubling the size of it. Astrid needs three pianos. Since it shall be Astrid's one day, we are doing a proper job now. The contractor is working overtime. It's late, they just left, but will be back tomorrow morning, early. In another couple of weeks it shall be ready. It took a little while to get the building permit," explains Father.

"Three pianos? Astrid!" I ask, exclaiming in disbelief.

"Yep! And both of you are guilty for that!" Astrid laughs back. "Remember the Earth, the Sower, and the Rainmaker? And they all are independently busy with what each of them has to do. Thus – three pianos!"

"Yes, Princess! I remember, you had to run away from the phone!"

"That's it! That's exactly it, Sis, and what I heard then was good. You'll see. It's not quite finished, the piano Partitures, I mean."

"Ingrid, Astrid has been working on a composition at the Conservatory. We had to remove all our instruments for reasons of safety and protection," explains Father. "Mother was lucky to find a good match for the two we have."

"Arne, darling! This has been a madhouse while we were busy with ourselves," I say to Arne, and put my hand on his shoulder.

"More than that, Sis! Much, much more than that!" Astrid repeats Mother's words to Arne. "If you only knew what awaits you both – with my approval – you would faint!" and Astrid looks at us with love and admiration. It must be something good, I'm sure.

"Well, you've had a long day and a tiresome journey. A special supper will be ready for us in about an hour. You certainly want to change and freshen up. So, I'll just take you up to your quarters – or should we all do that?" asks Father with a broad and knowing smile.

"Of course, Father! How else?" exclaims Astrid and takes Mother by the hand.

I don't recognize the upstairs of our home any more. It's a different world. At first, we enter our "study". Everything is his and hers: desks, bookcases, filing cabinets, telephones, even wastepaper baskets.

Then a door takes us to a large, beautiful foyer with a huge skylight high above and a well-grown hibiscus tree in full bloom underneath it. It is of the single, poppy-red, variety – the one Father knows I love so much. There are two very large and high plate glass mirrors opposite each other – one on the left, and the other to the right of us. We see ourselves and the blossoms reflected endlessly in both directions.

"Oh, yes, Astrid! This is it! Isn't it? Just marvellous! Thank you, Father! You wanted a free hand and now I see what you have done with it!" and I kiss him on the cheek, and Mother and Astrid too.

"Shall we continue the inspection?" asks Father. "Go on! Take Arne with you."

The door we came through is soundproofed on the inside – and so is the one leading us to our bedroom, presumably.

Not thinking much of it I take Arne's hand, open the door and, letting Arne's hand go – freeze – rushing both hands to my cheeks. Arne is still behind me and possibly has not noticed anything yet. I turn my head towards him and step aside. I know that my eyes are wide open; my mouth half open; and I am still holding my cheeks by my hands.

Arne looks, puts his arm around my waist, and we both enter our bedroom with ceiling and walls in continuous, large plate glass mirrors.

We turn around and see the faces of three conspirators. Astrid seems to be the happiest of them all. I cover my face and lean against Arne's chest, feeling his tender embrace. Then I lift my head and run to Father, kissing his cheeks and embracing him.

"It's okay Kitten! It's okay! It should be okay, isn't it? At least that's what we think – your mother and I and Astrid! Isn't it?" asks Father.

I nod my head in agreement, hold him stronger and rest my right cheek on his chest.

"Well, well, well! Then make a 'test run' and tell us all about it!"

I look into Father's eyes and then run to Mother. She embraces me saying nothing, as usual, just patting my back lightly. Then Astrid comes to us, embraces us and whispers:

"And when I grow up, it will be mine. That's where my approval came in, and now – my blessing!"

"Yes, Princess! Someday that will be your bedroom," concludes Father and, with his hand on Arne's shoulder, they both come to us womenfolk.

We also look in at the brand new nursery and nanny's quarters. Father has thought of everything with love and care, and his hopes shall be fulfilled – the Johannsens shall live through us.

The music hall is enlarged on a grandiose scale for a private residence. The latest in acoustic materials are used and movable sound absorbers and reflectors are yet to come. The hall itself shall be as tuned as an instrument.

As we enjoy the meal and chat – the main subject is our honeymoon and the joyful state of motherhood, the time, doctor and nanny.

The crate with eleven bottles of that extraordinary pink champagne has been received back and is in our wine cellar waiting for the appropriate time, perhaps next year, but not while I am carrying or breastfeeding my baby.

We also tell them of the trip we took.

"Isn't it a beautiful country?" Father asks Arne.

"Breathtaking in its beauty and variety! Although I have not seen the west yet – the east can stand on its own feet with its own variety and very distinct beauty," answers Arne.

"Next summer you shall see Canada for real when we go to visit our branches, if you would like that," assures Father.

"Of course! Of course, but it can wait! Ingrid comes first!" answers Arne, looking at me.

"Quite so! Quite so! If you have quintuplets – it may be a bit difficult! What do you say, Ingrid?" laughs Father looking at me.

"Oh, let's wait and see. We'll have a spring 'litter'. It might be best to stay put for a while," I answer, laughing, in the same manner as I was asked, all in good humor.

"Sure! Let's see when the time comes and decide then, shall we?" Father puts that question away.

"Well, here is something else new. You both have your own maid and chauffeur—"

"Thank you, Father! Thank you! I have been thinking about the same thing, but knowing how difficult it is to engage good servants, I held back. You have so much on your mind now with the remodelling," I interrupt happily.

"They are already here and waiting for your arrival, including your own limousine. As of tomorrow morning, they are at your service.

"It came quite easily and unexpectedly. Our cook is getting older. She realized the need, talked to me about it and recommended a married couple who were her relatives. They are in their early forties, but without children; they can't have any. She's reportedly a good cook. Her primary responsibility will be to look after your quarters. The rest of the time she will be with our cook and help her.

"Her husband was injured in an industrial accident, and who can live on Workmen's Compensation? His left arm is hurt. Our cook told us all about it, and it was just what we needed for you two, making our cook happy, and helping unfortunate people. They have safety, security and money for the rest of their lives. Both will be discreet, I am sure, knowing all about us through our cook.

"Her husband can perform all the duties of a chauffeur and has received training in that. He is very happy about it and so are we.

"Make them both feel welcome and appreciated, the chauffeur in particular, since you will have continuous daily contact with him.

"Make it right at the very start. Ingrid knows how. I am saying this mostly for the benefit of Arne," concludes Father.

"I have always treated others as equals or superior to me. Much is in your hands, Father – how we meet – how we are introduced to each other," answers Arne.

"Very true, son! Very true!"

"I have something very heavy on my heart," starts Arne slowly.

"In the decision on that Tuesday morning regarding the adoption, I did not think of something of paramount importance.

"My thoughts were only with Ingrid and the perpetuation of your family name. I completely overlooked that by adopting me, I am robbing Astrid. That is unacceptable. I can be your adopted son – as long as I am specifically excluded from your will as to any inheritance.

"This time I am saying something that has not been discussed with Ingrid. Please believe me, I am not a gold digger! I shall not inherit anything but Ingrid, and I have her already!" Arne tries to put it in light of his true feelings and the joyful atmosphere we have during meals.

"Over my dead body!" exclaims Astrid. "You are my brother and we both share everything equally, my sister and I. I told you that when we first met. Remember, when you kissed my hand and I kissed your lips? No! Not only your lips – when I kissed you!"

"Arne, you just confirmed that you are what we all think and know you are," interjects Father. "All the documents are ready. You are our adopted son, sharing everything equally with our daughters, just as soon as we all sign the documents tomorrow.

"You are in our will as a son – just as Ingrid and Astrid are as daughters. We cleared all this with Astrid and such is our wish, unless Ingrid objects," and Father looks at me.

"No, Father! No! I don't have any objections! How could I, with Arne as my husband? How could I?"

"Neither do I!" assures Astrid and looks at Arne dreamily.

"Son? Is this settled now?" asks Father and looks at Arne with his customary broad smile.

"Thank you all for the great trust and honour you have shown me. As long as you know that it was not intended that way," says Arne quietly.

"Now it's time for you all to know everything," I speak up:

"Arne asked for my hand in marriage thinking that I had a misfortune in life. He thought that I was pregnant, perhaps, and abandoned – and desperately searching for a saviour. He had fallen in love with me at the moment our eyes met – and so had I. He did not know of my wealth, but I knew that he was going to be my husband. He asked for my hand not knowing my family and my past. It was only I that mattered to him. That proves his honour beyond a shadow of doubt! It does to me!"

"Well, son! Do you accept our verdict?" asks Father.

"I do, Father, Mother, Sister and Wife! I do, and thank you again. I wanted to be Ingrid's saviour in shining armour. Now it turns out that she, in fact, is my saviour. She has opened doors that otherwise would have remained closed to me for life. I shall not let you down – not any one of you," assures Arne.

"I think that that settles it for life," concludes Father.

"I don't want to change the subject, but we will be making a pilgrimage to the lake – the first of many to come," say I, and continue, "We shall go just as soon as we can, in a couple of days and by ourselves."

"That is wonderful, Ingrid," Mother speaks gently. "We did the same – when we knew," and she looks at Father with a faraway look.

"Yes we did, in gratitude," answers Father and looks back at Mother for a long while. "So, you want to be completely alone. We were too, Gunilla. Weren't we?"

Mother just looks at Father. She does not speak. Everything is in her eyes.

"If we are successful, all of us shall see it. I better tell you of our plan. All over the east coast we bought wild red poppy seeds, and will get some more here in Toronto. We plan to sow them on the island, in its nooks and crannies, hoping that some will take root. If not this fall, we shall repeat it, hoping for the best."

"Excuse me!" and Astrid is gone. We all sense why. When she comes back, her face glows with an inner light – just what Arne saw when he first met her, and I know, somewhere idle staffs on a blank page have become part of a phrase – a sketch of a score of music – known only to her.

After supper, Astrid plays Brahms' Lullaby on my violin. So

tender is her touch and mellow the tone that I cannot resist, but ask her to play it with variations and improvisations. It is out of this world what she can do with it.

Soon enough I join her with the violoncello and we both are back on our well-beaten path of melodies that we have played together, now and then, since time immemorial – it seems to me now – since we both were kids. And then, in conclusion, I take the violin and play the same Brahms' Lullaby for Arne, with my heart and soul in it.

Homecoming is a true enjoyment of love, music and laughter – and for the first time, at last, I have played for my dear Arne.

★

Our first night in our unexpected and bewildering bedroom of mirrors is an indescribable experience – no matter how I look at it – in my mind only; or with my eyes wide open and with Arne in my arms.

Next morning, seeing myself in the ceiling spread out for Arne by full daylight – and him too – makes my blood boil, and we both have the time of our lives! The chalice of pleasure runs over! There seems to be no end to it all!

"Have I not been at an auction of race horses and ended up with the most desirable stallion?" I asked myself on that faraway Sunday evening – and remember it now again. Have I gotten myself a most desirable "Pet"? Yes, I have, and so has he. We shall share each other with gusto, no reservations. Father has made it possible and my dear mother and sister understand me. But won't all this wake up the woman in Astrid too early?

I wander in my thoughts while trying to regain my composure. There is so much to do today and we have to face our family shortly.

No! I can't tell Father about this test-run! I'm sure he will not ask. What he said was only a manner of speech.

This wedding present is worth more to me than the tiara… Much, much more…

That's what I shall tell Father…

It's the truth…

Getting Settled In

The documents are signed and social notices mailed. The university has been notified. I'm now Mrs Arne Johannsen, very officially. I have ordered my bras and a score of dresses.

Arne's huge walk-in closet slowly fills with suits, shoes and other things. His wedding morning suit is joined now by tuxedo and tails – one never knows when they may be needed.

Father has done a remarkable thing – our individual dressing areas are self-contained units adjacent to the bedroom, and contain dressers, mirrors and other facilities, and are connected to our walk-in closets as well as to our bathrooms.

Thus, our huge bedroom has no furniture, with the exception of a king-size bed, a few ottomans, a grand leather chesterfield by the windows, night tables and a round, marble table with a crystal vase and flowers. All is kept in warm pastel colours.

Arne has bought all the books he needs for the three extra exams. He wants to get them over with before Christmas. That's quite an order, but let it be. He studies continuously.

We were at the lake and did our sowing on the island and around places that have become close to us – some in our rock garden too, where we were married. Let's see what next spring brings and every spring after that.

I'm in my niche in the living room. It's cosy here. I made it so. Each one of us has, in accordance with our inner selves. Arne sticks with me in mine, now ours, and adds his personality to it. That's how it should be – augmenting each other.

Oh! I love him so, and with each passing day more and more. Our lovemaking is not as wild any more, but it is deep and so satisfying, body and soul. Body and soul.

Today is the first regular school day and Astrid is gone since early morning. Our lectures will start in a couple of weeks.

Mother comes in from the garden with autumn flowers for a few vases around the house. We chat a little and then she is gone again – slowly, imperceptibly as usual. She is still a young and beautiful woman, but so quiet.

When the music hall will be finally done, seasoned and the instruments back – she will play daily, again. That's where she does her talking, through the instruments. Arne's arrival and our wedding was just a short interruption of her routine.

I know of her love for Father and the quiet moments they spend together – just being together is quite enough for them. Talk is silver, silence is gold. That is how we grew up, but Astrid and I are more extrovert. Yes, Mother and her golden silence – yet, she's always there when need be.

Arne comes down the stairs:

"It is no good to be cooped up like that, day in, day out, Ingrid, but I must free myself – I must get those exams behind me!" and he joins me, stretching out on a sofa.

"You have undertaken a grand task. I hope you make it. It would be so nice to have my husband back again," I tease.

"Hey! Are you missing me?"

"No, dear, I'm not missing you – just wondering what are you thinking about while making love to me: The Balanced Budget Multiplier, or reconciling Monetary and Fiscal Policies?

"When was Canada born?" I ask quickly.

"1867, Charlottetown, P.E.I."

"Date?"

"That's details, Ingrid! Details are not important, the overall matter is what counts!"

"If I happen to meet your examiners, I shall tell them not to ask you details," I laugh.

"July 1!"

"That's better!"

"Hi, folks!" Astrid is home and Arne is up as if struck by a bolt of lightning.

"Hey, Astrid!" he exclaims.

"Yes, Arne?" and Astrid comes and sits down heavily with a huge load of new books.

"Ingrid! What does this get-up mean?"

"Oh! It's the uniform of our private school!" answers Astrid instead.

"But your skirt! It's so short!"

"That's the way they are supposed to be," and Astrid gets up and turns around, modelling it.

"Well, they are far too short – even now, while standing up, but when you sat down…" Arne stops, looking for words, perhaps.

"Oh! Yes! I know! My panties are white today!" Astrid comes to the rescue.

Poor Arne looks at Astrid and me in a way that makes us both laugh. Astrid falls down beside Arne and hugs him.

"Astrid! Do you mean that Ingrid was wearing a uniform like yours as late as this spring?" asks Arne.

"Shorter! She had grown out of hers, but did not want to change!" laughs Astrid in Arne's face.

"True, Arne! It was so," I agree.

"And when did you cut your hair?" Arne continues.

"Towards the end of grade twelve."

"Ingrid! With a get-up like that and your long golden hair, you were a walking advertisement sign!" he exclaims.

"Advertising what?" asks Astrid still in her laughter.

"'Open for Business', that's what!" answers Arne.

"What business?" asks Astrid and stops her laughter.

Then she explodes: "Oh, no! Arne! No! Is that how I look?" she manages to ask, fighting for breath.

"I was referring to Ingrid's long hair and even shorter skirt, at her age. But you are on the right track," mumbles Arne.

"Oh, my dear, dear, innocent brother-in-law! I adore you!" Astrid embraces Arne and squeezes him. Arne returns the embrace ever so lightly until Astrid lets him go.

"I have rehearsal time booked on one of the best organs in Toronto! Do you two want to come along?" she asks.

"I would love to! How about you, Arne?" I ask. He agrees and we go.

Astrid and I get into the limousine first and I see Arne's disbelief as Astrid's tights flash. Yes, she is only thirteen, but her budding femininity is obvious.

At the practice, we are with Astrid for a while watching her play, sitting on the very edge of the bench. Arne looks at her legs and turns to me with a big question mark on his face. I take his hand and pat it a little and look in his eyes, smiling. My dear Arne has so much to learn and get used to in this country – things and customs, new and foreign to him.

Astrid is gone... She no longer exists, nor do we, only the music does... The instrument has become just a medium... The organ in her hands and under her feet is born anew and responds accordingly...

We quietly walk away and find a spot in the cathedral. It's saturated with the vibrations of thousands of pipes – all awakened by the master at the console.

The organ submits to Astrid. She is the virtuoso master and commander. One senses that without fail. I put my head on Arne's shoulder and listen to the performance. No! It's not a performance! The very genius of the composer has been awakened through Astrid and it is truly the genius of the composer that we hear. That's the ultimate any artist in music can hope to attain...

The final chords of Bach's "Little Fuge" reverberate through this vast space. Then she stops, and my mind sees Astrid, how she sits with lowered head and slender fingers over her face.

Soon enough another composition graces this cathedral, and us too.

"This is new," whispers Arne.

"Perhaps her own," I whisper back, and we both listen intensely and in amazement.

It is very beautiful. So very, very beautiful, with melodies winding through and with each other. Quite different from Bach's fast mathematical configurations. It's melodic and sumptuous. Above the very low tones, there's a lark in the sky, singing its heart out over its nest! A deep river flows slowly past forest meadows with wild flowers in full bloom. It is an adoration to all that is good and beautiful. And then it ends with a dramatic crescendo. It was short. Too short.

On the way home Astrid is very quiet. Her body is with us, but not her mind. We do not converse. We let her mind return to us first.

"It is not finished yet... There is still a lot to do..." Astrid breaks the silence very quietly.

"Call it 'Miracle', Astrid!" says Arne just as quietly.

"No! Arne! It shall be called 'Glory' and dedicated to our parents. It will take years to complete. The choral part alone is a task in itself. I have only ideas about it, nothing concrete. It should be done by the time I am ready to graduate from the conservatory. Five years is a long time for me, but short for what I have to do," and Astrid falls silent again.

"I'm sure, Astrid, Father and Mother will be very, very happy, and they deserve that!" I add.

"I hope it turns out as well as I hear it in my head. If it does, it shall be one of my graduation works…

"Miracle! Miracle? Miracle," Astrid whispers and then quickly grabs some blank sheets of music and notes start to fly on empty staffs, filling them with life. It happens fast and furious.

We do not realize that at this very moment a symphony is born. It shall be called "Miracle" and dedicated to Arne, for he's the inspiration. It shall become another of Astrid's graduation works, along with "Glory"; and yet, a third one, dedicated to me, is to come as well – yet unknown to any of us at this time. It shall become an unprecedented graduation trilogy.

*

Later that evening, when going to bed, Arne is still in the grip of his experiences today: Astrid's short skirt and the grandeur of her music.

I try to get him down to earth by modelling my skirt of this spring. Arne looks in disbelief. He asks me to sit down and I do. He only shakes his head, but remains in his world.

"You have not been in Toronto during a school year. Private schools have their uniforms and it's a long-standing custom for girls to have short skirts. It's an unquestioned part of daily life here, but to you, of course, it's an abnormality. I agree with you and understand it – now that I am married, but remember, they start to wear them young and slowly grow up in them."

"I think that you are right, but that is not all that is on my mind, Ingrid."

"Arne! Share with me! Share with me your feelings, if you wish," I offer.

"Are you sure, Ingrid? Are you sure?" he questions me.

"Is it something that you would rather keep to yourself?"

"No! It is not that! I do not know how to put it in words. Perhaps there are no words to describe it.

"Could it be true that we live in a historic time when, right in our family, a new Beethoven is awakening?

"I cannot describe Astrid. It escapes my comprehension.

"As a woman – you, Ingrid, are a rare, juicy T-bone steak to a hungry man; Astrid, in the years to come, shall grow up to be an unattainable goddess – a dessert without a name. One can gorge oneself on T-bone steak, but not on dessert."

"One also does not eat salt, pepper, mustard or horseradish by the spoonful," I interject.

"You are right. I was thinking aloud. Let me… I may yet find a way to tell you what I think of her.

"When I first met her I noticed her pure white, unblemished face, reflected today in her thighs. She is only thirteen, but already a goddess-like creature on a pedestal to be known that she exists; to be seen, but not touched; to be enjoyed as a fleeting image, but never beheld for any length of time – unobtainable…

"Her music is that of an indisputable genius."

"How do you feel about her?" I ask.

"I do not know."

"I wouldn't be a bit surprised if you would desire her as a woman when she grows up." I say what I think might be troubling Arne.

"No! Ingrid! No! What are you saying? No! Not that! At her age? And having you! I am not a pervert, Ingrid! But what it is, I cannot explain…

"Awe? Yes, Ingrid! Awe! That is the best I can do – awe. I am in awe – a woman, child and genius in one body.

"Your unexpected question shocked me and the brain reacted accordingly. Awe. It is awe that is in me. Awe of her and her potential. Awe of what is, and what shall come.

"And there may be truth in what you said. My subconscious mind may have detected in her a desirable member of the opposite sex – when she grows up, but I had no such thoughts on my mind, though! *Just think of her age, Ingrid!"* explodes Arne loudly again.

I know that I have wronged him and am so sorry. I take my own short school skirt off, throw it aside, put my arms around Arne's neck and look in his eyes. He looks back, starts to smile and we kiss each other tenderly.

"Just think, Ingrid," he says quietly. "That skirt has a slit, leaving the impression that it can be thrown open at any time! Anytime at all! Do you see what I mean and understand my reaction?" he asks in a whisper.

"Arne, forgive me. My question was tactless. As far as I know, men desire pretty women, if only with their eyes; and there surely shall be women in our lives that would make me jealous if I would know what you think about them, even if only for an instant."

"I would be abnormal if my masculinity would become immune to provoking sights and instances in our lives, but I shall always be faithful to you, darling. Always. And do not apply such thoughts to children, ever," he answers, patting my back.

"Yes! I see, Arne, what you mean. I am used to her, but you were exposed so suddenly to all of it in one dose. Yes, I would probably have reacted just as you did. She is a marvel, isn't she?" I ask slowly and very, very quietly, but then I change my tone:

"Come now and have your rare, juicy T-bone steak!"

The Company

Arne has passed all of his extra exams and it is only the tail end of November. Now I have him back – body and mind.

The final designs of the jewellery we ordered at Birks have been approved, as well as cost, excepting the rock, of course. For that we will have to wait years, perhaps many. Christmas delivery is assured.

I helped Arne to catch up with philosophy in depth. He has attended all the lectures with me, but now he is studying the subject. Logic fascinates him. It's as if someone has put down his own thoughts in writing and in formulae. He's at home with economics, and psychology does not present any problems either.

Everything is up to date and I tell him the gossip at my faculty. All the girls are in a flutter, planning who is going to marry whom, in the "upper crust" of course.

I'm the only married one in our course. How happy I am about that! I would have been lost in that crowd of fortune hunters. I've my own fortune – material and marital.

They all are my friends, perhaps since I am out of the race – out of the competition. It does seem as if the majority wants to be in the faculty primarily because it's where the rich look for wives. Not me! I want knowledge only and am in it for the full two-plus-two-year term.

The music hall is finished, climate controls working and it is tuned for best acoustics. All the instruments are back, plus our new piano – a tremendous instrument. We positioned them so that we are face to face, two against one.

Oh, did we have a go at them? Mother, Astrid and poor little me. What a difference! Astrid was right; the third piano has created a depth otherwise unattainable! I'm sure that the new hall has plenty to do with it as well.

Mother plays daily again. We play a little before and after supper, and then – studies.

It's very comfortable and relaxing in our study, very conducive to a high degree of concentration. Arne had discovered that earlier and proved it by passing his exams. I'm sure that his capacity had something to do with it as well.

It's Saturday and we're in our living room. Father comes up to us and invites Arne to spend some time with him regarding the company and we all three go to Father's study.

★

"Let me put it as clearly and briefly as I can," starts Father. "The most important elements in our company are the employees. Regardless of their individual positions, they all have been selected with these four basic elements in mind:

1. Honesty; reliability; responsibility and trustworthiness. Note that these all are matters of character only.
2. Knowledge; ability; capacity.
3. Interpersonal relations; and positive outlook.
4. Sense of belonging.

"It is an inverted pyramid of four; three; two; and one element – all interacting and supporting each other.

"All new positions are filled with the best personnel available and at the highest pay. We do not raid other companies, but search the market for what is available, including those who still work for other companies, but have expressed a desire for change.

"It's a competition, best of the best. Our own employees have priority only if they are fully equal, or superior, to the best on the open market for any specific position at that time.

"This gives the employees incentive to attend night classes or take correspondence courses to improve themselves.

"The company pays all the fees for any course an employee wants to take – even if it does not appear to have any relation to the job they are presently doing, or conceivably may do in the future – until the employee has exhausted his or her capacity.

"One can't predict the future and one does not have the right to interfere with the goals an employee may have set for him or herself. That's where the capacity of everyone is determined, not

only for the benefit of the company, but also for the employee –
having satisfied the desire to learn, having reached the ultimate in
ability to absorb knowledge.

"Of course, they have to pass the exams in order to receive
further company funding.

"From the very beginning of our company, my grandfather
formed an employees' union with all expenses paid by the
company. It's not a 'run-of-the-mill' union as established in other
companies here. It's not for the purpose of strikes and wage
demands. We pay more than any other company.

"My grandfather saw another vision. Unions were not popular
in those days, but the need existed for social welfare for the
employees and their families and he wanted to help in as much as
he could. Why not let the employees get together, with their
families if they wished to do so, and discuss anything they
wanted, right in the plant after hours or on weekends? That's how
it started.

"It gives the employees, and their families, a forum where they
can discuss matters related to the company, as well as their social
lives and plans.

"We can afford to pay top wages and salaries because of top
productivity and top quality in every phase of our operations,
including the offices.

"Of course, the product has plenty to do with it as well:
Swedish steel ball-and-roller bearings of every kind. That's why
we were able to weather the depression without laying off any
employees. As long as there are wheels – there shall be ball-and-
roller bearings – unless square wheels are invented or something
else of that sort," Father laughs and continues.

"The employees remember that and also know that their high
income, bonuses and wage increases depend on productivity and
quality. It's a self-governing body throughout, including top
management on an equal footing with the floor sweepers and
maintenance men.

"Directors of the company are specifically excluded. We
participate in their meetings only when requested and only those
who are invited.

"Although we're a privately owned company, our annual

audited financial statements are distributed to each and every employee – including a letter stating the total capital investment; current rate of interest; and how much interest the capital would have earned if deposited in a bank.

"The total profit, after taxes, less such interest, is money earned by the operations of our company – twenty-five per cent of which is 'risk factor'.

"The remaining seventy-five per cent is analyzed as to reserves required for: wear and tear; updating; replacements; and expansions – with a timetable for that.

"Directors' fees are a nominal $1 per annum each. I'm on the payroll as is everybody else, serving as the President. All salaries and annual wages are known to everybody, including mine. They each receive a complete list, along with the annual statements and a Directors' Report.

"The rest of the profit is distributed to all employees in direct proportion to their annual earnings as their share of profit. It may be as a bonus, increases in wages and salaries or a combination of both. The employees decide that with, or without, the input of their families. All decisions are made by democratic votes, open or closed, according to their own rules – which may change from time to time in accordance with their own decisions. Of course, promotional or performance wage or salary increases are separate, over and above the annual adjustment based on profitability.

"Yes, I almost forgot! Two directors are allowed cars with all expenses paid by the company. Presently it is my limousine and Arne's Oldsmobile.

"Consequently, Arne, the employees are kept in the overall picture and satisfied that the owners do not take out of the company more than the equivalent interest the investment would have earned in a bank, plus the 'risk factor'.

"We pay all premiums for the protection of health and life for all employees and their families. We also pay all premiums for pensions at retirement.

"There are no payroll deductions with the exception of those demanded by law.

"It is all a common sense co-operation at all levels. Just like you two invited Astrid to share your limousine and chauffeur, thus greatly reducing the load on the other drivers and keeping yours fully occupied.

"All of that creates loyalty.

"For as long as there shall be wheels – there are going to be ball-and-roller bearings of one type or another. That's our business," concludes Father.

Silence...

"Father, the pension fund. How is it handled?" asks Arne.

"Through an insurance company. The same one as life insurance for the employees and for us," Father answers.

"Is it so," asks Arne, "that, let us say, an employee at age twenty-five is being told *now* how much the premiums are going to be for the next forty years, starting *now* – although the company pays them; and, at the same time – how much his pension is going to *be then,* at the age of sixty-five?"

"Yes! That's how it is, Arne. They all are like that!"

"It's no good, Father! It does not protect the purchasing power of the dollar. Valuable money is being spent now in premiums, but very cheap money received in pensions. Who can tell what the pensions will be worth forty years from now? A fifteen cent loaf of bread now may cost $1.50 *then,* or more!"

"It is happening, with inflation!" replies Father.

"I recommend a change, for your consideration," comes Arne so early in the game.

"Why not call a meeting of the board of directors?" I ask.

"True! Why not?" and Father goes to round up the gang.

"Astrid requests to be excused, after all, she is attending two schools at the same time and has to leave shortly, but she will participate for the formal orders of business," says Father, with Mother and Astrid in tow.

The law of the land has limits as to ages, etc., but we have our own traditions, and as long as we all are a family at peace with each other we shall continue to do so. First year at high school and of sound mind, is our prerequisite. So, Astrid became a director this spring and Arne upon our wishes.

We go to the library and Father calls the meeting to order. He is the chairman and Mother, vice-chairman and secretary.

After the approval of the minutes of the last meeting when

Arne was made a director, we proceed with the first order of business – the change of names for Arne and myself. Then I take over from Mother the title and duties of the secretary, with Mother remaining as vice-chairman. Astrid can go now.

"Arne has raised an important point. We all should hear him out. Please, Arne!" starts Father and turns the floor over to him.

"It deals with our employee pensions. Currently all employees know to the penny what their exact pension amount shall be at retirement, at sixty-five years of age, regardless of the value of the dollar when that distant time arrives, and for some employees it may be forty years, or even more, from now.

"There is no built-in preservation of the purchasing power of the dollar. What I am going to propose is not for the faint hearted, nor a short-term matter. It most definitely is a very long-term commitment, requiring a steady hand and strong nerves to carry it out.

"I request you to consider and, if seen fit, propose to the employees the following:

1. Give a thirty-day notice to the insurance company that we shall terminate our pension plan account with them as of December 31, 1948.
2. As of January 1, 1949, for the purposes of preserving the purchasing power of the dollar, we shall establish a new pension plan based on a Company Pension Trust Fund and administered as such with full participation of our union.
3. I further propose not to be greedy, not to stretch our luck, and stick with a uniform plan with fifty per cent invested in one hundred per cent secure bonds; and fifty per cent invested in 'blue chip', high-potential shares. This should be safe in case of another depression.
4. All employees should have the right to protect the purchasing power of their pension dollar by remaining in the plan even after retirement – at least those who wish to do so. After all, they may live another twenty years or more, after retirement, under the pressure of a constantly decreasing value of the dollar.
5. The amount paid in the Pension Fund shall be equivalent to the amount currently paid to the insurance company, thus not

decreasing their annual bonuses or wage and salary increases.

6. It should be understood by all employees and their families that the amount of dollars received as pension at age sixty-five cannot be predetermined, but is expected to be far in excess of what is now promised by the insurance company under the present plan.

"That's about it," Arne concludes, "but there is another matter I would like to discuss separately."

"Arne, how can an employee participate in the pension plan after retirement?" I ask, in awe of this completely new concept.

"First of all, each and every employee shall have an account, if you wish to call it that – or a card – showing all bonds and shares he owns, with fractions, of every purchase the Fund makes.

"On retirement the employee would state how much money he wants for the first year of retirement. Sufficient number of bonds and shares would then be sold at market prices to create the amount he wants, and reduce the holdings on his card by what has been sold for him.

"The remainder remains in his account and continues to participate fully with the rest of the fund; and so from year to year, for as long as he wants to remain in the fund. This does not apply to the estate of a deceased employee or former employee while still in the fund.

"Those who do not wish to participate after retirement shall receive total holdings at the market prices on that day – to do with it as they please. All, of course, in accordance with the laws of the land at that time," concludes Arne.

"I am for it, Father!" I say without hesitation and quite eagerly.

"How about you, Mother?" asks Father.

"What Arne told us so plainly about our present plan is very obvious! Just think of us spending money for our employees' pensions that would not be worth much when they retire!" Mother says with concern in her voice.

"I'm the one who knows best the inadequacies of our present plan. It has existed for a long time. What Arne warned us of has taken place in practice. The pensions our past employees are receiving now are growing in inadequacy year by year," Father admits and continues:

"I thought that the company, by paying all premiums for everything, was doing the corporate duty at its best, but I should have known better. Such a philosophy does not apply to long-term undertakings, such as pensions. It is clear that *what we do* is one thing, but *how we do it* is quite another!

"We've always been proud of our advances in looking after our employees, but as I see now – most, if not all, of the innovations were my grandfather's doings, and my father's. I've known of this inadequacy, yet I've not had the spark of originality to solve it.

"Ingrid! Do you realize now what you have done by snatching Arne out of the crowd?" and Father looks at me seriously.

"I also support Arne and express our thanks on behalf of all of us for having the guts to tell us that as early as he did.

"In order to give proper notice to the insurance company we must act quickly. There are only a few days left in November. Should we propose this to the union for consideration?

"All agree? Good! Monday morning it shall be in the hands of the union. On Tuesday, we must know.

"So, that's done! I feel better already. It has been depressing me for some time.

"Arne, you had something else to say as well, didn't you?" asks Father.

"Yes, but I am not as sure about this one as I was with the previous."

"Shoot!" says Father.

"I studied the financial statements and your last report to the employees, the package you gave me before I was made a director, but I do not know your financial wealth, and it is none of my business.

"For the purposes of what I have to say, may I assume that Ingrid is right? I do not question Ingrid's reliability, but it was a very informal remark she made, and now it becomes a most important detail.

"Is it so that, living as we do, we do not use up our income and we are getting wealthier year by year?" Arne asks.

"It is so, son!" Father replies.

"Now, what would you say if a part of the 'risk factor' would be set aside in a, let us say: 'Johannsen's Employee Future Fund –

in Trust'? At least as much as the total annual investment in the Pension Fund," concludes Arne.

"Why?" asks Father.

"Well, frankly, as a safety reserve if there is another major depression, or if the new pension plan does not perform as well as expected. To make sure that the employees are well protected."

"It shall work, Arne! It shall work. I made some quick calculations and have the proof that you are right. The pension plan will work – on a long-term basis, that is.

"Now! Here's something you didn't know. We are already setting aside *all* of the 'risk factor' – *in a special secret contingency account*. Only the directors know that and we forgot to tell you. We have accumulated in that fund a huge amount. Now listen carefully:

"Should we ever be forced to discontinue operations, we want to be able to continue paying our employees full salary, and provide all benefits as well, to retirement age, regardless where they go and what they do. Salary and cost of living increases are not included. Those considerations are incalculable.

"We are not far from our goal with the amount on deposit and investments. We shall be there in about ten years.

"How did it happen that I did not realize that the same could be done with pensions? These are the calculations that went through my mind while you were talking, and I realized that it would work. It's based on the same principle. You woke me up, Arne! Thanks!

"As I said, only we, the directors, know that. It's our intent, not an obligation nor a promise to fulfil. It's a promise to the consciousness of each one of us, including you, as you so amply proved just now," and Father looks at Arne with his usual wide smile.

"That is quite unbelievable!" exclaims Arne.

"Yes! I do not know of any company that is doing anything like it, and no one knows of our intentions either. Let's hope that such a day does not arrive, but if it does – in ten years we shall be ready for it and the news announced at a press conference.

"Our employees will be shocked in disbelief of their fortune, and the rest of the industrial world as well, in envy!"

"Well, then, I do not have a 'second point'. That 'Secret Contingency Fund' of yours is free and can be used as conditions permit – while mine would have been earmarked and held in trust out of our control," and there is great relief in his voice.

"That's right, son! That's right, but you were on the right track. The only difference is that ours, established by my grandfather, augmented to the unbelievable by my father and helped along by myself – is wider in scope and much more penetrating, as well as completely free and available to us.

"This availability is what made it incredibly flexible. Did Ingrid tell you about my father selling all his stock about a month before the stock market crash?" asks Father suddenly.

"Yes! She did."

"Good! So you know a bit about us?"

"What Ingrid told me about the family and you and Mother – was the ingredient necessary for me to forsake my family name to preserve yours," Arne admits rather shyly.

"That showed us the greatness of your heart and character. Mother was in tears. What you have done today gives me full confidence that in time I shall turn over the company to deserving hands. Nonetheless, for all of that, the most deserving is Ingrid. Without her we wouldn't have known about you – we would not have a son."

Silence... I look at Arne with a guilty smile... He looks back seriously...

"Well, if the worst comes to the worst, and someone invents a square wheel – I am sure we can produce square ball-and-roller bearings to match and still remain in business," says Arne in a light tone and continues: "But now seriously:

"Father, could you then incorporate in the release to the employees, that the company guarantees that the pensions under the new plan shall never be less than those offered by the insurance company?" asks Arne. "They have nothing to fear, nothing to lose, but stand to gain very much!"

"Yes! We can do that easily and even more. Would all of you agree to notify all past employees still alive and on inadequate pensions, that their pensions will be augmented to a comparable level of the purchasing power of the dollar, retroactive to

January 1, 1948?" asks Father. All agree.

"Knowing our employees, they will rejoice and be willing to absorb that extra cost in our non-operating, but legitimate and tax deductible expenses.

"The 'capital risk reserve' shall remain as is. In about ten years we shall reach our goal, and after that we shall truly be in a commanding position in industry and keep the 'risk factor'. That's what our employees think we have been doing all along! Nonetheless, we shall continue to update that fund from year to year.

"Mark my words, in about ten years' time we shall wake up the industrial world!

"Oh, yes, son! Whatever our wealth is – after we, Mother and myself, are gone – all of it, some day, will belong to you and Astrid, and your children and grandchildren.

"I hope that in the years to come it all shall be split many times and in many parts. That's a good reason to accumulate some wealth for ourselves, as well as for future generations.

"By the way, Arne, our family income is not dependent on the company only, but on investments as well. That is why we can afford to do all of this for our employees – for their security and future, as well as ours…

"I shall update Astrid as to our decisions today," Father concludes slowly and thoughtfully.

Having no other business to discuss, the meeting is closed and we disperse. Father goes to his study to write the report to the union.

"Father said, 'I hope that, in the years to come, it all shall be split many times and in many parts' – Arne – to our children, grandchildren and their children – and so on, and on, and on.

"Even Mother and I don't know our total wealth and it's not my business to know all – until I'm told. There is a very valid reason for that. Just think about me and Astrid; and now you too; and, of course, Father and Mother as well – and the possibilities of any one of us being kidnapped for ransom!

"Perhaps this is the best time for me to tell you that we all must be careful. Let's keep our eyes open and not talk about it again, ever," I plead, and Arne understands…

★

"I am fortunate... I am the Earth to bring forth life... And I have a sower worthy of his seed..."

Christmas

It's Christmas Eve today... The air is full of expectancy... After all, it is our first...

A Christmas tree arrives fresh from the forest in the afternoon and we, all three 'kids', are busy: Arne helps with his strength; and Astrid and myself with plenty of advice, quietly spoken in reverence...

It's a beautiful spruce, secured in a special stand with a large container of water to keep it fresh and fragrant. Only white Swedish candles decorate it – nothing else. Our ceiling is high, but our tree is usually less than eight feet in height. There's no need to destroy a tree well on its way.

As it begins to thaw, its fragrance permeates the house. The most beautiful night of the year is near...

We all gather in the music hall and play the melodies of Christmas. It's Arne's first Christmas in Canada and the Christmas carols of the English-speaking world are foreign to him, strange and disappointing. He heard them during the pre-Christmas season on the radio, in the streets and in stores – ad nauseam. He has complained since November. That is much, much too early – according to him – and I agree. Too much commercialism. The melodies become commonplace and worn.

Yes! He's right! "A red poppy on the lapel belongs to November 11 – not a day before and not a day after – let alone in October," he said when he first saw it. "On November 11, but then with all your being, with all of your heart and soul, and all businesses closed."

Nonetheless, there is true beauty in all carols, and when we play them now – it is as if he had not heard them before. That is true – *we* are playing them, and that does make a difference. He likes them now much better, and finds some quite original and meaningful. It takes time to adopt a new country...

Then we switch to the hymns of Lutheran Europe. Yes! That's

a different world! Of all of them he finds the harmonization of "Lo, How a Rose E'er Blooming" the most beautiful.

Now we have a brand new task upon us – to teach Arne Christmas carols as we know them here, but he still does not like the "tiresome" one with all the "partridges" in it.

Arne has a very mellow, beautiful, well trained and controlled base-baritone voice with a two-octave diapason, excluding falsetto.

There's still plenty of time till supper and the observance of Christmas Eve, and Arne brings down from our study a pack of sheet music – about five and a half by eight and a half inches in size. Every page is very neatly written with his signature at the bottom of all of them. Astrid goes through them, quickly fingering the melodies.

"This is a treasure chest, Arne!" she exclaims. "What are they? Where did you get them?" she persists.

"It's the full repertory of one hundred songs of our choir."

"Oh! The one Ingrid told me about?"

"Couldn't be any other!" Arne jokes back.

"Come, Arne! Select some. I will play and you will sing! Okay?"

They start with sacral and switch to secular songs. There is Beethoven, Brahms, Gruber, Abt, Schubert, Praeterus, Bishot, Spohr, Guno, and even Kennedy and Harr, let alone Richard Wagner. Yes, the same Praeterus who composed "Lo, How a Rose E'er Blooming"; and the same Gruber who gave us "Silent Night, Holy Night". But there are scores of new music never heard of before here by us. Astrid cannot hold back any more:

"Arne! These compositions! These harmonizations! They are out of this world! And the melodies, the melodies! Beautiful! Beautiful! *Beautiful!*

"And majority of them are related in a mysterious way! In a mysterious way. Like brothers and sisters.

"This exposure to an entirely different culture is an unexpected gift to me, and on Christmas Eve at that!

"I don't know, Arne, what you have for me tonight, but nothing can exceed the treasure of this. I would like to have them enlarged: photographed, plates made and printed in a very small number, for our use only. Could I do that, Arne? Please!" she almost begs.

"Of course, Astrid! Of course, but take good care of these originals. They mean a lot to me," and Arne puts his arm around Astrid's shoulders while she plays and he sings in Latvian, or German, if it's Wagner.

He need not look at the music; he knows it by heart – the leading voice and the second base partitures and all the words.

I sit with Father and Mother and hardly whisper a word. It is a revelation to us as well. We shall have a concert after Astrid has made the enlargements.

Supper is the traditional, roast duck. In just a few years Arne will introduce smoked wild boar's head as well – an alternate choice, with stewed sauerkraut – and we shall take to it like geese to water, but now we all enjoy our duck. We like duck much better than goose.

The family has decided not to touch alcoholic beverages of any kind during my pregnancy and while I breastfeed the brand new Johannsen. Well, that's Johannsens: one for all and all for one – if I can abstain, so can they. I'm so glad. I won't want to dull my senses with anything tonight, not even nectar.

Christmas spirit is with us – quiet, sacred feeling – full of reverence to the beauty and meaning of tonight, and the Christmas tree and its magic.

★

The candles are lit and they are the only source of light in our living room. The tree is our universe now – plain, green spruce tree, white candles – and light…

Nobody speaks… That's our tradition… The lights are in the centre of our visible attention, but our hearts and souls are with God – each of us individually – in our own way…

When the candles have burned about halfway down, Mother alone, and very quietly, starts to sing a peaceful melody with beautiful words dedicated to tonight, the night of Christmas Eve…

Peace… Peace… Peace…

I look in Arne's eyes, but all I see are two lit Christmas trees. I press his arm and knock my ring against his. He responds in kind and most certainly sees the same trees in my eyes as well. I put my arm around his waist. Our bodies feel each other and speak to each other, along with our souls, about gladness, belonging, home and future...

We celebrate our very first Christmas Eve together tonight. My God! What wonders have happened to me in one short year! Could I have thought of all of this last Christmas? No way! No... But it all has happened and I'm carrying a new life in me from a man I love so much – and I put my head on Arne's shoulder.

Silence...

Then Father gives us all his traditional blessing – different every year and so delightful in originality.

After that, we sit in silence and watch the lights go out – candle by candle; one glowing wick after another, until the last one leaves us in semi-darkness.

Astrid switches on a few table lamps. It's cosy. I look in Arne's eyes again, take his hand in mine, and pat it a little. He does the same and Astrid joins us. We are in a hand-holding game with smiles and snickers.

There's a multitude of sparkling colour under the tree: little boxes, large boxes, in-between boxes. Astrid takes them one by one and announces "to whom – from whom".

The "to whom" opens it slowly, enjoys it, says thank you to the "from whom" and lets it go from hand to hand until everyone has seen it.

Arne's cufflinks have come out beautifully and he truly enjoys them. He is wearing French cuff shirts, but these cufflinks will be for festive occasions only. He kisses me for mine and Astrid just cannot wait to get her kiss.

Then comes Mother to Father and the rest of us – and the other way around, just as Astrid happens to pick them up from underneath the tree.

The bracelet and necklace from Astrid are out of this world – my wedding and Christmas presents from Princess. They were not unexpected, but to see them done and in my hands is a different thing altogether.

It's a beautifully matched set of glowing emeralds in gold, rather than aquamarines in platinum. We made that change – leaving aquamarines and platinum as Astrid's jewels.

Underneath all the other presents are two very small boxes, unnoticed before and placed there with intention, perhaps.

"Arne to Ingrid!" announces Astrid and brings me one of them. I open it. In it is an unmistakable Birks blue box. What could be so small? I think – and then I almost shout out, but manage to hold my tongue. It couldn't be! It just couldn't! But there it is – my rock engagement ring!

I look up at Arne, Father, Mother and Astrid with eyes of disbelief. Astrid falls on her knees besides me and both of us have our noses in a velvet presentation case.

"Darling, how is this possible? How on earth did you do it?" I ask.

"With your father's money and connections, it was no trouble at all!" Arne laughs, but then becomes serious:

"Well, on your eighteenth birthday you had only a pair of diamond and pearl earrings to match your tiara, and our prayers that this ring arrived in time. It did and here you are!

"Ingrid, it is part of a special selection and we had the first choice. Thank your father for that. This one was taken for tonight – from me to you.

"Would this satisfy you as your rock version of our engagement ring? It's on approval. Now, let us all see it!"

"Thank you Arne!" and I run to Father and thank him, smothering him with kisses.

"That's all right, Kitten! It was a pleasure! Come now, come – simmer down. Tomorrow by daylight you may not like it at all."

And I let Father go and kiss Mother instead. I just have to kiss someone! Oh! Yes! Arne! I have not kissed him for it yet and I do and stay with him. I should have kissed him first, but my subconscious mind knew that it was all Father's doing and I reacted accordingly.

I look up to Arne and whisper that I am sorry, but he only laughs. He understands.

"Isn't someone going to kiss me?" asks Astrid in a make-believe, lonesome voice, and I rush to and kiss my sister, my

Princess.

We now look at my ring with all the lights on. It sparkles. Tomorrow we shall see it by daylight and Arne will give it to me. Let's hope that it is a sunny day.

"To Astrid from Arne!" reads Astrid, obviously not able to wait any longer.

"That's me!" she exclaims and starts to open her present slowly and carefully. It also contains a Birks blue box with an elaborate velvet presentation case inside. She opens it and her mouth also pops open.

There's a solitary, unmounted, large FL blue-white diamond, with twice as many facets as usual.

Without saying a word and very slowly Astrid walks up to Arne, lifts herself up on tiptoe, puts her arms around his neck and kisses him on the lips again – just like when they first met. Arne embraces her lightly.

"Astrid! Keep it as it is, or have it mounted if and as you wish, when the time comes for you to perform on stage in public," says Arne quietly.

Then she kisses every one of us and sits down stunned, with the diamond still in its case. She has not uttered a word to anyone yet. Arne walks up to her, sits down and, putting his arm around her shoulders, whispers audibly:

"Some day, Astrid, you shall be showered with them and this may appear small and insignificant by comparison, but always remember – it came from the heart and with the best wishes in mind; and, of course, with your father's generosity."

"I shall never, never forget this... Whose idea was it? Unmounted – like this?"

"Mine," answers Arne.

"I am so glad! Free to keep it as it is, or have it mounted as I wish... I am so glad," and Astrid just keeps looking at it and its brilliance shimmers with the slightest movement.

"It's a rare stone, Astrid! A very rare stone," says Father quietly.

"I can see that, Father, but the idea of giving it to me unmounted – is the greatest rarity there can be. At least for me. Thank you, Father!" and Astrid gets up, embraces and kisses

Father again. "I know! It did cost you a fortune, but that it is from Arne and unmounted means more to my heart, to my soul," and she is by herself again – just staring at it.

"It's a virgin jewel. It will have plenty to do with my life. Exactly what, I do not know, but I feel it. A new horizon is opening before me – as if out of the mist, from behind veils that shrouded it till now. Thank you, Arne! Thank you.

"May I be excused for a little while, please?" and she turns to go to the music hall.

We embrace and look in each other's eyes. Did we witness a turning point in the life of a genius?

And we hear a melody never heard before by anyone.

Johann

Master Johann Johannsen is having lunch, as I look at my little bundle of joy at my breast beside me in bed.

We're in the maternity ward of Women's College Hospital. He arrived according to schedule, May 2, 1949. Yes! It was on the rock. It was when I became a woman.

His hair is as blond as can be, and eyes – sparkling sapphire blue but closed now – in contentment.

I'm relaxed and very, very happy. The birth was easy and the boy, healthy. We shall keep him that way – Arne, the family and me.

I've plenty of time to think. My studies are up to date. I have heard all the lectures of my faculty and Arne kept me informed of our mutual courses.

My dear, dear Arne! When he was permitted to see me for the first time after the birth, he kissed me gently and I felt some of the weight of his upper body against mine. The kiss lasted, and lasted, and lasted. It was sweet, soft and deep. We got stuck and just could not separate.

He sank into my soul all over again and told me later that I tasted like mother's milk. That was only natural – I feel it too. My whole body has changed with motherhood. I am in unison with nature.

This man means so much to me! So very, very much! And I am still falling in love with him, deeper and deeper. The birth of our son has created feelings of love that I didn't know existed. We both have stepped over the threshold into a new phase of life – parenthood.

We all were invited to a gala formal ball and New Year's Eve party, but, in consideration of me, and Arne's twenty-fifth birthday, we stayed at home and enjoyed a wonderful evening of music and laughter.

The day will come when we shall go and dance, dance, dance.

By then, I shall not be nursing Johann any more, and I daydream of all that is to come – of all the beauty of life with Arne.

We had plenty of surprises on New Year's Eve, his twenty-fifth birthday – and the quite unexpected for both of us.

Our ruby and pink sapphire cufflinks got it all started. The rubies were glowing and Arne was flabbergasted about Astrid's idea. Birks had outdone themselves with the pink sapphires – pink rubies, in fact. It was their luck and our good fortune that Astrid could give Arne cufflinks with extraordinarily sparkling pink sapphires.

Birks advised me of obtaining them and I approved a very substantial increase over and above the original estimate. Oh! It was worth it! Arne could not take his eyes off them – almost like Astrid with her diamond.

Is fate bringing them together through my fortune? If so, let it be. We cannot, and should not even attempt to avoid what is written in the stars. There is a purpose in everything that happens.

From Father, Arne had an eighteen-carat gold pen and pencil set. Mother gave him a leather-bound album with pictures of our family: great-grandparents, grandparents, Father, herself, and us kids as we were growing up; and a fine Morocco leather wallet with a gold monogram.

And then the unexpected happened. From Father and Mother we received a million dollar cheque each! "To make you financially more independent," said Father. We were stunned, particularly since he insisted that bills for all of our purchases should still be sent to our accountants.

That's a lot of money and we decided to open our own investment funds to preserve the purchasing power of the dollar and earn good income on top of that. Let's see how we make out in, say, ten or twenty years.

I overcame the surprise readily since I am used to our level of luxury, but poor Arne, I'm sure, has not overcome it yet. Well, I shall still call him "poor Arne" just the same, whenever he's struck with something unexpected.

He has excellent taste and I am proud of him. His looks, his manners and his speech radiate confidence, finesse and handsomeness.

Yes! A man of stature and means, but gentle and wholesome at the same time. What a gain for me, the family and the company – and Astrid too, should it come to that. It probably already has.

Astrid? She puzzles me. Since Christmas Eve she has changed. No longer is she a brisk, bubbly, laughing and joyful kid. She seems to have grown up suddenly. She's more like Mother now – quiet, soft spoken; she studies very hard and is prolific in composing one theme after another.

We have played her "Concert for Three Pianos: The Earth, The Sower and The Rainmaker", even though it is not quite finished yet. It's unbelievable that a thirteen-year-old kid has composed it. I play "The Earth"; Mother, "The Sower"; and Astrid, "The Rainmaker" – by far the most difficult score, with gusting storms and large drops of rain – to gentle, gentle descending mist.

My part – "The Earth" – is the easiest, but very dominating, particularly in the lower scales.

"The Sower" walks with distinctive steps as he honours "The Earth" with seed. Mother has her hands full with them.

Astrid has plans to let it grow into a concerto for three pianos and orchestra, but she is not even touching the orchestration now, it's much too early. She must study, must know more.

The "Concert for Three Pianos" is dedicated to us as her wedding present and shall be performed on our first anniversary. She has given it Opus Nr. 1. All previous compositions shall be used, in one way or another, in her following works.

I'm sure we shall have a standing ovation from the entire audience – Father and Arne – and I smile to myself. Oh, yes! Almost forgot, maybe Johann and his nanny will be there too, but he will be too little to stand up.

Must give the youngster the other breast now and, with the assistance of my nurse, we accomplish that quite easily, without him knowing anything about it. Well, a breast is a breast to him as long as there's milk in it, and I smile again, thinking about Johann growing up to be a man like his father.

Now we know the colour scheme for the nursery too! Everything shall be ready and waiting. Yes, I have engaged a nanny for him. She's already with us in her brand new quarters, getting acquainted with the surroundings and our family.

She'll have her meals with us – with little Johann between her and myself. I must spend as much time with him as I can, and mealtime is an excellent time for me to be more permanently imprinted on him.

Arne and Astrid shall be facing us. Well, they'll be side by side, and Arne, as a gentleman, will assist Astrid if and when necessary, as he has assisted me. Arne will see me and watch his son grow up.

Where was I? Oh, yes, Astrid.

There's another change in her – she plays the violin much more often than before and concentrates on all famous violin concertos written. There may be a number of reasons for that – after all, violin is her love and hobby; wanting the knowledge for the purpose of her studies; or, perhaps, love? I wouldn't be a bit surprised if it is Arne.

She was a mild bobby soxer before Christmas and wanted to get a kiss from Arne at every opportunity, but not any more. She's maturing into womanhood. A couple of years yet to go and she may start to feel the pangs of passion. Arne, myself, our marriage, our mirrored bedroom, the baby and knowing the rock – all of it is speeding up that process – not slowing it down, that's for sure! She may mature too early.

Johann has had his lunch and is back in his "pen", and I keep on thinking about absolutely everything, when Astrid pops in. "Hi, Sis! Remember me?" would have been her bright and cheerful greeting, but not now:

"Hello, Ingrid! How's Johnny?" come her softly spoken words, with a gentle smile and a peck of a kiss.

"Ha, ha, ha! You have a nickname for him, 'Johnny'! Let's not confuse him at this age, the formative years. Let's call him Johann for now. Okay?"

"Okay, Sis, but how is he?"

"He's just fine. Had his lunch and burped a 'Thank you, mom'. And how are you, Princess?"

"Busy! Just stopped by from school to the Conservatory. I want to plant a seed in your mind – a question. You have plenty of time now, don't you?

"Requiems are beautiful expressions of music for symphony orchestras, but they seem to fall flat almost as soon as the choir cuts in, or very soon after. The choral part seems to destroy or, at least, puncture it. Not the words, the voices.

"Do you agree? Or am I wrong?" she asks and continues: "If you agree, why is it so? It could not be blamed on the choir every time, or the soloists, but the soloists do most of the damage! There must be something else. Can you think of it? No rush."

"Astrid, when I get home I'll listen. In the meantime I shall think about it. It's an interesting observation.

"Do you remember our discussion a couple of years ago about Beethoven's Ninth? Had it been instrumental only throughout? The answer may lie there, but, at least I do not know of anyone who has attempted to orchestrate the choral part properly and fully, and we do not know how it would have sounded! Do we?"

"I shall orchestrate it someday 'properly and fully', and then we'll know. Not so?" and she smiles.

Yes! Our family joke is back and Astrid is still Astrid, only growing up.

"There's something else. I am preparing for five pre-Christmas charity concerts in various cathedrals. Father will donate a huge amount as seed money for an 'Instrument Fund' for extraordinarily talented children without the means of obtaining their respective instruments. It will be administered by the Conservatory. These concerts shall be planned for every year while I am at the Conservatory."

"That's great! Whose idea was it?"

"The charity concerts? Mine. The seed money – Father's. It would apply to all qualifying, talented kids across Canada.

"The Conservatory hopes that other conservatories and similar institutions of learning will, in time, also participate and it will become a Canada-wide effort – Canada-wide assistance, with Canada-wide benefits. That's why my concerts shall be from coast to coast. Mother will come with me."

"Astrid, that's very noble of you to get something like this started – and most unselfish and generous of Father. You brought me great news. I am delighted just thinking about it – and that is how I should feel as long as I'm nursing the baby.

"As a matter of fact, that's the best way to be all the time! Don't you think so, Astrid?" I ask.

"Yes, Sis, it would be ideal, but life is not ideal."

"Astrid, what has happened to you since Christmas Eve?" I ask openly and sincerely.

"You have noticed? Yes, I am different. Arne's music and that diamond changed me. I'm no longer afraid of being wrong.

"Those melodies Arne gave us put my mind at ease. I was concerned that the music I hear and compose may be out of place, but now I know better.

"Now it's full speed ahead with what I hear, unconcerned about when, where or how I may use it in my life. The future will most certainly show me that. There is no escape from one's self.

"Since Christmas Eve, I'm the master of music, and it shall help me serve mankind – just as the diamond does – sparkling for everyone around it.

"My destiny is taking shape and I am to obey it.

"But now I have to go. Think about my question, please," and with a quick kiss, she is gone on her way to her future.

"…sparkling for everyone around it…"

At The Lake

It's summer. August. We are at the lake, all of us – Johann and his nanny too.

Our wild poppies have germinated and some are in bloom. It's quite obvious that we have sown different varieties, blossoming at various times. This is the first summer for them and some may not blossom this year at all, but next year they shall be prolific all summer long. In our rock garden, we can pretty well see how it looks here.

Father and Mother were pleasantly surprised seeing the island in bloom, even sparingly. They had not expected much. Astrid's eyes are glued to it, now and then. Poor Astrid! How is she imagining it all?

Oh, what memories! What beautiful memories of our first year! We made a pilgrimage to the Toronto Islands on the day we met, a year ago, and to Queen's Park to "feed our kids", the squirrels. We have been there a number of times, in all seasons.

We retraced our steps to the Royal Ontario Museum. The magnificence of the mineral exhibit hall engulfed us again.

Oh! What a difference between our thoughts and feelings then and now! Then and now. What is now? Now? Here we are, with Johann to show for it!

The blossoming island confirms the founding of a new dynasty of Johannsens – all thanks to Arne and his big heart. And his big...? Oh, I'm a naughty girl! I couldn't help. Ha, ha, ha – and my famous exclamation: "It's shrunk!" and I start to laugh in earnest all by myself. It's good that nobody sees me now.

We spoiled Father's and Mother's vacation last year, but they have it with gusto this year.

Arne has seen Canada now, from coast to coast. Father took him on two trips to show him the company and Canada at its best.

They went west first: Winnipeg, Regina, Calgary, Vancouver

and Victoria. Spring is earlier on the west coast, much earlier. They told us that Stanley Park was in full spring bloom already, and so were the other parks too. Then they went east: Montreal, Quebec, Saint John and Halifax. Arne was very pleasantly surprised with the city of Quebec.

Father is enjoying himself immensely, for now he has a pal, a friend, a son – Arne. Most of the time he is with Father, going fishing: angling; casting; spinning; and fly-fishing. Arne enjoys all of it – spinning in particular. Yes! Father has a companion at long last. Theirs is more than a father-and-son relationship – they have become fast friends.

We, the womenfolk, are so glad. Mother shows it the most. There's a reason for that. When we, the girls, were growing up, we didn't know what Father was missing, but Mother knew only too well.

Johann and his nanny are doing just fine. She blends in with our family very well. I chose her with that in mind. I still breastfeed him. It's the fourth month. There are, perhaps, two more to go.

We had a splendid and heartfelt wedding anniversary – all of us – the family. Arne gave me extremely beautiful diamond earrings – as the pearl ones were for our wedding day. The "family" – a diamond and pearl necklace (a choker) and a matching bracelet. Now I have everything to go with my tiara. Whenever I wear these jewels, I shall feel the family around me, always.

I took Johann and put him in Arne's arms and said, "Here is my wedding present to you!"

Arne promptly put Johann in the hands of Father and said, "And here is Johann Johannsen to you both!" and we all had a good laugh.

We gave ourselves a splendid concert of Astrid's Opus Nr. 1 and had, as predicted, a standing ovation from Father and Arne. Johann's eyes were wide open, but not a sound came out of him. That would have spoiled it somewhat. His nanny was holding him on her lap.

Yes! Astrid had finished her "Concert for Three Pianos: The Earth, The Sower, and The Rainmaker. Opus Nr. 1", dedicated to us: Arne, Johann and myself. It is breathtaking in its conception and configuration as well as the distinct differences between the scores for each piano. It's a masterpiece and, yes, in time – it most certainly could form the core for a concert with a symphony orchestra.

Astrid is fourteen now and has grown considerably, including in her femininity. She sports a mini bikini with a ladylike grace, but it's so revealing! "It's the coming fashion," she told me, "and I don't have to hide anything from anyone. Don't you remember how grown we were and still running around here with nothing, or next to nothing on?"

When I asked about Arne, she said, "Oh, he's entitled to see his family in its entirety!" and laughed sincerely.

She's still so full of innocence, but I think I know what it is. Astrid wants to confirm what she said when they first met, "I have no freckles at all anywhere…"; and his reply, "Your face is so fair and clear…" "You are a piece of non-existent art…"

Since she burns so easily, even in the shade over a prolonged period of time, just as easily as Mother, they swim and sunbathe just a bit and spend the rest of the time in the shade or indoors – Astrid with her ever-present piano.

Father and Arne got up early today to go trout fishing. Now they are having their midday nap.

I'm alone with my thoughts in our favourite spot that we selected last year in the shade, but with a full view of the lake, our island and the house.

My hair has grown some six inches and the change is getting to be noticeable. Astrid has also let her ponytail grow and in a year it shall be just above her waistline. The curls of her ponytail are just gorgeous – various shades of red – just like mine are in gold.

Oh! Yes! On her birthday Arne gave her a platinum ponytail ring adorned with many very small aquamarines and told her that she shall get one on every birthday, but with different gemstones, for as long as she keeps her hair in a ponytail style. Arne got a shy and quick kiss for that, but still on his lips. I'm sure that is where her kisses shall always be.

Ponytail has been her only hairdo for some time now, securely held by a ponytail hair clasp or a ribbon or a bow. That accentuates the beauty of her face and her fair skin.

Yes, Astrid has changed and shall continue to change. It was only last Christmas when she put her arms around Arne's neck and stretched out that kiss of hers. That, probably, was a goodbye kiss to the innocence of a kid. She's maturing and it shows.

My memories, plans and thoughts are travelling long distances when I see Astrid coming. She's a very beautiful young girl – not a child any more, not in my eyes at least. Her face is classic art and she has a body to match. It's a rosebud well on the way to opening. And a beautiful one at that.

I'm not surprised – we both come from the same assembly line, but, as Arne said in so many other words: "You, Ingrid, are a down-to-earth, sexy and most desirable woman; Astrid is a goddess!" Those were his words – or at least the gist of it, the meaning.

And here she comes, my dear, dear sister – in a gait so ladylike and feminine. I am excited about her beauty and very, very happy and proud of her – even if she is destined to love Arne. Perhaps she already does...

I went through that too and I didn't even have such a splendid specimen dangling in front of my nose all the time! I can't, nor shall I ever deny Astrid the fulfilment of her destiny – even if it means sharing Arne. Then he shall become *our* destiny – if willing – and he might not. Time alone can tell that, and shall.

"Sis, may I join you?" she asks sitting down.

"Sure, Princess!"

"Only while Father and Arne are having their siesta. I'm ready to play now, but do not want to disturb them and Mother.

"Do you remember the bit of 'Glory' I played for you both at the end of the rehearsal last fall, on the first day of school?" she asks.

"Of course I do. It was breathtakingly beautiful!"

"'Breathtakingly beautiful'? Was it? If it was – I want all of it to be as you just described it. Therefore, there shall be no choral part in it. The organ must sing instead – and more beautifully than any voice could.

"Consequently, 'Glory' is in its final stages of completion now – not in five years as I had originally thought. It shall be Opus

Nr. 2, and, as I said, dedicated to Father and Mother. I shall play it at the end of each concert this coming season, the last composition.

"After you came home from the hospital and gave me your views of 'pros' and 'cons' regarding requiems, I have done a lot of thinking.

"I know that I am still very young and inexperienced, but here it is:

"I'm not talking about recordings of music. Recordings can be manipulated so that every listener can feel to be seated 'front-row-centre', and that's how most of the music was composed then, for the nobility sitting in the most desirable position to hear it.

"I'm talking about the average listener stuck somewhere in a huge cathedral – hardly seeing the choir, if at all.

"The organ is the most powerful instrument there is. It is made for the cathedral and can make the last cubic foot of its space reverberate accordingly. A choir, no matter how large, cannot do that.

"Organ and choral music are almost at the opposite ends of the scale. For a choir or a soloist to be heard in a meaningful way – the organ must stop, for all practical purposes. Just when the music must blossom at its best – the organ must tone down, to give way to the choir, and the choir, unfortunately, is unable to bring the music to its fulfilment.

"Now, there are exceptions. For example, the conclusion of Part 2 of Handel's 'Messiah' – the jubilant 'Hallelujah' for which King George II stood up in reverence and thus started the custom.

"Well, it's Handel's very best chorus – an oratorio – and written in an incredibly short period of time. For three days he did not open his door and took no food, so they say. It's born in a burst of mental explosion. Nonetheless, notice the sonority of each syllable of each word, mostly 'Hal-le-lu-jah' where the voice can open up in full blasts. That's impossible to maintain and even then, the orchestra must pull back its power.

"I've played the choral part on an organ, and from where I sit – the most disadvantaged place to be in most cathedrals – the organ alone exceeds the voices by far: in beauty, strength and positive assurance. That's if one gives the organ a free hand to utilize its true potential.

"I shall compose for voices in time, but never in a combination of primarily organ music. It's different if the choir or soloist is in the centre of it all and the organ or orchestra only an accompaniment. Yes, it's different then – like Mozart's 'Hallelujah'.

"Look at 'Finlandia' by Sibelius, with symphony orchestra! See the goose pimples on my skin! See? That's just from thinking and hearing the 'Finlandia' chorus in my mind. What a perfect marriage! I can assure you that sooner or later in my life you shall hear such beauty in my music too!

"That's why my Opus Nr. 2 shall be ready shortly. I know the organ and need not know anything else to complete 'Glory'.

"Instrumentation and voices will come by the time I graduate. Even well before that, but now I do not need that knowledge. Not for 'Glory'.

"The organ shall be a great help for it has stops corresponding to various instruments in an orchestra and I'm completely familiar with them – the stops, I mean."

Silence...

"Astrid! Just a year ago you were still an energetic kid. You clawed at the piano or organ as if were part of your body – in full control of the infinite—" I break the silence, but Astrid interrupts spontaneously.

"I'm still that, Ingrid, when dealing with known works of other composers, but lately I have been more involved with composing myself, and that takes a different approach. A year ago, I was not sure of my own work. Now I am and it will show – just as it did with Opus Nr. 1.

"It's true that I do not run around as a whirlwind any more. I guess I am growing up..."

"Is there any one thing in particular that motivates you?" I ask.

"Yes! Arne inspires me! I got the idea for 'Glory' when we first met, but I couldn't dedicate it to him – ignoring Father and Mother. It's only through you, Sis, and our parents that he is with us. Father's and Mother's acceptance of him gave me the full spectrum for Opus Nr. 2. The beauty of nature and our family is reflected in it.

"Well, you know that your honeymoon phone call inspired me to Opus Nr. 1 and I had to be true to myself and dedicate it to you, Arne and Johann – the future of us all.

"The theme that I heard when I met Arne shall be used as a leading motive to a composition dedicated to him alone. He reinforced it by suggesting 'Miracle' for my 'Glory'. Do you remember?" she asks. "It was in the car."

"Of course I do, Princess! What shall it be?"

"A symphony, but only when I am good and ready for it. At the present, there are only sketches.

"You, Sis, shall have a violin and violoncello concert with orchestra. I have the theme. You gave it to me when I was told that you were going to be his wife – that I would be near him all the time. This also shall come towards the end of my studies, although the violin and violoncello parts may be ready well ahead of time."

Father and Arne come carrying our swimming caps. We all shall go swimming now. Mother comes too! We get up and hurry to meet the main body of our family.

I suddenly see the future! What a happy family this is going to be: Astrid's music reflecting her love for Arne, and I blossoming in his arms and our children!

How can I deny that to her?

Organ Concerts

The cathedral is slowly filling with people... Quiet steps...
Hushed whispers, if any...

We all arrived early and Astrid showed us where to sit and
with a quick airborne kiss off her slender fingers she smiled,
turned and was gone...

Now, the same fingers are giving us all a quiet soothing
background music and then I notice bits of melodies here and
there, quite unknown for an organ. Soon enough, I recognize one
of them. It's a bit of a Latvian folk song – and then another, and
another. Astrid has woven a masterpiece of a prelude from the
music Arne gave her. It's refreshingly original and beautiful, to say
the least.

I take Arne's hand. We look at each other and are thinking
about the same thing. Even Father and Mother turn their heads
and Arne nods in agreement.

In time, the music becomes stronger and the lower registers
repeat the same melodies that we first heard high up, a nightingale
on midsummer's night.

While listening, I look at the program again. It's a standard
eight and a half inch by eleven inch folded over to form an eight
and a half inch by five and a half inch size. An artist, by the grace
of God, has created a drawing of an organ on the front page – just
some bold outlines, but that's what makes it so masterful – just a
few strokes and, there it is.

I studied it all in detail at home, but here, in the cathedral, I
feel as if I have been taken by a hand and led to an eternal spring.

It took us all by surprise. Astrid's "Glory" has been changed to
"Glory to God" and it is printed here: "...by Astrid Johannsen.
Dedicated to Father, Mother and the family..."

It's simple, but looks expensive, and above all, in very good
taste. Some day it shall become a collector's item, perhaps. Little
do I know that that "some day" will be tomorrow or even today,

right after the concert.

There's a pause and then the concert starts. It's entirely Johann Sebastian Bach with Astrid's "Glory to God" at the very end. I close my eyes and in my mind I see Astrid at the console – unafraid, masterful, bold, and in places even forceful. Yes! It is Bach at its best.

Then comes Astrid's Opus Nr. 2 and takes our breath away. We had heard parts of it in the composing stages, but now... Now it is a masterpiece and, put against the background of Bach, it's overpowering in its interacting and transposing melodies as well as huge contrasts. Gone is the mathematical precision and comparative restraint of Bach, imposed on him by the instruments of his day and the pleasure of his masters for whom he had to compose, as well as the attitudes of those times.

Here and now is the modern instrument with all its subtleties and awesome power, and Astrid uses it all to the limit. I can see her at the keyboards...

And then, suddenly, after a forte, forte, fortissimo – there's only the resonance of space. The quiet is deafening...

I feel tears running down my cheeks and here is Arne again with his handkerchief. Through the corner of my eye I see him passing another fresh one to Mother. Oh, my Arne, he's always prepared for the possible and, I hope – for the impossible as well.

No one stirs... No one gets up... No one knows the end... Perhaps there's more to come? But it was the end. Astrid has made her statement and it shall live for all generations to come. A powerful statement it was and that's only the very beginning, in her youth... It's awesome to think of her works in the future...

Then, very quietly and melodically, we hear Brahms' Lullaby the way Astrid wants us to hear a true lullaby.

It shall become Astrid's trademark – the very last encore: whatever the instrument, whatever the concert with its numerous encores, the Lullaby shall become her lovely goodbye or goodnight and the audience shall know – "That's it folks!"

Then the Lullaby fades out slowly, but people still remain sitting as if dazed, and so they were, as we later found out – just as overcome as we were... Then, slowly, some rise and go, or just rise and look around. Some, like us, do not even get up.

And here is Astrid. Nobody knows her. Nobody pays any attention to us.

"Folks! I feel as if my soul has been laundered!" she says to all of us.

"And so do we!" we reply through each other.

"And us too!" mentions an elderly couple innocently passing by: "And us too!" What would have happened if people knew that this youngster here was the one who played?

Some notables saw our little group, but respected our privacy within the walls of the cathedral.

Nonetheless – it was different outside, on the steps. They were waiting to congratulate us. That caught the attention of others and suddenly the press was all around, and behind them – the public. Flash bulbs popped and voices asked questions. The Conservatory officials eventually arranged that there should be no answers tonight, but a press conference was agreed upon for tomorrow afternoon.

*

Tonight we celebrate! Do we ever! Johann is long since asleep and his nanny is with him.

We open the first bottle of our pink honeymoon champagne and toast Astrid, individually and all together. We then put down the glasses and go to embrace and kiss her. Arne first kisses her fingers and as he reaches for her cheek, Astrid turns her head and kisses him on his lips.

"Arne, we are not in the cathedral any more!" she laughs very happily, still holding on to him.

More bottles follow with our festive late supper – filet mignon with green peppers and mushrooms being the main course. Father does not make a speech, just smiles. We all do and laugh. Our happy little family and our darling Princess.

After supper Astrid walks up to Arne and, with her pointing finger at his chest, pushes him:

"And this man here is responsible for all of it. The main theme you heard tonight – I heard in my mind just as I saw him at first. At the very first glance!" and she pushes him harder, but

Arne does not retreat. He takes her finger and kisses it.

Astrid takes another sip, toasting Arne and then she turns to me, walks up, kisses me on the cheek and with a smile full of love, embraces me and says:

"My darling Sis! It's all because of you, by catching him for both of us!" and we toast to that. "For both of us", she said, and I toasted to her in agreement. "For both of us!" She spoke the truth.

"Folks! Let's make a circle!" invites Astrid, and we do, with Arne between us and Father and Mother before us.

"Now!" Astrid continues: "Let's all raise our glasses as high as we can and together, like this!" and Astrid lifts her glass and so do we – letting them meet in the centre with various pitches of sound as crystal meets crystal.

"And now the toast – to all of us and the future that awaits us! Now! Once more!" invites Astrid and crystal meets crystal again.

And the late evening turns slowly into early morning...

"The game is over! Now, back to life!" says Astrid. She puts her empty glass down, walks over to Father, embraces him and whispers audibly:

"If you only knew how dizzy I am!"

"That's all right, Princess. That's all right. I guess it's the first time for you?"

"Father! It's you! I thought that you were Arne! No, no – don't listen to me! It was a poor joke. I knew that you were you and shall always be my daddy!"

Mother goes, embraces both and tells Astrid:

"Astrid! Come with me, I will help you," and Mother holds Astrid as she is taking her to bed and waving a silent goodnight to us.

"See, Ingrid, what you have done – brought home Arne and created a genius," says Father with a broad smile and sits down.

"Father, Father! Have you had one too many as well?" I ask with a naughty smile.

"Sure, Kitten! It's the right occasion, isn't it?"

"It surely is, and you may not be entirely wrong. The genius was in her all the time, but the presence of Arne may have given her fertile ground."

"That's true, Kitten. That's true. I was also trying at a joke."

"But with me between all of you! What do I do?" asks Arne.

"Son, just keep on doing what you're doing – making all of us very, very happy!" laughs Father, as he jumps up and they toast and empty their glasses. Father turns and, as if remembering something, looks back and asks:

"Not so?"

I sputter a laugh, trying to cover my mouth.

"Yes, Sir!" answers Arne in the voice and manner of the military.

We do not realize how true all of this will be.

"Keep us all happy! Yes, Sir!"

Ball

The ceiling is twirling before my eyes. Not any kind of a ceiling, but the one in the grand ballroom at the Royal York Hotel.

I'm waltzing with Arne. Our very first dance of our very first ball. The whole floor is ours. We're alone and take full advantage of it.

I'm sure of Arne's hand and lean back as far as I can. With a smile of utter happiness, I throw my head back as well, in full submission to him. My long, golden hair is freely responding to the laws of physics. The lower part of my dress is full and fluffy. He partly disappears in it. We may seem welded together below the waist, but the legs do three-quarter time continuously.

We are like a blossom, floating in an endless, slowly turning current. It's a slow "Blue Danube" at my request.

I know what I'm doing. It's a full formal ball. Gentlemen in tails and ladies in spectacularly elegant dresses for the occasion.

I know what I'm doing. Father is giving this ball for his daughters' debut and I'm not going to let him be disappointed. There's elegance, formality and grandeur in everything – and our waltz must fit into it all. I'm so happy and proud of Arne, as he is with me, I'm sure.

It's contrary to our custom of no glamour, but this is our debut and when we do come out in society, we do so in style, befitting our family name. Only now, I truly realize the importance of preserving the Johannsen name. Thanks to Arne – it should live on.

Me? My dark red dress has a daring décolleté and a low, low back. The full skirt gives me freedom for legs to do any kind of dance and makes me look like a blossom. Yes! This is the place for the rock, the tiara, and everything else. It's my pearl and diamond set, the works.

And would anyone believe what Arne has done? There's an emerald cufflink on his left sleeve and an aquamarine on his right one. I'm so happy about him not forgetting the feelings of Astrid.

Much too soon this ecstasy is over and we are walking back to our table. I feel as if I'm on a cloud, my feet do not touch the floor. It was enough. Arne, probably, couldn't have held me on his arm much longer. It wasn't only the weight, but the centrifugal force as well. Only now, I begin to hear the applause from all around us. I start to wake up and have a quick look at Arne.

No! It just couldn't be that this man is my husband. I'm awe struck, just as I was at home seeing him in tails for the first time.

He is the very embodiment of Swedish aristocracy. At home I froze in disbelief: tall; slim; broad shouldered; most handsome and masculine facial features; university fraternity tricolours over his chest below the vest; and matching fraternal pocket watch and fob, a most elaborate piece of jewellery in itself. Now I walk with him like a crowned queen. It could not be – but it is – and he also is a Johannsen! How can the family ever thank him enough for that?

At our table, Father rises until I am seated and then we are our little family again. Mother touches me and tells me how beautiful we looked and how proud they all were of both of us – and suddenly a thought hits me: And I fished him out of the lake! And I laugh, and laugh, and cannot stop. Then, at the end, I tell everybody just what I thought, and now they laugh and I join in again.

Finally we manage to come to some kind of order and simmer down, but all we have to do is to sport a certain smile and our table is liable to explode again. No, we shall never tell anybody what we were laughing about. Shall we? Of course not!

While we were dancing, Astrid had arranged with Father that she will start her dance with Arne, and after a while Father would cut in. A slow foxtrot starts. Astrid puts her hand on Arne's and they go. Astrid is in a white dress and her best jewellery, including a diamond only tiara as a thank you from the family for her accomplishments in music, and to remember this ball by. It's a bit early, but she has earned it.

Oh! December was a hectic time, starting with the first day after her first performance: roses; newspaper headlines from across the country; and reporters.

Besides the scheduled concerts, she had two more in Toronto as well as in Montreal, each. Then, our birthdays, Christmas, and New Year.

For Christmas, and for some time to come, Father had managed to secure for us many cases of a very rare port wine. All of that particular vintage was bought by France and served at a state dinner for King George the VI of England and Queen Elizabeth on a state visit to Paris in 1938. What was left became available to mere mortals and we have a good share of it.

Astrid is now an instant celebrity, known to all and adored by all, but one thing the Toronto establishment had to learn: Christmas Eve; Christmas Day; New Year's Eve; and New Year's Day are ours – ours alone – not to be shared with anyone – regardless of how noble the invitation may be.

The togetherness of this family is more important than any glitter made by man. That means that we shall never be at any New Year's party, but our own. What a relief! But we might invite others to ours, in time, perhaps.

Yes! We were a quiet, unassuming family, but Astrid has put us in the limelight and there is no way to avoid it – short of hurting our little Princess. We are her family and have to participate in her successes.

She now has her own limousine and chauffeur – our chauffeur, a tested and reliable man. We have a new one now and he's good. Life goes on…

Having seen what we did with the waltz – Astrid selected a slow foxtrot to give Arne some rest. She's a good dancer and they dance close together, but she's too short yet to dance cheek to cheek – she just looks up and her natural ponytail hangs down in a most adorable display of multi-tone red – a true and most adorable sight.

Father gets up, walks over and taps on Arne's shoulder. As Arne walks back, I see him for the first time in tails at such a distance. What a man! I look at him reverently… And only now, I hear the applause for him and Astrid, their dance. Oh, if Hollywood would only know what they have missed! Well, their miss, my gain.

My king, prince, master and pet is safely beside me again and our hands meet, but something is missing! Oh, no skin contact, we have gloves on! I look in his eyes. We both look and press our hands a little tighter. If anyone noticed this small, but so meaningful exchange of love – it does not matter. It was in good taste.

The music stops and Astrid returns with Father following, bowing and thanking her. Then Father dances with me.

The whole invited company had an excellent banquet before the ball and now – having seen us, the Johannsens' daughters, introduced – we all shall dance.

After a little pause, the Master of Ceremonies takes over. He's our Vice-President Public Relations and Dance Master for tonight. Father gave a short speech after dinner. There shall be no speeches here.

To start with, there must be a formal polonaise, and it begins. It's a splendid opportunity for every guest to see all others present a number of times – at the discretion of the Dance Master and his weaving of the dance. He is Astrid's partner for the polonaise – the first pair. We follow and then come Father and Mother, watching over the brood.

I make a point of observing other ladies.

Well, when we were walking toward our table at the banquet, there were three ladies standing and quietly conversing. As one noticed us, she hushed and all three turned. They inhaled, but did not exhale. Their eyes were locked on Arne.

Now, during the polonaise, there are no such shocks, but only admirations. I know what I am talking about. I, as well, have inhaled and forgotten to exhale.

The polonaise concludes with a waltz, and from that point on the ball goes into full swing.

So, this is our debut, a little late for me, due to the baby; and a little early for Astrid, but that is okay, considering her very recent prominence all across this land.

Father has invited the Who's Who of the Conservatory; the world of music and arts; industrialists; educators; politicians; and the press – with the understanding that photographs may be taken, but discretely and no questions asked. All in good taste. And so is the music – popular classics for dancing now and, of course, background music during the banquet.

Then a break. Supper and refreshments for the orchestra. When they return there's an announcement that the next dance shall be a "ladies' waltz".

With the first notes of "The Voices of Spring", a young lady, dressed in gold, comes from nowhere and invites Arne. He responds without hesitation, as a gentleman should.

I decide to let this waltz pass. As a very happily married woman I shouldn't go and, maybe, create false hopes in someone's mind, as I remember my promise in the canoe on our wedding night. Yes! I've learned a lot. Mother asks Father and they're gone. Astrid and myself are alone at our table.

"I didn't even have a chance to get up when the 'lady in gold' was already here! Who is she?" asks Astrid.

"I don't know, Princess. Let's watch them – her, that is. Okay?" ask I.

"Okay," replies Astrid.

The lady in gold has a very elegantly styled and expensive dress. It's on the conservative side and so is her jewellery. The dress makes her steps look very sexy. She also knows what she's doing. Her hair is very light blond, done up in a modern coiffure. There is a distinct elegance about her.

Arne does not talk while dancing unless invited to do so by his partner. They talk. There are smiles and some laughter, but we see them very seldom and even then, just briefly. Father and Mother return before the music stops and we ask Father who that lady in gold is.

It turns out that she's one of the best artists in Canada at the present, a painter – mostly landscapes, and famous for her portraits – a class by herself. Independently wealthy. For her to enjoy life is to paint. A born artist. She could live a life of leisure, but she must paint. Not married. By the time Arne returns, a new dance starts.

"This is mine, Arne! You were stolen from me!" exclaims Astrid, and they are off. It's a tango.

I look at the beautiful solitary red rose on our table and think. We both shall be graduating this spring. I shall continue my studies at the faculty and Arne will go for his MA in Business

Administration. After that? A Ph.D. for each of us in Philosophy, but that is many years ahead, four at the very, very least... By that time we should have a couple more kids...

1950 shall be a memorable year: Johann will be a year old on May 2; Astrid – fifteen on June 23; Father – forty on December 13; and I – twenty on December 15. Arne and Mother will be twenty-seven and thirty-seven respectively... Little do I know of the unexpected!

The lady in gold is coming and passes by, but Father stops her, introduces her to Mother and myself, and asks her to join us for a while, if she can. By the time the dance ends and Astrid and Arne return, we are good friends. Astrid and Arne are introduced as well and we all know her as Rita.

Father wants to commission the painting of portraits for all of us, but she politely declines, saying, "People get tired looking at themselves! No, not for homes!" she adds.

"How about for the boardroom of our corporate offices?" asks Father.

"Oh, yes! That's different! That is fixing history at a time and place! I would be glad to!"

"There shall be one extra of Astrid – for the Conservatory," adds Father and it is agreed upon – after our exams this spring. Since Father and Mother have no exams, she will start with them in her studio only. And so we part, for the time being.

We dance and dance and dance... Almost every man wants to have a dance with Astrid and she obliges... I know that I have to dance with some of the gentlemen, within reason – no more than one dance with the same man, excepting Arne, of course... And Arne fulfils his "obligations" with the advice of Father...

There's one exception. Arne returns the favour to Rita and they do a sexy tango, after which he does not return for a while. Good reason for that. He was invited to sit down and spend a bit of time with a group of artists at Rita's table, and it was his obligation to do so...

*

The ball is over... We are going home, but a nagging question follows me: When Arne's time comes, shall it also be: "...in my studio only?"

Violin Concerts

The phone rings. I answer it. It's for Astrid. She takes it in her bedroom. In a little while she comes down the stairs in a hurry.

"Sis, I've been asked to play tonight! Violin concertos. Not less than two. Perhaps three, and maybe even four. It's unprecedented, but I accepted."

"Tonight! We all have tickets for Massey Hall tonight!" I exclaim.

"Well, that's where I'll be playing!"

"No! What happened to—?"

"He's hurt," she interrupts me.

"Who called? Why did they come to you?"

"I don't know why, but his manager called and Massey Hall assured me that it's true. They know our family…"

"But there's only one violin concerto in the program – Beethoven's?"

"The rest of the program has been scratched. I can't do it."

"But you can do the violin concertos?" I say with quite a natural question mark in my voice, although I did not mean it to sound like that.

Astrid comes up to me, puts her hand on my shoulder, looks in my eyes and asks me very quietly:

"Would I have accepted if I couldn't?"

"Forgive me, Princess! I was, and still am, dazed and concerned!"

"That's okay, Sis! I've very little time. There's some rehearsing to do. Please tell Mother and ask her to tell Father and Arne. Come up to help me with my dress. Could you come with me now? Wait, call Rita and tell her that we now have a spare ticket, if she hasn't got one. I'll call the chauffeur to make sure he's ready. Help me, Sis, please!" and Astrid rushes back to me, kisses my cheek and up the stairs she goes. All of the whirlwind is not quite out of her yet.

What just happened is beyond my comprehension. In a couple of months, she will be sixteen only. There's no time to reason it out. I must do as she said and I realize how quickly she has taken charge and is in complete control of the situation – just like Father. Soon after we are in her limousine and gone – taking my violin. It's fortunate that we didn't forget it in the rush.

★

"You shall follow me very closely," says the conductor. Astrid taps her fingers on the conductor's forearm:

"I'll neither see you, nor know that you exist," she says very slowly. "When the orchestra starts first – I shall join it. If the violin starts first – you and the orchestra join me. Whatever you do – follow me – my tempo!"

"Do you mean that you have the entire partitures in your head?" asks the conductor.

"There are those whose heads are in the partitures, and those who have the partitures in their heads. Mine are in the head," she answers quietly.

Some in the orchestra start to snicker and I notice that the conductor has an open partiture in front of him.

The program crystallizes quickly and in accordance with Astrid's wish. It shall be Bruch, Mendelssohn, Tchaikovsky – in that order – and then Beethoven.

While sitting and watching, I have plenty of time to reflect.

We received our first diplomas last spring. It's "neither here nor there" according to Arne. There's one more year to go for the MA's.

Father's plans at the lake were also carried out last year – including the saunas and proper washrooms, on the other side of the drainage divide. A proper road was built first.

We have become good friends – the family and Rita, and we two in particular. The portraits are excellent. She did two of Astrid, as planned, and also of Arne – one of him for herself.

Oh! Yes! Johanna arrived on August 15 last year. Johanna? That little bundle of femininity! Well, the next one would, probably, have to wait until after we get our Ph.D.'s.

The audience starts to arrive. Rita is most elegantly dressed. She knows how to paint as well as how to dress. She has something in her that I don't have – elegance and presence. I, probably, have presence as well, but different – the down-to-earth, sexy kind. Well, today, I'm lucky to have anything on me at all. I arranged that Arne sit between us – at least during the first part of the program.

Someone comes on the stage with a microphone, addresses the audience and announces the unavoidable. A shock runs through the hall, but with news that is not serious – sighs of relief settle in.

Then come the unprecedented changes in the program, but when Astrid's name is mentioned, along with the organ concerts she is known for during the past two seasons – there's applause.

Should anyone be unsatisfied with tonight's program, full refunds will be made, but the audience seems to be pleased that tonight, at last, they shall have a chance to *see* Astrid play, and not just listen to her. The response to her organ concerts has been phenomenal.

Astrid is greeted with tremendous applause. She bows her head for a little while, then looks up to the conductor; she's ready, and we hear Bruch.

In Bruch, the melodic is contrasted with sheer power – relenting towards the end, soothing. Perhaps that's why she chose it for openers – the contrasts. The applause is very, very good.

In Mendelssohn, the melodic is followed by smarting and yearning moods and then joyous, dance-like lightness. The smarting, burning expressions come so naturally and deeply felt that one forgets oneself in it all. The applause is even grander.

Astrid's red ponytail against the pure white dress supplements and balances the violin. I have never seen Astrid play so. It's an impressive start. I can hardly believe that on my mellow violin a master can create moods so demanding, penetrating, loud – and yet – mellow.

It reminds me of dark heather honey. Yes! This is Massey Hall! Astrid has immersed herself totally in her play. One can see and feel the mastery we are witnessing, in depth. We didn't fully realize it. It is history in the making.

After the intermission the announcer comes on the stage again and asks quite openly and frankly:

"Now! Ladies and gentlemen! Shall we have Tchaikovsky and then end with Beethoven? Or should we skip Tchaikovsky and go to Beethoven now? It's your time that we are concerned with.

"Tchaikovsky! Tchaikovsky! Tchaikovsky! Tchaikovsky!" an enthusiastic audience demands and they get it as they, probably, have never heard it before. They show their appreciation by a standing ovation.

The second intermission. I am relaxed now and change seats with Arne. Nothing can go wrong with Beethoven. I would like to chat with Rita about this and that, but she's overwhelmed by Astrid's performances and I become a patient ear to her "chatting wishes".

Beethoven! There's nothing else to say, but wipe a tear or two out of our eyes. Now Astrid is in her element as deep as she could ever get. The violin and her soul speak and are being heard and felt the same way.

A standing audience overjoyed by her art, and one can feel that the applause is in tune with how each one of the listeners has been touched by what they have heard.

Then come the encores. There seems to be no end of the demands. Then she plays a string of Latvian folk melodies transcribed for violin and masterfully arranged as to sequence.

At the end of this encore, the audience is still very receptive and, at the same time, completely stunned at what they have heard. Very loud applause comes from here and there – probably Latvians – and soon enough others join in with some hesitancy.

Astrid turns to leave the stage, but after a few steps – walks over to the microphone, switches it on and a very quiet and feminine voice says:

"That was a string of pearls and jewels – wild flowers in forest meadows, from a land far, far away. You do not know them and are confused. Now I shall play a men's choir song from the same land, not a folk melody."

It is: "Here! Brothers!" as we in the family know it. It starts with the most sorrowful and pleading languor. In answer to that – suddenly comes a stunning forte, forte, fortissimo – relenting ever so briefly to ff and then it ends abruptly with a burst of another short fff... Astrid bows, turns and is gone.

What an outbreak of applause! What applause! A standing audience again.

All are still standing when she returns. Her gait is very slow and thoughtful. She does not hurry. With her feet securely apart, she places the violin under her chin, looking down until there is absolute silence. Then she raises her head and the bow and then there is an explosion – the most difficult piece ever written for the violin – and it's not Paganini! I can't remember just now who wrote it.

We are all on our feet – including the orchestra! What a roar! What applause! At the back the younger generation is jumping up and down and a chorus starts: "Astrid! Astrid! Astrid!" The audience is in frenzy. Whatever they expected – they could not have expected what they just got. Most unusual for the sophisticated patrons of Massey Hall.

While we all are still standing, Astrid comes out and gives a signal to the conductor that is passed to the orchestra and they start to sit down. The public follows. When everything is quiet, she plays Brahms' Lullaby in its simplest, most melodic form, and mellow. How very, very mellow.

Then she curtsies to the audience – slowly and deeply – with the violin in her outstretched left, and the bow in her outstretched right arm. As she rises and lifts her head – she transfers the bow to her left hand as well, and with an airborne kiss, off the very tips of her fingers, waves goodbye and goodnight, au revoir – and slowly walks off the stage. My dear, dear sister – the violin is yours now! I say to myself. I'll just borrow it, now and then.

The applause is too long to be ignored and the announcer comes on stage again and, after the people have settled down somewhat, tells everybody that Brahms' Lullaby shall always be Miss Astrid Johannsen's "so long everybody, until next time – au revoir" as her last encore after each and every concert.

There's a general applause for the announcer and then we all start to look around and are getting ready to go. It has been an extremely long evening. I would say "over saturated", but for

Astrid that's good in every respect. A new and bright star has risen!

Only I try to go to her dressing room to help. What a crowd! But Massey Hall has experience in this. I am recognized and only I am allowed to get to her.

It's havoc at home the next day and for many other days to come. Roses, roses, and more roses – and cards. Mother is now her manager and protector, with separate telephone lines for both of them.

★

On her sixteenth birthday, Astrid receives a mysterious and expensive-looking leather case. Inside that is a most expensive violin case, and inside that – what else, but a violin, of course, along with a birthday card.

Astrid takes the violin right to the front windows and looks at it slowly and carefully. Then she notices something on its back and quickly turns it around and looks inside:

"Stradivarius! Mother! Ingrid! It's a Stradivarius! A Stradivarius!" she exclaims and puts it back into its case very carefully. In the birthday card there is only one handwritten sentence: "A thank you from your admirer!"

Oh, yes! A huge bouquet of red roses came with it and the messenger has a letter. He asks as to whether it is possible to have an answer now. A limousine is still waiting for him.

Astrid opens it and passes it to Mother and me. "Would you, Miss Astrid Johannsen, consent to give us all the pleasure of a concert devoted entirely to Paganini? It would be the closing concert of the coming season."

While we were reading and looking it over, Astrid has already written on the enclosed RSVP card:

"Yes!
Shall do!
Thank you!
Astrid.
June 23, 1951"

She gives it to the boy. He thanks, leaves and the limousine is gone.

We three women, not counting Johanna upstairs, are alone again. It's Saturday, and the menfolk, Father and Arne, are in the garden "on a secret mission", they say – preparing for the festivities of the summer solstice this evening.

What a coincidence – Astrid was born on this, most festive, day in the Latvian calendar. We all slowly become used to the customs of Latvians, as Arne is to Swedish. Midsummer's night is here...

I bend over and look at the instrument – not daring to touch it. Not because of its monetary value, but in awe of its rare availability. Now Astrid has her Stradivarius.

Amati and Guarnerius shall follow...

Astrid

Father and Mother are up at the lake with Rita. It's autumn and at this time the fall colours are gorgeous, at their very best up there. Rita will surely return with a load.

We have a number of summer landscapes, including one of our island. It's a wonderful painting. In a most artistic way, some of the poppies stand out individually and close to the viewer against the background of the dark and distant forest. As Arne predicted, true art is starting to show up in our home with everyone participating in the decisions.

We shall see what the autumn has done to her – or, rather, she to the autumn.

"Sis, do you have time?" asks Astrid.

"Yes, Princess!"

"Lots of time?" she asks quietly and somewhat shyly.

"All the time you want," thinking that she might want me to go to the music hall with her.

"Then come," and she takes my hand and leads me to the library, closing the doors, and we settle down in a cosy corner.

"Sis! What I'm about to say is not easy, but here it is – all thought out ahead of time.

"You're married and extremely happy with Arne. Are you not?"

I just nod my head in agreement, realizing that what I've been waiting for has arrived.

"Well, I'm married too and just as happy as you are. I'm married to Music.

"Practicing Paganini in depth, and finally realizing the complexity of his soul and then – understanding him – feeling completely at home with his genius, I thought that I shall never be able to give myself away completely to a mortal man. Not the way I've given myself to Paganini and Beethoven. Never, as you have given yourself to Arne.

"Every composer, sooner or later, would become my lover when I cross the threshold as I just did with Paganini, when I'm in unison with him.

"I presume that, what otherwise would become my unrelenting sexual desires, are channelled into music, playing and composing it. That's where all my energy goes. I've nothing left for anyone else. I do not have time for a husband and children. I cannot afford them. So I thought.

"Sis, I have a premonition that I shall die young – I may have ten years left, at the most. It came as a vision and a warning. Whatever years I've left – I have to live intensely for music only. Let's not tell Father and Mother. It would be a needless worry. Besides, as I said, I do not have a craving for sex as such, only knowledge and experience of it – a curiosity…"

"Only as long as you have not been awakened!" I interject.

"That could be, but, up till now, whenever the subject of a man or men came up – anytime, anywhere – only Arne came in mind and deep in the soul. It's automatic, out of the subconscious mind and very, very real. He represented to me both, believe it or not, both: the apex of Platonic love, and also the physical man, the physical love – the passion that I do not know anything about yet…"

"And that's what you need most," I interject again: "You must burn in its hearth – for your music to reflect it!"

"I do not know what life shall bring, but my desire and goal is not 'a bed with a man in it'…"

I explode in laughter and Astrid joins me. It was very well put and fitted me perfectly.

"All this time I felt that I most likely shall have relationships with men, but I will not be on anyone's list of conquests – another 'cherry', so to speak.

"I would pick and choose – not the other way around.

"No stranger shall have my virginity! The family doctor could do it surgically – but, at the same time, I feel that deep in me I need to know a man for what he is – the physical aspects of him and our lady doctor cannot give me that. I want to know and feel that I have belonged to a man and have become a 'complete' woman…"

"And that's where Arne comes in," I say quite unexpectedly and look at my sister with an understanding smile.

"I guess you expected that and tried to beat me to it," adds Astrid shyly, "but it isn't so.

"Arne was, is and shall always be, my first love. The love of a girl, of her dreams, but now I have been swept off my feet as a woman. Young, but nonetheless – a woman," and she looks in my eyes. I know instantly that something great has or will be happening. I do not interrupt – just look in her eyes.

"Sis, I'm in love with a man. It's mutual, and this is where you come in, not Arne."

Silence...

"What I am about to disclose is unbelievable, but true. I need your advice desperately. At least I have to tell it all, aloud, and listen to my own voice. That in itself may help, and I know you will also. Perhaps I do not need help, but support. I'm all mixed up."

"At the conservatory I was introduced to the most famous composer of today. He is another Verdi and a master of the violin. We all know him. He's on a business visit to Toronto at the present. He's Tomasini Cavotti."

"Cavotti! But he's three times older than you are!" I thoughtlessly exclaim and am sorry even before the sentence is finished. Then add shyly: "Older even than Father..."

"Yes. That – and his fame – has confused me, but in my heart I know that I love him. Only my mind is puzzled out of focus. How can all of this be reconciled? And to the public, on top of that?

"There is a tight lid on all of this at the present, but an untimely leak may spring and we would not want that.

"I'm sixteen. He's fifty-two – a widower. No children. The world knows him. He's been in all the newspapers with that prominent grey head of hair.

"But to meet him is quite another thing. What magnetism! What personality! I was instantly engulfed by his presence. I was swept off my feet..."

"Have you thought about yourselves some ten or twenty years from now?" I ask.

"He does not know yet that I love him. Ten years would be okay and I shall not live twenty."

"Oh, he doesn't know! But how do you know about him?"

"He told me. He asked for my hand."

"And you?"

"I asked him, how come so quickly? And then he told me that he has been a widower for five years. He knows me and of me. He's followed my progress. It was he who suggested that I replace him at that concert at Massey Hall. Remember? He's the one who sent me the Stradivarius and arranged for the Paganini concert I'm preparing for now.

"He's been waiting for me to grow up. He asked me not to regard him as a 'lecherous old man' after my body. Quite the opposite. He wants my mind to join his – and the physical shall follow in piety, when I'm ready for him.'"

"And then?"

"And then I told him that he has honoured me greatly. That, as a woman, I'm receptive to him, but that I also have to sort it all out in my mind.

"Ingrid, I had to be positive right then – I had to make a decision and I have invited him to our home at 2:00 p.m. on Monday. He has to fly back to Europe in a week. He most likely arranged our meeting and the introduction. It was not a coincidence, I think. What do you say, Sis?"

"Do you love him, Princess?"

"Yes, I do! But not only that. We are so compatible! As his wife, I would feel on top of the world. We belong together! If anybody does, we do, not only as husband and wife, but as composers and performers with identical minds, dreams, voices in our souls! Maybe that's why I love him – if what I feel is love? It's not adoration... I felt it in my heart and soul the very instant he was introduced to me.

"If there is such a thing as 'animal magnetism' – that was it – as a woman to a man – and that's what counts, I think..." and Astrid stops.

Silence...

"Well, Princess, as an artist he flies all over the world. You shall have the best of both – a husband that does not take up much of your time, but a husband nonetheless. Knowledge of becoming a complete woman – and a secure home in a congenial atmosphere with a man you love and I know, respect. We all do.

"If he's so kind, as I gather he is, and so patient in waiting for you to grow up, you would make him very happy, and be happy yourself…"

"There's one problem though. We would live in Italy," says Astrid quietly. "He has a number of residences around the world, but we would live in Italy – on an estate by a mountain lake. That would be our official residence, not that we would be there all the time. That's where he knows I would be waiting for him when he can be home," and Astrid stops.

"What if he wakes you up to the point of having to have a husband handy?"

"I would wait for him more ardently and he would come home more frequently, but there shall be a change in his routine. After the conclusion of the current season, he shall discontinue giving performances. In the meantime we may travel together and, perhaps, even perform together – as well as me giving some impromptu organ concerts myself.

"If I travel with him, it would affect my studies, but I can get back on track starting next fall – when we may live in Toronto for the winter, in this very home…"

"Hey, Astrid! You already know that your answer shall be 'Yes'! Isn't it so?"

"Yes, Ingrid! That's how I feel, and Arne shall become a beautiful, beautiful memory of my girlish childhood and youth… and all the composers shall not become my lovers…"

"Well then, Princess! Introduce him to Father and Mother on Monday. Confirm today that 2:00 p.m. appointment you made and ask him to be prepared to stay for supper, if at all possible.

"Ask him to visit us today and tomorrow – if possible – just us and Arne. That should give you enough extra exposure and time, under the circumstances, to give him the answer you know to be true."

"That's the same conclusion I came to just now while talking to you! Thanks, Sis – I shall!

"By the way, he's of the Piedmont-Lombardy nobility of

Turin, Milan and Genoa, but he does not use his title. I shall become a countess, but use Astrid Johannsen-Cavotti only."

★

Astrid said 'Yes'. Their wedding shall take place in the cathedral of Milan between Christmas and New Year. They both are too famous to escape notice and they also have their obligations to the public. Well, this is the year the Johannsens shall not be home over the Christmas season. The only exception so far.

★

The wedding was a once-in-a-lifetime experience. We all were exposed to something new and magnificent.

That sumptuous cathedral! The Italian, Spanish and French nobility! For that is Tomasini Cavotti's family tree, and I realized – if not for the public – he had to have a formal wedding for them.

Although it was winter, we enjoyed seeing their castles and elevating splendour of a lifestyle foreign to us. We rubbed shoulders with aristocracy and received various invitations to visit them. We thought that we are rich – and we are – but what is naked money, even if it is hundreds of millions? They have traditions and depth of life going back hundreds of years – even to the first millennium.

Rita was with us as Astrid's best friend and I saw her in her true element. Her aristocratic deportment blended in with the nobility – just as Astrid did. I first noticed that in Astrid when she came to visit me and Johann in hospital, and she has grown since. Arne had it all along and accentuated it at the wedding. Perhaps in Arne, Astrid observed it first and emulated him? As for myself? I was just a simple, sexy woman and Father with Mother tagged along – all of us in a distinguished and cool Swedish–Canadian way – the people of the north.

The elegance of Rita's dress surpassed those around her. It was not overbearing and presumptuous. It was not outshining the other ladies. It was there in depth and was recognized as such by all, who had eyes. Perhaps it was a blend of both – her regal deportment and the simple artistic elegance. She received a number of invitations for next summer. Who knows? We may have opened a new chapter of life for Rita as well...

The wedding banquet, which we call reception, was beyond description, in a castle beyond imagination, with guests beyond count – I mean numbers – for there were princes, dukes and counts in uniforms covered with decorations – and so was Astrid's Tom, an honorary colonel of a regiment. It hardly ended with the New Year's ball. I do not think that I shall ever be in a ball such as this... Never... unless through Astrid, back there again...

★

Well, their engagement was front-page news. Astrid and our family have been engulfed by best wishes and congratulations. The wedding only accentuated it all, for it has not ended yet. High decorations have been bestowed on Astrid and Father by Italy, Spain, France and Sweden, of course.

Rita is presently completing her commitments so that she can be free next summer to respond to the invitations she received – and do some painting over there as well.

★

Astrid calls him "Tom" and he calls her "My White Orchid". He shall continue his concerts of this season only and Astrid her studies. For the rest of this season their base is Toronto. We have relocated to the larger mansion.

The Paganini concert is still to come, but after graduations this spring – a new life shall start in earnest for all of us.

Astrid and Tom? Not only husband and wife, but voices, voices of their souls...

Paganini Concert

The quiet murmur of expectancy creating a festive background for our own whispered small talk. We are at Massey Hall again, before Astrid's all-Paganini concert. Tom is between Father and Mother then Rita, Arne and myself.

Oh, dear Rita! Her autumn landscapes from our lake and its surrounding area are breathtaking. I fell in love with that small maple tree that I know so well, growing on the bank of our trout stream. A small branch reaches a way over it and there they are – at the very tip – some of its leaves in most glorious autumn colours. Again – these leaves in gold and red are just patches of paint, boldly and masterfully applied. How they stand out and make the whole painting three dimensional, even from a close-up view!

She's our kind of people and we keep in touch. For tonight, nobody could get the seats we have, and Rita is with us – an integral part of us.

Astrid? Astrid glows in her love for Tom and Tom worships her... But now, back to the concert.

The program Astrid has chosen departs from the traditional again. The first part is Paganini's "Concerto Nr. 1 in D Major for Violin and Orchestra". The second, The Famous; The Difficult; The Beautiful – of his various compositions – concluding with "Etude VI", the last one in the series, based on a folk melody from the British Isles, "The Last Rose of Summer". The third part is "Concert Nr. 2 in B Minor for Violin and Orchestra" – and encores, of course.

There's a well-executed notation on the program that Mrs Astrid Johannsen-Cavotti shall perform this entirely Paganini concert on a Stradivarius.

I know what Astrid will be wearing. It's a one-piece black bodysuit fitting her skin tightly "from top to toe". With small black boots with high heels, it'll look as if the boots are part of her. She'll wear no underwear at all. Tightly around her neck is a narrow pleated white collar, and the same around the wrists.

For this occasion, the family gave her a solid platinum rectangular nugget type waistband. On its clasp is a huge aquamarine. The clasp has another foot, or so, of nuggets hanging down and ending with many very fine chains constantly in motion. Its weight is appropriate for the purpose – heavy. We all approved her get-up. I can't wait to see how she'll look on stage.

And here she comes, greeted with exuberant applause and even some shouts, but her waistband is plain! Where is the aquamarine clasp? Nonetheless, she still looks divine and devilish.

Her red ponytail is almost down to her waist, counterbalanced by the violin. Her face is so fair and accentuated against the all-black bodysuit! Her ponytail clasp and aquamarine earrings are in good taste and glitter. Yes, she is Tom's "White Orchid"!

She's perfect, in looks, and I quietly pray that her performance shall surpass her dress, otherwise it would be a disaster, but I also know Astrid – she wouldn't do it if she was not sure of herself.

After her curtsy she just smiles and bows her head in acknowledgment.

Concerto Nr. 1. Paganini wrote it in 1811 to exuberate the violin and his art. The orchestra has little to do in it and Astrid takes full advantage of this composition, and the Stradivarius obeys her.

The most outstanding aspect of this first part is the flashing and dominating virtuosity. Astrid does not let Paganini down, nor Tom, who trusted and invited her. It's a brilliant start, with the audience reacting accordingly.

She turns around and leaves the stage with that huge aquamarine sparkling on her back and the nugget "tail" hanging down – dangling. The audience goes wild! Tom explodes!

When she comes out for the second part, the aquamarine and the "tail" are on her belly. Her mimicry of Paganini is confirmed. She has read all about the composer.

The second part throws the audience from one fascinating extreme to another: one string only; guitar effect; flageolet; staccato; pizzicato; plucking; double fingering; etc. It shows her mastery of the instrument and knowledge of Paganini.

She has won the hearts of the audience and has to repeat "The Last Rose of Summer". We still won't let her go, but, eventually, must.

Then she comes out for the last part with the belt loosened so that it hangs down with the aquamarine over her left leg – and its pendant hanging down in front of it – an age-old custom. This is how it was supposed to be worn to start with. That is where the weight of the belt comes into play.

The audience stands up to receive her. It must be, at least in part, because of her play with that waistband as well, not just the violin, I suppose?

Concerto Nr. 2. All is not over yet. Could she still "spill the beans"? I do not think so.

This concert is different. The orchestra is allowed to play too – meaningfully, that is – and the violin even more brilliantly blends in the overall concert, much more than in Nr. 1.

Astrid's ponytail gets tossed about and part of it lands over her right shoulder and arm. She becomes a mystical firebird of some non-existent place in a non-existent time.

With the large aquamarine flashing, the end of her waistband swinging about, her face in translucent peace and classical beauty – no matter how difficult some passages are – one sees that she is the master of all that is around her. It's not theatrics, that, in some instances, she bends over the violin – and, yet, at other times, the violin is lifted high and she looks at the heavens – as it were – or is she mimicking Paganini again? Soon enough Concert Nr. 2 and the program are "well done".

She stands still with lowered head and arms. Then she looks up, puts her hair back where it should be and with outstretched arms makes an appropriate deep curtsy – bringing, at the end, her Stradivarius and the bow just below her chin – bows her head once more and leaves the stage. Her ponytail looks gorgeous – it is all over her back.

Then, after many and various encores, a piano is rolled out. Astrid plays Franz Liszt's transcript for the piano of the last part of Paganini's Violin Concerto Nr. 2 – the "Rondo", "Rondo à la Clochette", the "Campanella". Well, that was not expected and the audience is in awe to hear these pieces head-to-head – in the same concert.

When she comes out again, she stands still until there is absolute silence, and then comes Brahms' Lullaby – à la Paganini d'Astrid Johannsen-Cavotti.

The concert is over and Tom, in tears...

They have been married for almost five months now and in her playing I could hear a passionate change. Tom has awakened something in her that was not there before... Tom? Tom is everything to her! Astrid told me, he's a wonderful, sincere man and a genius...

★

There's no end to the roses, thank you cards, etc. Mother is in for it. As Astrid's manager, she channels everything effectively and according to etiquette and protocol.

The newspapers! Oh! The newspapers have a field day! It's all positive, and loud accolades also for the play with her belt – so they say – and her "dress".

Yes, we have seen and heard Paganini again – teasing the audience and giving it a lot more than could be expected of a lady so young – not yet quite seventeen! I wonder what the audience, the newspapers and the people on the street would say if they knew that her waistband was solid, brushed platinum? But so was her play – a matching set...

★

Her fourth and final year of organ concerts bring a new and unexpected surprise. On the initial program, the drawing of the organ was very simple. With every year it has become more and more complete and now, the final one, has only bold shades added, to anchor it, and it has the artist's signature – Rita... *It's our own Rita!*

The whole family is excited when we receive some advance copies from the printer. We call Rita and invite her to dine with us. It's a very memorable occasion. She brings the original. It is large, expensively and elegantly framed. It's a gift to Astrid. For

Arne and myself, she brings a self-portrait – the first one she has ever given anyone.

It is in a class by itself: original, bold, and yet, submissive. It's not only her looks that speak, but her soul as well... There is an underlying message – well hidden, but there – nonetheless... Should we ever see it revealed? Life shall answer that, if there truly is anything to reveal... Perhaps my imagination is seeing things that don't exist, but the painting holds me in its grip...

It brings tears to our eyes when Astrid promises to write a symphony dedicated to her, but she must wait.

After her graduating concerts, Astrid reigns supreme in the world of music along with Tom.

"The whole world shall be mine with my compositions, Ingrid! Performers die – composers don't..." she said some five years ago...

"The whole world"!

Graduations

This is the year we all have been waiting for since I met Arne. All three Johannsen "kids" are graduating in 1954, one way or another.

Last year Astrid added violin and composition to her keyboard instruments. This year she gets her MA in music. Her doctorate is to follow.

Arne and me? We got our Ph.D.'s in philosophy. Arne is very close to what he predicted during the first week of our honeymoon at the lake. His thesis, or dissertation as he calls it, is: "The Individual; The Family; The Society; The State". Mine – "Humanity". What Arne wrote for his MBA: "Employee Benefits", is now a standard handbook on that subject.

Defending his doctorate, Arne takes us apart and then puts us together again – creating an idealistic society in the process for the future, and all of that well within the framework of feasibility and practical considerations. Our dissertations support each other and the world has taken notice of them. A strong family is the foundation.

Astrid's compositions are works of beauty and she's composing continuously, but not for its own sake, or forcing it – only what comes naturally, and that's more than she can handle. Thus, many sketches are accumulating for use in the future – just as she now uses some sketches that she wrote years ago.

We still have our meals together; Father and Mother, and Astrid and Tom walk over to our place.

To Astrid, Tom is everything and her love for him is so obvious in her music – he's her lighthouse now. They are departing for Italy next month. Life goes on…

★

During the festive aura of our graduations, Father received a very serious and rare tip that opened the doors to penny-stocks. Grandfather sold his stocks at the right time and Father says that this is the time to buy. He invests all but the land, and we – our measly two million plus.

We tell Rita what we've done and that gives her the courage to do the same. On top of that, Father guarantees that in case of loss, he will stand behind her to the extent of such loss.

It's an old rule that one may invest in such risky stocks only as much as would not be missed if lost. We have plenty of real estate around Toronto in reserve and, on top of all that, the company.

Three years later, Father gives the order to sell, March 1957, and suddenly we are multi-billionaires via mines we never heard of before, in a place we did not even know existed – right here in our Ontario.

Everything has multiplied sixtyfold. Our two million in three short years has grown to 120 million. It's not a dream, but a tangible fact.

Rita follows suit and just in time, before Easter 1957. She can hardly believe her wealth now!

The time has come to call a press conference and announce the unheard-of news in the presence of our union executive. Father offers a choice:

1. Everyone's pay is guaranteed to age sixty-five; or
2. The ownership of the company is donated to current employees on payroll as of now, and retirees. The whole thing: "lock, stock and barrel" – right across Canada.

The response is enormous. The press can't believe it, but, nonetheless, it's done. When questioned – Father answers that it is the result of four generations of planning for it and never doubting.

The employees decide to accept the company. That releases Father and sets a new course for Arne.

He will write…

*

Our kids! How could I forget our kids? Rita was born on

November 18, 1952; Henrick – on September 11, 1954; and John – on our eighth wedding anniversary – July 24, 1956.

We pretty well decided that he should be the last. Five is enough: three boys and two girls. By the time we sell the shares, John is already nine months old. Yes! Aunt Astrid has her very own "Johnny" now!

★

Aunt Astrid and Tom are on a visit with us when Tom receives a phone call from one of his distinguished relatives and promises to accompany Rita to France for a special visit and festivities, then fly back again. Rita has decided to "paint Europe" again.

Father and Mother will go with them part of the way and "paint the world" – just travel and enjoy life. They are only forty-seven and forty-four years old, enormously rich and free as the birds…

Free as the birds.

Tragedy

TRAGEDY! Incomprehensible tragedy!

Oh, Death, where is thy reason? Oh, God, where is Thy love? I wanted to scream, but how can I accuse God for what we have done – for what we, as people, have brought upon ourselves? All of that flashes through my mind in a fraction of a second – just as soon as I comprehend what has happened. Just as soon as I realize the terrible truth.

I fall on my knees, for my legs cannot support me. I cry with hands over my face and tears seeping between my fingers. A jolt of electricity runs through my body and a strange scream comes from my mouth – animal-like – a mortally wounded animal... There's blood in my mouth and I fall to the floor...

★

I wake up in a hospital... A nurse is beside me... Arne and Astrid too... A doctor comes and tells me that I have had an epileptic seizure, but it is not serious and may not happen again...

I look at Arne and Astrid... They do not know! My God, they do not know yet! How could they? How could they possibly know what struck me down?

I lift my arms and motion them to come closer. I embrace them and ask them to be strong... They both back off and look at me as if I have lost my mind... Perhaps I have – at least some of it...

I'm weak... I'm sedated... I beckon again, embrace them again, pull them closer, and say very quietly:

"Father and Mother... Father, Mother, Tom and Rita are dead... Their plane crashed over the Atlantic... No survivors..." and I feel both of them embracing me...

Astrid is trembling... Arne takes my hand...

"Do not be weak as I was... Do not let it destroy you," I

whisper and their tears mix with mine...

"Do not be weak as I was..."

★

A month has passed in mourning... I have changed a lot... From now on I shall be strong... Nothing can shake me now, I say to myself, but just as soon as I think of Astrid, Arne and the children, I know that the sudden and untimely death of any one of them may strike me down just the same – maybe even more – for now I have a lot less left to lose...

A courier delivers a letter to Arne. He has to be at some lawyer's offices tomorrow, alone. He signs for it and the courier departs.

That was the first outsider we have received. With that, we slowly start to return to the living – for life must go on... They would have wished it so...

We start to open the pile of accumulated mail and sort it out. There is a letter from the same lawyers Arne just signed the receipt for. He did not open it, although it was registered – thus the courier.

Astrid wants to be alone most of the time. She is not wasting away in bed. No! She is ardently composing – even in the middle of the night or early morning hours – whenever her genius calls her.

I go and bring her over for meals, if I can persuade her to come – if she is not in the trance of composing.

Arne tries his best to console us both, but I see how deeply hurt he himself is...

There is one relief though – on top of all of this – we do not have to worry about the company any more. I couldn't, but Arne would have had to.

Arne! How much love and happiness he brought to Father and Mother in every respect: to go fishing with, or just be their "lost" son. He has been the source of so much happiness in our family – and shall again – once we get over the shock and tragic grief.

★

Arne goes to the lawyers the next day and returns looking pale. In her last will and testament, Rita has left him everything, plus an unopened envelope specifically marked:

"For Arne's eyes only!"

He has not opened it yet and goes to the library, closing the doors behind him. It is some time before he comes out and, without saying a word, gives me the opened envelope and the letter from Rita that was in it.

Arne!

It is not easy to write this letter. I want to write it and I need to write it, but am puzzled as to why I find it so difficult, considering that you may not even see it, ever.

My mother was Danish-Norwegian. My father was born in Norway of Latvian parents. He served on an ocean liner. He was a handsome dashing officer. They met during a crossing and the captain married them, thus me – Rita KALNS.

At the outset of WW II, my father predicted what would follow and sent me here – to Canada. He was not rich, but my mother was and they could afford it. Father was killed while fighting in the Norwegian underground. His body was, unfortunately, identified and Mother arrested. She died in prison.

After the war, I did not return home. I sold everything there and had enough to live well and paint here, in this beautiful land called Canada.

Your family, inviting me as a friend into your home and sharing its genuine and generous warmth, not to mention the tip and even guaranteeing the investment, made me rich beyond my wildest dreams. Now I am truly free. How can I thank you all? How can I? It is not only the money, but the friendship and trust above all!

I am going to Europe to paint. Considering my present wealth, I left my last will and testament with a firm of lawyers, naming you as the sole beneficiary and executor.

Please consider this letter as a codicil to my will regarding the following: Nothing to be donated to anybody, nothing. Otherwise you may use everything as you see fit. Knowing you, I have no doubt that you will carry out my last wish, for I could have given it away myself in person or in my will.

I was sent to Canada as a Danish-Norwegian girl and I left it at that. It was and is the truth: My father's Norwegian and my mother's Danish passports counted. Bloodlines were not asked.

I know that you are Latvian, but for a number of reasons, I did not reveal myself to you as being half-Latvian. I have not revealed that to anyone, waiting for maturity in my art and undisputed recognition. Then, I wanted to surprise everyone by announcing that I am also Latvian, thus bringing honour to my father's land – Latvia.

I fell in love with you at that ball. Do you remember how quickly I snatched you for that "ladies' waltz"? It was "The Voices of Spring". I requested it and was ready for you. As a gentleman, you returned the favour with a tango called "Domino" and spent a while with us at the artists' table. Remember?

I did not want to attract your attention as a fellow Latvian – only as another human being of the opposite gender. The fact that you were no longer available did not help me. I still love you, but not for an instant did I want to show that, and I hope I didn't.

I know of Astrid's attraction to you, and for good reasons. Ingrid told me. How would it look if I too showed my affections – and as a family friend? That would have destroyed everything I hold sacred and so, I continued to love you in secret. I am blessed with good fortune. As a friend of your family I would see you now and then. You all are rare people and very, very dear to me.

Should you pass away before me, this letter shall be committed to flames unopened. It would be too painful to read, even for a rickety old hag. Should I pass away first – you are reading it now and may show it to Ingrid. She is a good soul and will understand me. I was late. My ship had sailed, but I still wanted to love you in secret, and keep my pride and self-respect in the open.

Now, when all is said – place the portrait of you that I painted for myself – beside my self-portrait that I gave you both. It may reveal something very dear to me: the friendship of your family towards me shown in many different ways; and my love for you, dear, dear Arne – not once revealed to anyone, but to you – now…

With my first and only kiss on your lips –
Rita

[Lipstick imprint of her lips.]

P.S. Should it be Ingrid's wish – she may show it to Astrid as well and, perhaps, Mr and Mrs Johannsen.
R.K.

I return the letter to Arne, with my eyes wide open – I'm sure. He looks in them and they lock again, we know of our love and responsibility to continue to live for each other, Astrid and our kids – last, but not least...

"Arne, did you return Rita's kiss?" I ask.

"No, I didn't."

"Kiss her lips now, please! That's the least we can do," and Arne kisses the imprint on her letter.

I now realize why her self-portrait held, and is still holding me in its grip... It was her language of love and I, as a woman, intuitively felt its power, but did not know what it was...

Arne has made an almost instant decision. None of Rita's money shall be touched by any of us. He alone shall inspect her studio and living quarters, leaving everything as is, but removing anything personal. Then we both shall put it in good order, but the studio and adjoining exhibition hall shall remain untouched.

Beside her studio, a museum shall be built for her works and all paintings repurchased, if at all possible – regardless of cost.

An inexhaustible "Rita Kalns Memorial Endowment Foundation" shall be established for scholarships to gifted artists – painters and sculptors of true art – not decadent perverts. We shall establish the criteria. It is not a donation – it has to be earned.

The rest of her fortune shall be held in trust for ongoing acquisitions and perpetual preservation of her works, the museum, her studio and the grounds. Her apple orchard around it shall remain as part of her legacy – developed as a park, perhaps, in time, after the apple trees die out.

I offer an idea of a monument for Father, Mother, Tom and Rita in our family plot at Mount Pleasant and Arne agrees.

"It is very generous and unselfish. You are not jealous?" he asks.

"No, Arne! How could I? She only confirmed what I saw and still see in you. There may well be other such women!"

We spend a few moments in a tender embrace with only a few words spoken – now and then – remembering our lives together and the blessing of five healthy, good-looking and bright children.

We decide to order a bronze bust of Rita for her museum – with a copy incorporated in the overall monument in the cemetery. The subject ends with bronze busts for all four of them in the cemetery, and a statue of her in the park.

Let those who passed away be in peace, we are returning to the living.

"…for life must go on…"

Visiting

Ashes... Cold ashes...

Oh! Where are the years when we all sat around this campfire at the lake barbecuing steaks or sausages and eating them with French buns and having cold beer or ale? Where are those years long ago when we did that, just the five of us: Father, Mother, Arne, Astrid and me? Then, where are those with the kids at different ages? And then, with sorrow and no laughter, but reflections after death had paid us a visit? Where are they? In our memories, I answer myself...

Now Arne draws mystical signs in these ashes.

"What do these signs mean?" I ask.

"Oh, I was only doodling."

"What were you thinking about?"

"You'll never guess, Ingrid! Never! I was having a question of physics, philosophy and medicine answered by logic, but it defies logic.

"As you well know, a cane would be helpful in walking, but it is an extra object, weight and pain in my hand. Would the benefit to my legs be greater than the trouble for my hands?

"Can you answer that by logic?" he asks.

"No!" I reply. "The same as it is with the wheel – extra weight, but great help! A cane may well be a hindrance at this time while you still have me to lean on."

We smile at each other and continue to make wreaths of autumn leaves for everyone: Father, Mother, Astrid, Tom, grandparents Ulf and Ulla (nee Swenson), great-grandparents Anders and Matilda (nee Ibsen), and Rita as well.

Arne was hurt badly during the war and is suffering now from fibrositis syndrome and other related conditions. "...Horrible memories of war are the price a soldier pays for surviving it... The price for life is high..." he once said, and I can well see – not only horrible memories, but, with aging, physical afflictions as well.

★

I wake up as if from sleep, but I was not asleep – my mind had travelled long distances and has just returned to me. Funny, my body was sitting right here, beside Arne, yet I was not here at all.

It has been thirty-three years since Father, Mother, Tom and Rita perished; and thirty since Astrid died suddenly and quietly – without pain. She was only twenty-five then. Her vision was true – as predicted. There is a world we do not know anything about. Perhaps we shall see it when we pass on…

We are visiting them all now at Mount Pleasant on a beautiful September afternoon… It's 1990… The wreaths we made up north and the flowers are beautiful.

I look at Rita's bust and think of her beautiful and grand memorial museum. Arne found her journal, listing all paintings in numero-chronological order, giving essential particulars and owners. That helped a great deal, as we then knew the maximum space required.

Our former company donated all of our portraits. We also donated all the works we had. The response from other owners was very positive and generous. In her biography, it is disclosed that she was Latvian, on her father's side.

Father and Mother… Their busts and memorials are in a close, family-like configuration. Who can count the times I have been here? Who can count the tears? After Astrid's death, I changed. She came to me in a dream and asked me not to cry – not to weep…

Astrid's larger-than-life bronze statue is a monumental work of art commissioned by the Conservatory and the family. It has become a place to visit for many. Thus, these elaborate surroundings and massive Canadian cedar benches. The same statue is also in front of the Conservatory – the new and most modern buildings that the family built for it. Inside is her memorial, with her portrait by Rita, bronze bust, her violins and the piano she liked best. It has become a tourist attraction and a major source of revenue for the Conservatory.

For Father and Mother she composed "Requiem" for organ only, and "Requiem Symphony" for orchestra. Both are works of beauty and immense love. Astrid composed them with tears running down her cheeks. Perhaps she died of sorrow...

For Rita, a symphony as promised, the "Tragic Symphony", dedicated to her memory. It's a beautiful, melodic composition with a few measures of frightening dissonance at the end and abrupt silence, and then – a short instrumental cry – her letter from beyond the grave. Yes, Astrid read the letter to Arne. I showed it to her. She wept...

The Conservatory has been requested to accept trusteeship of her works in perpetuity. Our children, grandchildren, etc. are the owners of all her works – now performed around the world. Such beauty cannot die!

She passed away before Tom's statue was completed. Now she is part of the memorial to Tom in Milan.

Her mission has been completed – her destiny fulfilled...

As I look at Astrid's statue, I think of us. It was many years after Astrid's death, when a new Nobel Prize category in "Humanities" was announced, and we, Arne and myself, were the first recipients for our doctorate and post-doctorate works in writing and deeds in life. How Father, Mother and Astrid would have liked to experience it beside us in this life, but they know it there, in the life hereafter.

Now I know why Arne's life was spared: Not only for what he did, but for what he has inspired in me as well, and for giving to the world such brilliant ideas and children. He has done a lot of public speaking, but written much more: poetry, plays, essays, as well as memoirs, etc., published around the globe in the free world. His works are forbidden in the Soviet Union, but known in Latvia. Right now, Latvia itself may well be on its road to freedom again. It will be a long and difficult road, Arne tells me. The convulsions of collapse will be excruciating for the Soviet Union – a state of terror, torture and death.

I realize now – Arne could write about philosophy of justice, good will, freedom and love of "the individual, family, society and state" because he has experienced the opposite. Even his suffering had a purpose – it moulded him, and he gave all that depth of insight to the children and the world...

The children? Yes, our children have found their own niches

in their lives – in science, arts and business, besides being fathers and mothers. The huge inheritances helped a lot. Father was right when he said: "I hope that in the years to come it shall be split many times and in many parts – to our children, grandchildren, and their children, and so on, and on, and on…" – and we have plenty of them all.

Our dear children! I remember Arne telling me how I looked when preparing our nine-month-old Johnny for our regular visit to the doctor:

"You were in tight-fitting, fine leather black trousers and boots. You bent over Johnny, fixing him up and looked completely submerged in love and the fruit of it. Your red lips were slightly open; cheeks rosy; a most serene expression on your face, with love, engulfed in what you were doing. You were the very personification of love – all there is – kids, home, husband, love; spiritual and physical – a woman at the apex of her fulfilment…"

Yes! I was and still am very much in love, and that brings me to that faraway weekend when everything happened – the islands, Queens Park, our cathedral!

Oh! Our cathedral at the Royal Ontario Museum with the mineral exhibits! It has been destroyed… The ceiling is low now in the Mineral Hall. Of all things – they have built bleachers above, for children to watch movies! Just imagine, movies! As if we did not have enough movie theaters already?

*

I wake up again… No one can control thoughts – they come and go with double the speed of light. To be sure I do not drift away again, I turn to look at Arne and put my hand in his side pocket. He turns to me with a question mark on his face.

"Did I disturb you?" I ask.

"No! Not a bit! It was just about time you returned to the living," he smiles back.

"Yes. I was far away. All through the endless space around us," I reply very quietly, "but now I'm back beside you again."

"Astrid has thought of everything regarding her final resting place. I was just thinking about her."

"Yes, Arne! In death, as in life, she wanted to be beside you, by your right hand, and so she is resting and waiting for you. After the loss of Tom, she gravitated back to you for support – the man of her dreams as a girl, but she remained faithful to the end to Tom, in body and in mind.

"I shall be by your left, as always," I whisper. "'…We share everything – my sister and I…' Remember?" I whisper in his ear. "Oh, that was so long ago!"

"But Ingrid! After death, I have a standing appointment. After I empty the last goblet of the wine of life, I am to be Death's lover in her kingdom. Don't you remember the poem I wrote long, long ago, before I met you?"

"Oh! Yes, Arne! I remember! That was your deal with her!" and I start to snicker sincerely, thinking of the racket all those bones are going to make.

"Now what?" asks Arne.

"I'll tell you later – not in this sacred place."

"You are a naughty girl, Ingrid."

"Yes, I know," I answer thoughtfully remembering the life of beauty we have had. The life of sheer beauty. After a bit of silence I exclaim:

"And Rita waits too! 'Oh, well, we can't have everything!' as one of us said once. Do you remember where? No! Do not answer that. All four of us shall share your love," I say with a smile.

"But notwithstanding that, 'You are my favourite wife!' – remember?" Arne interjects.

"Oh, yes! I do! In the canoe on our lake! On our honeymoon! But I'm your 'guardian angel' too."

"That's right! The one and only!"

"And Astrid and me will be on either side of you! Neither of them can claim that!

"Even in death you shall be between a pair of emeralds and a pair of aquamarines.

"Even in death we shall be with you."

"Even in death – the ashes of life…"